tuesdays at six

kj lewis

Editing by Anna Esquivel
Cover Design by: K Yarwood and KJ Lewis
Interior Design by Champagne Book Design
Proofing by Monique Tarver

also by
kj lewis

Taylor Made

Taylored to Perfection

Sunday Love

Mondays with You

Dedication

To my KellBell.

tuesdays
at six

chapter one

"Excuse me," I murmur impatiently, bumping into the person in front of me. My customary curt disposition prods me to ask why they feel the need to stop directly in the doorway. By now, one would think I would have come to anticipate it. This lobby is a showstopper after all. "A new and oxygenated breath of fresh air," I believe were the words *Architectural Digest* used to describe our newest building in its coveted September edition. Since my name is one of two on the building, I bite my tongue and make my way around the obstruction. I pull up short some steps later when, in my haste, I realize I have forgotten the little hand gripping mine. Unable to match my 6' 3" stride, Poppy's little legs are barely hitting the Italian marble tiles as I drag her across the lobby. God, I'm a daft prick.

"Sorry," I grumble. It's the first time I'm acknowledging that I've practically slogged this poor girl across several parts of the city, and it's only nine o'clock in the morning. This is not the first time she's had to run to match my haste. She looks up when I apologize but doesn't give me the pass I've grown accustomed to—the sweet look telling me I'll get it right one day. I wonder briefly if it's because she's not feeling it or if she finally realizes what I've known all along: I have no idea what the hell I'm doing.

Her brown curls bounce haphazardly around her round face; her small hand is wrapped securely in mine to ensure she doesn't trip. I slow my pace, but it's no longer necessary. We're at the private lift my brother Finn and I use to access our offices and our residences.

What Poppy is feeling today is a fever and a sore throat, which means a trip to work with me instead of the elite school where I have her enrolled. Fever. I mean, unless you had an appendage hanging from your body and were losing copious amounts of blood, you didn't stay home when we were growing up. I'm certain I never missed a day of courses until I was in university and even then, it wasn't because I was sick, but because I was arseholed from the night prior. British stoicism for the win.

The lift doors close and Poppy and I ascend the twenty-seven floors up to my office. Our routine, as are our rituals, are smashed this morning. Usually I am on my mobile already checking emails and Poppy is dancing from one corner to the other, commandeering the lift as her own personal ballet studio. Today her head rests against my lower thigh, her hand still encased in mine.

The doors slide open onto my brother's office. Finn and I have an impossible day scheduled that began with a teleconference with our affiliates from China a little more than an hour ago. My instinct is to hurry about, but I make an effort to slow down, conscientious of the infirm little one at my side.

Nelson Financial has been our family business for decades. Our grandfather started the business in 1953. When he passed away a few years ago, our father who had been groomed to take over, should have, but rather abruptly decided he didn't want to die like his father, an old man who never lived. Instead, he opted for the backseat and became Chairman, making me the CEO and Finn the President of the company after he graduated from Oxford. Dad and Mum have since been traveling, taking art classes, and learning to speak German. They even started a small farm together. I thought he had gone barmy when he greeted me in overalls on my last visit. *Overalls.* This man, who ruled the financial world and wore ten-thousand-dollar suits every day of the week. Our parents are very different people now than the ones I knew growing up.

Poppy and I enter the holding area outside Finn's office. Par for the course his PA is not at her desk. I honestly don't know why he keeps her on the ledgers. She's never where I think she should be. Helga, his PA at our home office in London, is the epitome of structured efficiency. I'm pretty sure the changing of the guards at the palace is set by her watch.

Rolling my eyes in frustration at Samantha's absence, I push open the heavy lacquered door, finding his private office empty. As I expected, he's not in here. Based on the clock on the wall, he should be leading a tour of our facilities right about now. A tour I was originally slated to conduct.

"Poppy, I'm going to leave you here while I locate Finn." She coughs, and I cringe at the sound, like sandpaper against metal. I deposit her on the couch and pour a glass of water from the bar cart. She takes a small sip, wincing as she swallows, and sets it on the table. Her deep blue eyes implore me to stay, but she doesn't say anything, and I despise the part of me that is grateful she chooses to stay quiet. She tilts her head in what I think is censure, like she knows my thoughts and is disappointed by them. I'm still learning to read some of her cues.

She's pretty easy to forecast most of the time, but the look she's giving me is new and I'm not sure what she really wants. She knows I won't stay. I can't. Instead she sits back like a trooper. I feel like a prize idiot, once again reminded that I have no idea what Everett and Jenny were thinking.

Five years apart, Finn and I sometimes struggled to have the same interest, but I knew the moment my brother was born that he was mine to protect and look after. If I hadn't known it from my parents engraining it into me from the moment they found out they were expecting, I would have known it the moment he was placed in my arms. This was my baby brother. I've adored him ever since. Not that it's difficult or taxing. Finn is nothing if not lovable. I quite believe he's the only one that needs reminding of that.

I remember the conversations my mum had with her friends. They had tried to have another child for years after I was born, but they never thought it would happen again. When it did, they were determined to appreciate that one. As early as primary school, I first understood Finn was the favorite and I was not living up to my potential.

Or so I felt.

I can chart my life based on my parent's disapproval. In year six, I was caught smoking behind the field house. In year ten, my buddies and I dropped our trousers during a rugby match, each cheek with a letter telling the other team they were daft pricks. Countless more times where I seemed to disappoint them, but none like the ones playing out now.

University came easy to me. Numbers have always been my first language. I see equations and formulas in my surroundings. Because learning was intrinsic for me and I didn't have to work at my courses, I had plenty of time to get into misadventures—a feat made definitively easier with the Oxford Five.

We shared a flat together starting our first year. I was the rugby captain. Pierce, the American, the hard-core guy who seemed aloof to everyone but us. Quade, the Canadian, grew up playing hockey and would cut his arm off to give to a mate in need. Colin with the panty-dropping Scottish accent. And Everett.

Everett was the other Brit. Nicest lad I knew. Everett was genuine, intelligent, caring. He met Jenny, an American, our second year and despite all our merrymakings and the revolving door of women in our flat, Everett never strayed. Never so much as glanced at another girl after Jenny.

They found themselves pregnant their first year. I had to give it to Jenny. She stuck with university, even when it wasn't easy. She was determined becoming pregnant at nineteen wasn't going to keep her from the life she had mapped. Her parents stepped up and Everett was a great father, even without an example of one growing up.

They married when Zinnia was two, finished their education and made a life for themselves in New York. Poppy was born several years later. There are exactly ten years between the girls. Everett's life was simple: he loved Jenny, he adored his girls. He had achieved his life's calling before we all turned thirty.

It was Everett who convinced me and Finn to consider a second office in the States. We were already partnering with him and several other companies, and after a little research we went bi-coastal. Until four months ago, Finn and I were mostly in London, spending only a couple of months a year in New York.

Four months ago to the day, Everett and Jenny were killed on their way home from a customary Oxford Five dinner. It was late, and we tried to persuade them to stay in the city. We wanted to go dancing, but they didn't want to leave the girls alone overnight. Just over the Connecticut state line, a driver crossed into their lane. We were still gallivanting when I received the call that our group of five was now four.

The days following were a blur. They still are. I hardly remember anything over the last four months. The four of us shifted into autopilot and ensured things were handled the way we knew Everett would have expected.

Until the attorney contacted me, I had no idea I was the one he and Jenny chose for the girls. In fact, I didn't believe it at first, convinced Everett was pulling one final prank. His mom died a couple of years after they were back in the States, and he had no father to speak of. Jenny's parents love the girls and would have taken them in without question, but said Jenny had a long conversation with them about their wishes when she and Everett made the decision. And while they would step in and help if and when they were needed, they wanted to honor their decision. It was only then I realized this wasn't a prank.

Within those days since, I have picked up my mobile no less than a dozen times a day to ring them to tell them it's not going to work. But the letter on my dresser and my desire to honor my friend keep my thumb hovering over the button, never connecting the call.

"I'll be back as soon as I can," I tell Poppy. "Try to rest. If you need anything, push the button on your bracelet, alright?" I point to her panic button disguised as a charm. She nods, and I feel like a heel leaving but my options are limited. I pull his office door, ensuring it latches. No one without fingerprint access will be able to open it. It's not ideal, but she is safer here than she would be anywhere. Our office security rivals the Queen's.

I fall back into my usual brisk stride and report Poppy's location to my security team. I locate Finn on the 18th floor trading room. Most of what we do is kept under lock and key, but we have an area for prospective clients that showcases each of our projects.

"I apologize gentlemen." Finn cuts his eyes in my direction, irritated but relieved. I greet our clients in Mandarin and Quade raises a brow. The businessmen are his clients; he is the one that brought them to us. Quade can speak Chinese better than I can. In fact, he can speak at least a dozen languages fluently, but you'd hardly know it, he doesn't seem like the sort. And it's all self-taught. He's had more than one client unknowingly reveal their hand by assuming Quade didn't understand the what they were saying.

"I hope you didn't give anything away, Walt," he teases before he directs the clients to the next area. Finn and I hang back.

"I was about to send out the guard."

"Poppy is sick," I mumble. "I put her in your office. The school wouldn't keep her. Zinnie scared off another nanny, so I didn't have a backup."

"Camilla?" he asks. I roll my eyes. My fiancée isn't exactly Mary Poppins. In fact, I'm surprised she's been as patient as she has while I sort this out.

Quade comes to a stop at the next project and I take over the meeting. I mistakenly assumed I would have the floor to discuss the A28 project. While I *am* the one speaking, the men in the room, which happens to be everyone in attendance, divert their attention to Samantha when she enters. Jotting a note down, she's oblivious to her audience and comes to a stop in front of her boss. Her heels must be five, maybe six, inches high. I've never seen her in anything less. It occurs to me

just now she does it to be within whispering height to my 6'3"
brother. When she edges up onto her toes and he tilts his head,
she can just reach his ear.

I wonder if Finn is aware she does it. He probably is.
While I have always felt Samantha wasn't up to task, he only
sees the good in Sam. *Sam.* What proper lady would want to
be called Sam?

Finn has always had a soft spot for his PA. Human
Resources sent her up as a temp when we first opened our offices here. We weren't here often enough for her to be a major
consideration, but now that this is our primary location for
the foreseeable future, I've tried more than once to have him
hire someone with more education and ambition. Sam never finished university. At twenty-seven, I would say she's had
more than enough time.

Seeing it's no use, I halt my presentation to await the spell
to which the other men seem to have succumbed. With her
back to the room, her lithe legs flex as she raises onto her toes.
Finn bends his head forward, their cheeks touching. He nods
as she speaks. She sways slightly, and his hand gently but firmly lands at her waist to help her balance. He whispers back, her
heels fall back to the carpet, and all eyes follow the path of her,
admittedly pleasant, backside shifting into place. Other than
the fact she has blonde hair, there is nothing about her features
I can really speak to. This is the first time I've taken notice of
her arse. I've had too many subjects needing my attention as
of late.

Finn nods for me to continue and I catch the barely per-
ceptible tick in his eye. He doesn't like it one bit that these men
were eye-fucking his PA.

I'm finally relieved of my misery when the meeting comes
to an end ninety minutes later. Thirty minutes past schedule.

The only silver lining is that we got the account.

"We had another hacking attempt," Finn tells me as we exit on the 13th floor, our IT department. Evidently, it's common in the States to omit the "13" in the numbering of floors. There's no lift button for this floor in our building either, but not because we are superstitious. Every piece of intellectual data is stored on this floor, so it's only accessible to a select few.

As expected with any organization of our caliber, we've dealt with nuisance attacks, but when an anonymous person started a run on our stocks, someone simultaneously started a cyber war with our IT team.

"How much damage did they cause?" I ask, sliding my hand onto the pad outside of the main room and placing my eye against the scanner. When the yellow light comes on, I state my name; the voice recognition turns the light green. Finn and I enter and are immediately greeted by our head IT guy.

"This one was sneaky," Brad says.

"Aren't they all?" I ask.

"They're getting sneakier. We found the code only after it emptied an account. We were able to stop it and put the money back where it belongs."

"And if we hadn't stopped it?" Finn asks.

"It wouldn't have tripped the system until all of the accounts in Malaysia were empty."

"An oversight I assume we've repaired?"

"Yes. My team has a patch in place until we have the code written. That should be sometime tomorrow."

"Have they been anywhere else?"

"No. Like I said, we were lucky."

"How soon 'til our luck runs out?" I ask, even though I know I'm not going to like the answer.

"It might have already," he admits.

"If there is anyone you need to bring in, do it. I don't want us caught with our knickers down and our tallywhackers blowing in the wind. We've been chasing this fucker for too long."

Brad starts snapping his fingers as if I've said something intelligent. I haven't, but he leaves without a word, like a man on a mission.

"Are we sure he's the best?" Finn asks as we leave thirteen and head into a meeting on twenty.

"He is. Everyone else is underground."

"Maybe we should meet with Elise again, give her some more information. What good is it to hire her if we don't give her all the data we have? We either trust her or we don't." Elise Donovan is a fixer. Some of the things she fixes are visible, others remain a mystery.

"Fine. You're right. I'll ring her again. Who do you have to screw to get a sandwich around here?" I ask, taking my seat at the table. Less than a minute later, a plate of food is placed in front of me by a guy I've never met before. I lean over to ask Finn his name, but he's too busy looking at his arse to answer.

The next time I look at the clock it's five-thirty in the evening. I have not been to my office once today. The day was stacked with consecutive meetings, all designed to finish the deal with the Chinese clients. If one meeting had a hitch, the rest would fall like dominos. Thankfully the only glitch was running behind schedule, something we were able to repair by mid-afternoon. We had all items settled before the trading floor closed downtown at four.

In the last hour and a half of the day we finalized the press release and held interviews with the top financial shows on CNN and CNBC.

"I'm exhausted," I admit, sinking into my office chair. I could sleep right here if given a moment of peace.

"Why don't you skip the dinner? I'll make an excuse."

"No. It would be monumentally offensive, and even though they signed today, we still have three platforms we want them to partner on. I'll just run up and check on the girl—Fuck!" I jump up and make a run for the door.

"Poppy isn't in my office."

"What? Where is she?"

"I told Sam to take her to your place this morning."

"Jesus Christ, what is wrong with me?" I collapse onto the couch. That kid would have gone without a lunch today if it had been left to me. Would have spent the day alone in an office without me even thinking of her.

"Cut yourself some slack," Finn says softly, taking the seat across from me. "You need help. No one expects you to handle this all on your own."

"Everett did."

"No. He didn't. I haven't seen one piece of communication from the lawyers that suggested Everett had branded you as Superman."

"He was."

"No. He wasn't. He had a wife, in-laws, and a community of parents at the girls' school."

"I'm fine." I make to stand, but he easily pushes me back down.

"I'm not finished." He gives me the no-nonsense stare he's known for. "I agree it's not fair to the girls. None of this is fair. Their lives were destroyed in a single instant. Then they were uprooted from the only place they knew and moved to a city that never stops."

"Don't you think I know that?" I shout in frustration.

Defeat. Sorrow. Pick one. Any one of them would only describe a fraction of what I am feeling right now. "What the hell were they thinking? Me? Why me?"

"I don't know why. None of us do. But we're here now. Why don't you ring mum and dad to come stay for a few months?"

"No!"

"Just until you have your footing."

"I know I was the wrong choice. I don't need them reminding me every day."

"They would never say that." My brother's eyes are filled with sympathy for me and I hate it. I'm supposed to be *his* protector. Not the other way around.

"They think it and you know it. They never miss a chance to tell me I've screwed up."

"They kept you on a tight leash, I agree. But you needed one. You were always too smart for your own good. Mum and dad didn't want you straying too far from the line. They love you."

"Not an option," I say with finality, closing the topic.

"Well, we need to figure out something. You cannot continue at this pace, and the girls need stability."

"What I need is a nanny who won't bail."

"Zinnie is just acting out because she's hurting."

"I know that. You would think a ten-thousand-dollar-a-week nanny would understand it, too."

"Let's go, Superman." Finn pulls me up and we take our private lift to my residence, a floor above his.

"You need to thank Sam when we get in there." He narrows his eyes at me. He is more than acquainted with my opinion of his PA. "She set aside her entire day to take care of Poppy."

"Fine. I'll play nice, although you might want to talk to her about her wardrobe. Every bloke in that room was eye-fucking her."

"Caught that did you?" Finn chuckles, plowing into me when I stop abruptly.

My home is...tidy. There's no trace of the chaos that has become the new standard. We walk through the living area to find Zinnie at the table. She's never out here. She and Sam are having a conversation. She has a smile on her face. As soon as she sees me, it disappears.

"I need you to keep your sister tonight while I go to a meeting. I shouldn't be too long."

"That's what you always say," she says under her breath. I choose to ignore it as usual.

"Zinnia," Sam lightly chastises.

Zinnie rolls her eyes. "Fine. I'll watch her."

"Would you give us a minute, please?" Finn asks Zinnie, who goes to her room.

"Sam, I know Friday is your last day." *It is?* "I'd rather like to keep you on."

I roll my eyes. I just don't understand his attachment to this girl.

"We talked about this, Finn." She is exasperated. "I make too much to keep my financial aid and too little to work and afford school. I'm having to move out of my apartment just to afford books."

"Since when? You didn't tell me." My brother is not pleased with this news.

"Of course, I didn't. I knew what you'd do, and I don't want a handout. You're not paying my rent and my school. Plus, I don't want to listen to you go on about Queens."

"When have I ever *gone on* and why do you have to be

so stubborn? And you are *not* living in Queens." He slices his hand through the air in a show of finality. "Unless you plan to be inside by seven. You are not taking the tube late at night."

"Oh my God. It's like the same conversation on repeat. I'm living Ground Hog Day. I'm over having this same argument with you, Finn. And there's nothing wrong with Queens. Plenty of people live in Queens. Good people."

"Do I need to be here for this?" I ask dryly.

"No. Sorry." Finn releases a frustrated breath. He's considerably silent for a moment. I know that silence; he's scheming. A sly, Cheshire grin spreads across his face and he says, "Sam, I want you to meet your new boss. Walt, meet your new nanny."

"What?" Sam and I respond at the same time.

"The new fellow—Josh—filled in today while you helped out here. He isn't you, but he'll do. You were already planning to work for me part time, and Walt needs you more. Now that I know you also need a place to live," he gives a disgruntled look to his PA, "there are nanny's quarters that come with the position. Two birds, one stone."

Sam and I both start to protest, but Finn cuts us off.

"You can get the girls off to school. Do your courses on the days you have them, work with me on the days you don't. Then while you are doing your coursework at night, the girls can do theirs."

"Thank you but no. I can handle this on my own," I say through gritted teeth. I'm afraid of the tirade that will let loose if I release my jaw.

"Plus, I'm not sure this would be a good fit for me. Living here," Sam says.

"What's wrong with living here?" I snap, totally missing the point that she and I are on the same page. This is not a good fit for either of us.

"Nothing. It's beautiful. It's just…well, you're a little high strung, and you don't like me very much."

"I neither like nor dislike you. I don't think about you enough to come to an opinion on the matter. And, yes, I am currently high-strung. My entire fucking life has been flipped upside down," I growl. Finn's look tells me I have crossed a line. It doesn't matter, though, because the woman in front of me does not give a shit what I think about her.

"All you ever talk about is what this has done to your life," she spits back. "Do you ever stop to think about what it has done to theirs?"

Her words are like a feather falling from the sky and when it lands on my back, it's the last weight it can take. I snap.

"Who the fuck do you think you are, standing here in my house lecturing me on something I already know? Do you think a day goes by that I don't worry about what I am doing to these girls? I was never meant to raise kids. Fuck you if you think for a minute I would have chosen this…" I search for the words and when they don't come I regrettably land on, "*hell* we're all living in." She blanches at my words and I can feel the bile rising in my throat. I finally admitted the words I've been choking down since the day I found out I was a guardian.

The three of us stand there in the acrid silence of my words. My body is shaking. Finn wraps his arms around me, but I just stand there.

"You're alright," he says quietly. I wish I believed him.

"I don't feel so good." Poppy appears at my feet. My face pales at the thought she might have heard me.

I squat down and touch her forehead, she's still running a fever. Her eyes hold mine and they look hazy. "Go lie down and I'll bring you some…" She vomits. All over me. I can feel it running down my shirt collar, onto my chest. Vomit that must have been living inside her stomach for days it is so retched.

Vomit.

I hate vomit.

She immediately bursts into tears. Sam pulls her pajamas off where she stands and leaves them on the floor. Picking her up, Poppy rests her head in the nook of Sam's neck. It's an image that confuses me: how she can pick Poppy up in those heels and how she can stand that stench of vomit so close to her face.

Sam places her hand on my arm and uses me as a brace so she can kick her shoes off. "Shower and go to your meeting. I'll take care of her and stay until you are home."

"I'll cancel." The defeat in my voice is evident to everyone in the room. And even though I'm expecting it, seeing the pity in her eyes is worse because it's a mirror of how I'm feeling.

"You can't. There are people's livelihoods depending on this deal," she reminds me.

"They won't let her at school tomorrow. She has to be fever and vomit-free for twenty-four hours."

"I can keep her," Finn offers.

"You can't," Sam says. "Tomorrow has all the rescheduled appointments from the day you took off to care for West." At just the mention of Finn's new friend, his eyes flash with desire, confusion and a hint of uncertainty.

"I'll stay with her tomorrow," she says. "I can check in on Josh. Like you said, he made it okay today, he'll make it okay tomorrow."

"Go. Shower," she says with a flick of her hand, dismissing me.

Guess it's settled then.

chapter two

I like being in control. I like calling the shots. But something about Samantha taking the reins just now is enough to have my dick waking up.

Hello, fella. It's been a while.

For the first time in four months, my mind is completely blank. No problems to solve. No wondering how I am going to maneuver this meeting and Poppy being sick. Nothing. Just me and my hand. It's glorious. Did I mention it's been a while?

By the time I'm showered and dressed, the scene of the crime has been cleaned and the only person in the living room is Finn, waiting for me to go to our dinner meeting.

I thank the gods we're meeting at the restaurant next door, so we won't have to deal with traffic. We would have been late otherwise, something I loathe.

I knock lightly on Zinnie's door. When I open it, she's sitting on her bed with her earbuds in. She's on FaceTime with someone. She's not happy about it, but she takes one out and acknowledges me with a glare.

"Sam is staying until I get back, so you don't have to watch your sister." She nods as if she couldn't care less and puts her earbud back in, resuming her conversation. Alright then. Guess ours is over. This fifteen-year-old has made me her bitch. She is never going to come around. Shuffling down the hall, I open Poppy's door.

The lighting is muted but I can see she's unsoiled and in bed. Sam is rubbing her back, and I faintly hear her humming a song I don't recognize.

Despite having this problem temporarily solved, I'm still frustrated with my brother. Half of me is angry with Finn for making a decision of this magnitude for me, while the other half is relieved at the idea of having a nanny who isn't going to walk out in two weeks. I don't know how much longer I can keep this charade up. Can it even be called a charade if everyone already knows the truth? That I am fucking this up. I'm the only one who's refusing to admit defeat.

"Ready?" Finn calls from the end of the hallway where he waits, watching me. He knows I'm going to protest before I even open my mouth.

"I don't think this is a good idea. I can do this. I can make this work. I appreciate your offer, but it's not necessary."

"I love you, brother, but you are too close if you think you can do this on your own. You've wanted—correction, *needed* a nanny all along. How is hiring Sam any different?"

"The nannies I hire come from Willingham Society, the most prestigious firm in the world. The Royals use this firm. You're telling me a twenty-seven-year-old college dropout is going to outperform nannies who attended the best universities and have had world class training? Somehow I doubt Sam is what Everett thought I would provide his girls when he entrusted their care to me."

"Everett just wanted his girls to be loved. *That* is why he entrusted them to you," Finn says over his shoulder as we walk to the table reserved for our meeting. He greets the gentlemen already seated and it takes me a moment to gather my wits about me.

Is Finn right? Is that what Everett wanted?

If so, why didn't he choose their grandparents, or friends that have children the same age? I shake my head. Everett wanted his girls to be raised by someone with the financial means to give them everything they needed. To ensure they would have the best the world had to offer. That is why they chose me. I have more money than God.

Dinner drones on and by the time we leave I am more than ready to be home. It's ten o'clock by the time the lift stops at Finn's. He invites me in for a drink, but I don't have it in me. In the short ride from his floor up to mine, I start to feel the dread that has become second nature. It will take me at least an hour to get the girls down, then another hour to prep for tomorrow. I still have a thousand emails to tend to. The first is a request to the Willingham to send a new prospect for review. It usually takes a few days for them to arrange travel; with any luck they can have someone here before the weekend.

The doors open and when I step into the foyer, I notice that something is amiss. I can't tell if I'm in the right place. It's quiet. There aren't shoes and clothes and Barbies strewn about. The table isn't covered in iPads and laptops and earbuds. For the first time in four months it looks and sounds like the home I always had.

Walking down the girls' wing, I crack open Poppy's door. It's dark, but the pale light from the hallway illuminates the room enough that I can see Poppy asleep against Sam. Quietly, I maneuver the darkness and place a palm on Poppy's forehead. She still feels feverish, but she's sleeping for the first time in a couple of days. Sam's bare feet are propped on the otto-man, so I shift the blanket she has draped over Poppy to also cover her toes before stealing my way out.

Zinnie's room is surprisingly dark and she's in her bed sleeping. The first time since she has stayed here that she's asleep before midnight.

Today was just a bad day, I assure myself on the way to the refrigerator to grab a water to take to my office. *Maybe* I can do this after all. *Maybe* we are going to make it. Everyone keeps telling me that one day you look up and you're over the hump. Maybe today was our hump.

I smile at the thought, but the truth slams into me like a wave when I open the refrigerator door. There's a lunch made for Zinnie. An actual lunch. A thought-out, pre-planned lunch. Made the night before.

She had both girls in bed before ten and a lunch made for the next day. A feat the nannies from Willingham have yet to accomplish. The difference isn't that we've made it over some hypothetical hump. The difference is Sam.

I'm an hour into emails when there's a light knock on the office door casing.

"I'm going to sneak down to Finn's place for a minute," Sam says groggily. "Wanted to let you know. Both girls are asleep, but Poppy is still running a fever and coughing. Do you know if she has any allergies?"

"She doesn't. I spoke to her pediatrician after the accident to get some history on both of the girls."

"See. You're better at this than you realize." She smiles and for the first time I see the girl standing in front of me. I've always registered her as pretty, but I would go as far to say she's beautiful. Her blonde hair, matted from sleep, hangs just below her shoulder blades. Without her heels, and based on where she's hitting the door frame, I'd venture she's around 5'7". Her silk blouse skims over her ample breasts like silk draped over highlands. She has an hour-glass figure, show-cased by the black pencil skirt she's wearing. Her stomach is flat, but her hips, thighs and bum have a noticeable curvature to them. I suppose she would be considered 'thick' compared to the women I am usually attracted to. My size-zero fiancée, Camilla, can wear designer clothes like a runway model. From every angle, they hang perfectly.

"Pardon?" I ask reeling in my revelries.

"I was saying, you are better at this than you realize. You could stand to cut yourself some slack."

"I don't have that luxury. I have two little girls who depend on me getting this right."

"You do," she agrees, "and you will." She says it like it's a given, like she believes it.

I wish I had her confidence. I'm seconds away from asking her how she knows, and can she guarantee it.

"I ordered some cough syrup," she continues, oblivious to my turmoil. "The front desk will call as soon as it arrives. I should be back by then."

"You're leaving?" The thought brings a surprising level of panic with it.

"Just to Finn's for a few minutes," she politely reminds me.

"Right. I'll listen for the girls." I gather my footing and straighten the fuck up.

She nods, and I hear the lift ping seconds later. True to her word, she's back in less than ten minutes, but not alone.

"Thanks, Finn."

"You're welcome, Sam." He nods to me when I enter the foyer.

"I brought Sam up. She doesn't have access to your floor,

so the lift wouldn't open."

"She has access to yours?" I ask surprised. Finn has strict rules when it comes to his privacy.

"Of course. So will Josh once I know he's not a crazy person."

Sam laughs and hits him on the arm. "Josh is a nice guy. I hand picked him to look after you. Be nice."

"Fine. I'll be nice."

"Not nice like you were to me the first month. True niceness."

"That's not a word." My brother winks at her and I notice they have a camaraderie about them that I haven't observed before. This girl means something to him. I don't know how I missed it.

"If you say so. Thanks for the clothes." She yanks the edge of the T-shirt she has on. She's changed into one of his white undershirts and a pair of his joggers from uni that have Oxford screen printed on the upper thigh. She's rolled them up where her ankles show so she won't trip. On anyone else the ensemble would look ridiculous, but she pulls them off, looking comfortably familiar.

"Anytime, love." He kisses her forehead and the doors close.

"We met the doorman on the way up," she says, holding up a white paper bag. "I'm going to wake her for a dose now and again in four hours."

"I can give her the second one," I offer, exhausted at the thought of waking up in four hours when I have to be up in six.

"Nah." She waves me off. "I'm going to sleep in her room. If she's still running a fever in the morning, I'll run her to the doctor. Good night." She smiles. There's mascara smudged around her hazel down-turned eyes. She has a few freckles on the bridge of her up-turned nose and full rosy-pink lips. Other than that, she is fresh-faced.

"Good night," I reply.

I sleep through my alarm the next morning. A bit of a bad habit lately. Having only been asleep for a few hours, it takes some effort to drag my arse out of bed and to the shower. I implore the fall of warm water to revive me, but it's simply not up for the task. I wrap a bath towel around my waist before stepping up to the mirror where I find a tired man peers back at me.

I don't know how Everett managed it. I'm feeling every hour of my thirty-four years, and in the reflection staring back at me, I feel like you can see each of them.

I give a silent thanks to God that my body still has quite a bit of athletic definition, even though I haven't seen a gym in months. Finn and I have the same sea-green eyes and angular jaw, but he has our mother's nose and cheeks while I favor our father. Hard and intimidating.

My skin ruddier and more textured from the sun, unlike Finn's whose skin reflects our privileged lives. Rotating my face from one side to the next, I decide to leave the growing stubble that has become a common presence over the last few months. Anything allowing me to be out the door earlier. A lazy splash of cologne and I'm ready.

While everything else in my life has changed, my closet has been my one constant. It's still an organized shrine to the suits housed here. I slide into a Saville Row suit, a gray pin-stripe, one of my favorites. I button my waistcoat before grabbing my suit jacket and starting the morning ritual.

I'd caution anyone not to mistake the word ritual for organized. Or planned. Or controlled. No, ritual for us simply means constant. The chaos, disorder and confusion are all constant.

You can do this. I lift my shoulders and crack my neck from one side then the other. I take a deep breath and go.

I release a lung full of air and head into the living area. The 30th floor is approximately six-hundred-fifty square meters. Not small by any standards, but not as large as some of my counterparts would expect. The floor-to-ceiling windows in the living room open onto a terrace that wraps around three sides of the building and adds another 200 square meters of outdoor space. That's more than big enough. Anything larger would be vulgar.

Fastening the cuff on my sleeve, I stumble over my feet taking in the scene. Zinnie is at the kitchen bar eating breakfast. This is a first since she's been living here. Poppy isn't eating but is sitting at the bar, reading a book. Do kids read at this age? Either way, she's flipping pages.

"Maria said you like two sugars," Sam says, handing me a steaming cup of coffee at the same time she sets a plate of toast with butter and jam on the island next to Zinnie. My usual breakfast. Another piece of information my assistant must have bestowed. I take a bite, noticing that Zinnie is eating yogurt with fresh fruit.

"How do you feel Poppy?" I ask the little one.

"Pops." Sam commands her attention when she doesn't respond. "Walt asked you a question." She's still standing on the other side of the bar. She eats a spoonful of yogurt before leaning across and tugging Zinnie's earbuds out of her ears. Zinnie shoots her a disgruntled look to which Sam replies,

"Not during meals."

"My throat feels like growls," Poppy says, turning the page.

"Gravel," Zinnie snaps. "And if you pass it to me, you're gonna pay."

"But I only have two dollars." A sheen comes over her eyes and there's a slight lip quiver.

"It's an expression, honey. No one is going to make you pay." Sam smiles then gives Zinnie a scolding look.

"So, tell me girls, was it your mom or your dad who had a thing for flowers?"

Poppy stops a page in mid-turn and Zinnie sets her spoon in her bowl. I hold my breath. We never talk about their parents. I don't want to upset them and I figured they'd talk when they were ready. Yep. Time for Samantha to go home. She doesn't understand the little rules we have for survival, that help us make it from day to day.

"Mom," Zinnie says quietly. "Zinnias and Poppies were her favorite."

"I wish I had a cool story about my name like you guys, or Walt for that matter." She nods in my direction.

"You were named after a flower?" Poppy asks, her page finding its spot against another.

"Writers, actually." I look to Sam and she gives me a reassuring smile. "I was named after my mother's favorite poet, Walt Whitman. She named Finn after her favorite book by Mark Twain. Do either of you know the name of the book?"

"Huckleberry Finn," Zinnie says with a genuine smile. It's the first one since before the funeral and it's breathtaking.

"Daddy read that to us!" Poppy exclaims with a slight bounce.

"That's right, Pops. He did," Zinnie says to her sister.

Breakfast is quiet after that, but I feel like a small chip on the mountain was made. It's the first time we've had a conversation that didn't seem perfunctory and forced. Maybe Sam would be a good fit with the girls. She is the first nanny they have had a response to.

"It's eight, you need to go," Sam tells Zinnie. "Dishwasher," she says when Zinnie heads to her room.

"There's a maid who does that," Zinnie and I answer.

"Not anymore. Rinse your breakfast bowl and place it in the dishwasher please," Sam insists, setting the example with her own dishes.

Zinnie walks heavier than necessary to the sink, following directions.

"I'll take you to the lobby." I stand pulling on my jacket and go to grab my briefcase.

"Walt."

"Samantha?" I look over my shoulder to see what she needs.

"Dishwasher," she says, pointing to my plate and coffee cup.

I'm this close to telling her that I pay people to do these things for me, but I don't. She raises a brow in censure at the attitude with which I handle my dishes. I check my watch and call the lift, holding it for Zinnie while she takes an inordinate amount of time getting her items together.

"I'm coming," she snaps when she observes me checking my watch. I hold my tongue. By the time she makes it to the lift, Sam is waiting for her with her lunch. Zinnie mumbles a thank you and before she anticipates it, Sam wraps her in a hug and kisses her cheek, wishing her a good day. Zinnie quietly hesitates and steps into the lift. She doesn't speak, but I catch her wiping a tear from the corner of her eye as the doors close on us.

"What's wrong?" I cringe just asking the question. There are so many unpredictable ways she can answer this question. I can't say that I'd be prepared for any of them.

"It's just the first time since Mom." She says softly.

"First time?" My voice just as soft as the doors open to the lobby.

"That I started the day with a hug," she says exiting the elevator as it opens to the lobby.

I watch her walk to her security detail waiting to take her to school.

That I started the day with a hug.

Instead of exiting myself, I punch the button for the 30th floor. When the lift doors open Sam is in the kitchen pulling items out of the fridge.

"We need to talk," I command.

"I know. Listen. I love Finn, but he tends to want to fix everything for the ones he loves. His heart is in the right place, but sometimes his mouth writes a check it can't cash."

"He's right."

"What?" She looks at me with perplexity and surprise.

"Finn is right. I think you would be a good fit for the girls and I would like to do a trial run to see if we can make this work. I'm a big enough person to admit that I am not winning this like I would like to." I clear my throat. "Especially when it comes to doing what's right for the girls. I only want the best for them."

"That's how you know you're going to be okay," she says with a conviction I have yet to find when it comes to being their guardian.

"It's going to take me a while to get a replacement. Zinnie has maneuvered her way through five."

"She's hurting."

"She is, and while I have tried to give her leeway, I'm running out of options."

"And I'm an option? You didn't seem very keen last night."

"I wasn't. I'm still not keen on it, but already the girls had breakfast, spoke actual words, and Zinnie talked in the lift. All of these are new."

"I have some stipulations."

"Fine. Negotiate your terms up front. I don't like to make amendments."

"I need one night off a week to do as I please. Preferably Friday."

"You can have Thursday." I have no preference what day she takes, but I don't want to lose the upper hand before this even starts. She has no idea that she already has me by the bollocks.

"I want you to support me in front of the girls, as I will you. If you disagree with something, you need to pull me to the side and let me know. If they think they can play us against each other, they will."

"They wouldn't."

"They would, and they will."

"Fine."

"I'll be here before the girls start their days and stay until they are in bed."

"You'll stay here. There are nanny's quarters."

"I don't need you nor your brother—"

"Let's address this now, shall we." I cut her off, crossing my arms. "I am not my brother. You work for me, not Finn."

"I'm working an IT project for him."

"He can oversee your projects at the office, but if you accept this job, you will be my employee here. Finn and I handle things very differently. I cannot have you thinking *you* can play us against one another." It's a prick move. A purposeful one.

"I wouldn't."

"As I said, you'll stay here. The girls might need you in the middle of the night." I honestly don't care where she stays, but I know Finn will feed my dick to me if I don't make it so she doesn't have to go to and from Queens at night.

"Fine. Room and board and five hundred a week. I'll move in next week."

"I'll pay you three thousand a week, room and board, and you'll move in this week."

"You can't. I'll lose my financial aid."

"I'll cover your school then."

"No. I already had a budget set. I don't need handouts. I just want to be paid fairly."

I'm just about to tell her the former nanny was making ten thousand a week so three would be more than fair, but Poppy takes our attention.

"Sam, will you lay down with me?"

"I'll be right there sweetheart." She glares back at me. "I'll move in this week, but the pay is non-negotiable. My IT work is counting as credit hours. They are considering it an internship. You can't control me by throwing money at me."

If that's true, she would be the first.

"Fine. I'll stick to your salary requirements."

"Then I'll move in this week."

chapter three

"All the cable networks carried the deal with the Chinese this morning. And the yen was up four when their markets opened," Quade says, closing a folder and sliding it across the boardroom table into Finn's waiting hand.

"And they agreed to the three-year stipulations?" Finn asks him, glancing through the signed contracts.

"They did. We had to give them first rights at the solar project you're working on, but Pierce built in a protection clause that gives you the right to refuse if you see fit."

"I don't imagine we'll need it, but it's nice to know it's there. What's the latest projection date on the solar panel that's in production now?" Finn says, sliding the file to me.

"Next prototype is due any day now," I answer as I review and initial each page, and sign the last.

"As we expected, IT stopped another hacking attempt this morning," Finn says.

"Well, you guys were expecting that, right?" Quade asks. "I'm telling you, you need to bring Elise Donovan into the circle. I've used her services before. She can be trusted, and she can get things done. Plus, the chap she has working for her has a way of 'cracking the nuts' so to speak."

"Hear that, Finn?" I smirk at my brother who promptly gives me the finger.

"What? Hold up. What's the story, Junior?" Quade teases. My brother winces at the nickname he has hated since these guys became my pack.

"*Junior* likes a boy," I tell Quade, who claps his hands, flutters his eyelids, and says in a high-pitched voice, "Do tell."

"The boy is in love with Elise's guy."

"Blake Thomas is gay?" Quade says sitting up, shocked into his regular voice.

"Did Walt tell you he hired Sam to be his nanny?" Finn fires back.

"No shit? Finally. You're getting your footing with this guardian thing. You're starting to make smart decisions." Quade looks genuinely pleased with this turn of events. Stand in line man. There's a long list of people who know I'm fucking up.

"It's on a trial basis," I mumble, looking through the messages Maria handed me this morning and pretending to read them. There isn't anything the guys wouldn't do for me, but they are as at a loss as I am. And even though no one has said as much, I get the feeling they are trying not to crowd me, hoping that if I have some space to sort through things, I'll finally get us moving in the right direction.

"Well, it's a good move," Quade says, standing and buttoning his suit coat. "Plus, that girl can 'supercalifragilisticexpiali-docious' me any day."

"Quade," Finn barks.

"What? I'm serious. I've had a thing for Mary Poppins

since you hired her as your assistant. We have an understanding. She's playing hard to get, but really she wants me."

"Stop asking her out," Finn demands, making it clear that he's not messing around.

"Simmer, Junior. I'm always a gentleman," he says, tussling Finn's hair.

"Walt," Finn snarls, fingers combing his locks back into place.

I exhale a deep breath. Finn knows that when I have to choose between my brother and my guys, he always wins. He sometimes likes to take advantage of that fact.

"Quade, leave Samantha alone. There's too much at stake now that the girls are involved." It's a low blow, but one I know Quade understands. He's as invested in these girls as I am. All of us are. He would never do anything to fuck this up.

"Like I said, it's a good move. I'm proud of you." Quade leans over to hug me in my chair. He's always been the hugger of the group. Him and Everett. Zinnie's words come hurling back. *That I started the day with a hug.* Everett was a hugger.

My phone beeps, pulling me from my thoughts.

Finn's PA: I took Poppy to the MD. She had to get a shot and has to take an antibiotic for a week. Should be back to normal in a couple of days. No fever so far today.

She's attached a picture of Poppy napping. Her curls are splattered to and fro on her pillow. Her arms are tightly wrapped around Edward, her blue elephant.

"Pops is better?" Finn asks reading over my shoulder.

"You too, with the Pops?"

He shrugs. "When Sam came to get something to wear last night, she said that Poppy told her Jenny and Everett called her Pops and that she misses it."

"Sam changed at your place last night?" We suddenly have Quade's full attention. "Did you see anything?" He waggles his brows and I swear I see a droplet of drool on his chin.

"I saw *everything*," Finn goads, slapping his hand down on Quade's shoulder.

"You're shitting me, aren't you? Are you serious?"

The look of sheer anticipation and jealousy on Quade's face volleyed against the look of utter detachment on Finn's is enough to make me laugh. For the first time in a long time, sadly.

"And for God's sake, her name is 'Samantha' or 'Sam'. Don't list her as 'Finn's PA' in your phone, knob head," Finn shouts out before the door closes behind him and Quade, leaving me with a much-treasured moment of peace. I take in the picture of Poppy. Even in her sleep Poppy looks content.

Me; Thank you for taking her. Let me know if she needs anything.
Sam: Happy to. She ate lunch and kept it down. She's been sleeping most of the day, so I really think she's on the mend.

My thumbs float above the keyboard. I'm tempted to reply but decide I'm better off not engaging Samantha. We are not friends who text. I am not Finn. I am her boss.

The next two days fly by without incident and already there is evidence of an established routine. A routine that has fallen into place with shocking ease. Now if I can get my business life to follow suit, I can maybe catch a breather.

Every corner I turn there's another crisis to be managed. Thankfully the China Organization parted amicably, and we have a bit of down time in between projects. I really want to nail down this solar project.

"Mr. Nelson." Maria's voice crackles from the speaker phone. "You need to leave now if you are going to make it to your lunch meeting on time."

I glance at my watch and finish the email I am sending to Brad about the hacking attempts. I'm concerned our luck is soon to run out, and I'm not convinced we have enough safety traps in place.

The lunch meeting is at a restaurant around the corner from our offices. Being that, at our core, we are a financial company, some thought it made more sense to locate our building in the Financial District, but Finn and I both wanted the convenience of having our living spaces above our offices. In London, we both commute to work. At the time we were only here a couple months of the year at best and we enjoyed the idea of home being only a few floors away. Given this was going to also be our residences, we decided to build in the Flatiron District, specifically near Madison Square Park.. A hindsight decision I am especially grateful for now that I have the girls. This area lends itself to a family setting more than the Financial District.

"Thank you, Maria." I nod to my assistant who is holding the lift for me. Before the doors close, she hands me a couple of phone messages and reminds me the meeting is at Phillipe's. The lift opens a few floors down and Finn and his new PA enter.

"Walt, I don't believe I've introduced you to Josh. My new assistant."

"Nice to meet you," I respond without looking up from my messages.

"Walt."

Inwardly, I roll my eyes and look up.

"Sorry, chap," I say with a bit of sarcasm, but still offering my hand. "Nice to meet you." He's nice looking. Young. Looks eager to please. I'm sure my brother has already beat the bishop to the thought of Josh's rather large lips.

He pushes his black frames onto the bridge of his nose before tripping over his greeting, obviously nervous. Thankfully the doors open, putting me out of my misery. Josh scurries in an opposite direction and I use the opportunity to chastise my brother.

"You hired him because he's pretty, didn't you?"

"I didn't hire him, Sam did."

"You know you can't fuck the help. No matter how big his lips are."

"I swear mum left you in the sun too long when you were a tyke. You are so crude."

"I'm just reminding you nothing good comes from it. Hierarchy serves a purpose."

"Crude and a prude. We're not aristocracy for Christ's sake. And his lips are rather plump, aren't they?"

"I mean employer/employee hierarchy arsehole. What are you doing?" I ask over my shoulder entering the restaurant.

"Having lunch."

"I'm meeting someone." I pull out my phone. To be honest, I didn't even look to see whom I was meeting with. I just went where Maria directed. If I needed to have prepped before coming she would have given me the necessary information.

"I know. I'm expected at the same meeting. Nelson," my brother tells the maître d' who informs us our guest is already seated.

"Samantha?" I look around to make sure we are at the correct table.

"You look lovely." Finn plants a kiss on her cheek and takes his seat.

"You're my lunch meeting?" I ask with incredulity, even though I don't know why.

"Yes. Didn't Maria tell you?" She seems confused by my displeasure.

"She did not. The morning got away from me and I hadn't looked at my meeting schedule today. Why are you here?" I ask my brother as I finally take my seat.

"Sam scheduled it with Josh." He shrugs and opens his menu, perusing the lunch section.

The waiter brings a glass of scotch to the table and sets it in front of Sam.

"Thank you but I didn't order this."

"From the gentleman at the bar," he informs her.

Finn's head shoots up to see who he is and frowns. "How does he know we aren't together?"

"Maybe because I was sitting here for ten minutes before you came in. He probably thought I was lunching alone." She turns and gives a polite smile to the man, and when she turns back around Finn has emptied the glass.

"There's a side to you that most would find surprising," she chides.

"But not you," Finn winks, going back to his menu, but Sam isn't done with him yet.

"You act like you're my brother."

"You *are* like a sister to me and you could use a brother, so it works out for both of us."

It's fleeting, but there's something akin to a flash of pain in Samantha's eyes. It's gone as quickly as it came.

"Do I really need to be here for this?" I grumble.

The waiter again interrupts us. We place our selections

and Sam squares her shoulders. She switches to corporate mode. I see it in my mates when we're doing business. I just never expected Sam to have the same quality.

"I scheduled this meeting because I wanted to talk to both of you about the girls and I felt like doing it together was best. A lunch meeting seemed like the optimum time."

"You chose a public place, so you must have concerns we aren't going to receive this well," I say.

"I have no ulterior motives, if that is what you are asking. I wanted to eat and knew you needed to also."

"So, let's eat."

"I also want to discuss my position."

"I told you the other night that I don't like to make amendments to closed deals."

"Walt, let her finish."

"I don't wish to amend our decisions from the other night, but, naturally, raising two girls is going to be an organic experience. A one-size-fits-all deal is not going to work here. We are going to find ourselves constantly evolving our approach."

"Our?" I say with more provocation than intended, which she insightfully ignores.

"I want to take the girls out of summer school," she blurts, then waits.

I look at the table wishing Finn hadn't finished off the scotch, picking up a water instead. I take a long steady drink to calm my rising agitation before responding.

"You want to take the girls out of a school I had to use every connection I could to get them into? A school that provides consistency and discipline, something I'm sure even you can agree they need."

"*Even I* can agree they need those things, but it is not the school's place to provide consistency or discipline for that matter. It's yours."

My blood pressure hits an all-time high. Who does this bint think she is, telling me what the girls need? She's been with them all of forty-eight hours. She either is unaware of the detonation about to happen or she doesn't care, because she continues as if I'm not on the verge of imploding.

"And it's mine and it's Finn's. We all have a role to play here. I need the girls home over the summer if I'm going to help. Plus, they need some down time. They've been through an incredible amount of change. They need time to adapt. I think being at home for a few weeks will encourage that."

The slow as fuck waiter finally brings our drinks and I tap into every part of my control to slowly twirl the amber liquid in my glass before taking a sip. That I didn't throw mine and Finn's back and demand he bring the bottle is a clear testament to my business prowess.

But this girl. There's something about her. She's learned more from Finn than I have given her credit for. She's not the stupid girl I painted her as earlier. She's in a restaurant where the glass of scotch some tallywhacker sent her is more than she makes in a week. She's across from two formidable business men who rule the financial world, and she is not intimidated in the least. More than that, she fully expects to win. I see it in her expression. She seems to be approaching this as a hostile merger and doesn't appear to be the slightest bit out of her comfort zone.

"Finn, you aren't doing enough. You really need to start stepping up."

"Excuse me?"

"You heard me. These girls are your nieces now and you're still behaving as if they are Everett's children."

"They *are* Everett's children," I caution her.

"Not anymore," she says gently. "He is and always will be their father, but they are now your responsibility. But they need an uncle, too. Someone who lets them have dessert for dinner. Someone they can make fun of Walt with." She holds up her hand to stop my protest. "They need to know there is one constant in their life right now and that needs to be Finn."

"I really think it should be Walt. He's the one Everett chose," Finn says softly.

"He is. But Walt is not in the position to be that person. Not yet. He has to be the guardian. Don't you see? Walt is the one that had to handle everything. He's had to move them to the city. Pull them from the only school they knew. Everything about him right now is the exact opposite of constancy. He represents all the upheaval."

"Despite what you might think, I'm not a monster. I talked to the girls before I made those decisions. I wouldn't have pulled them from the only life they knew without having a conversation with them."

"You think I don't know that? The girls know it too, but they can't allow themselves to be angry at their parents, so for a while it's going to be you. It's not fair and I know it's hard, but that's the reality."

"I'm perfectly capable of handling it." I run my fingers down my tie in a move to calm my nerves.

"Capable and not affected by are two different things. I know it hurts when the girls act out. You gain nothing by pretending it doesn't. We all want what's best for them and we can't accomplish that if we aren't honest about where we are starting from." For a moment I think she is going to reach out and touch me, but my countenance must have alerted her that would be a mistake.

"Finn, these are your brother's children now. You're still

behaving as if they're some friend's kids you see on special occasions."

She's right. I haven't processed it until now, but she's right. If I had kids, Finn would be loving them from every angle available to him, and he wouldn't allow anything or anyone to stand in his way. At best, he's kept the girls at arm's length.

"Jesus Christ. You're right." Finn solemnly sits back. "I've been so focused on running the business, so you could handle what you need to do, that I haven't even tried to form a relationship with the girls." When he looks at me, his eyes hold regret.

"There is no manual on how to handle this, but being with you all for these two days has confirmed what I've suspected for a while now. You and the guys are trying to care for Walt, but the best way to do that is to care for the girls. Walt can care for Walt. What he needs is help with Zinnie and Poppy."

Fuck. Me. I'm dumbfounded. And pissed. And frustrated. Because Mary Poppins is right. For the first time since the accident, I feel like I have my bearings. Yes. If Finn and Samantha can help with the girls, I can handle the estate side.

"Done. Handled," Finn says with finality. He's made up his mind. He understands.

"Now. The girls and summer session," Samantha says, plowing forward like she's just checked something off a list.

"I don't think it's a good idea," I say, but with more diplomacy this time. "If they need consistency, how is pulling them from school going to provide that?"

"They can have a routine without having to give up their summer. They want to be at the park with friends, not stuck in a summer school program."

"How do you propose to occupy their time?"

"I've changed my second summer classes to online classes.

I can be with the girls during the day and study at night."

"What do you have to lose?" Finn asks me.

"Their spots at their school, that's what. What if she leaves like the other nannies? What will I do then?"

"I won't."

"And you have a way to guarantee me that?"

"I'm giving you my word. I am not going to leave these girls."

I want to believe her. I really do.

"Take the chance. If Sam buggers off—she won't, but if she does—I'll take holiday for the remainder weeks until school starts and keep the girls myself."

Our food is delivered, and we eat in silence while I digest the proposal on the table.

"Why?" I ask.

"I told you why."

"I mean why are you doing this? It's easier for you if the girls are in school. What's in this for you? You know the girls can't access their accounts until they are twenty-five." I know it's a shitty thing to say before it even leaves my lips.

"I'm going to pretend that's the stress talking and not something you meant to say."

"That's a dick move, and you know it," Finn growls.

"Fine. Remove the dick remark at the end. It's still a valid question."

"I understand these girls and they need someone to stay. I want to help them."

"Out of the goodness of your heart," I say snidely and immediately regret it. The pain in her eyes would bring any man to his knees. I turn away because the only option is to see it and for some reason I try to ignore, I can't.

"Alright. You can take the girls out of school," I relent, but

I'm not sure if it's because I agree with her proposal or because I feel the need to atone my ill-spoken words. Neither reason sits well.

"Perfect. Just a couple more things."

I drop my silverware loudly onto my plate, staring at her with unbridled exasperation. "More amendments?"

"Let's call them agreements."

This girl.

"Fine." I go back to cutting my steak. "Let's get it all out now. I mean it when I say I don't like amendments."

She ignores my insolence. "I'd like to redo the girls' bedrooms."

"What's wrong with them?"

"Nothing, if they are a 35-year-old Englishman."

"I asked the girls if they wanted to bring their bedroom suites from their house. They didn't want to."

"Which I think is okay, but they need a space they can each claim as their own. A space that reflects them. I think it will help them feel like this is their home. It's also a summer project. Something for them to do."

"Fine. But you will use a designer and you will have a budget. I don't expect my home to look like it came from a box store."

"You are so…"

"Careful…"

"…out of touch. I agree to your terms, but I choose the designer."

"With my final approval. Next."

"I would like you to schedule a vacation with the girls before they start school."

"No. I don't have the time."

"Make it."

"I have Everett's items to close out. We are in the middle of being hacked every time the market opens. I don't have the time to take a holiday before school starts." She can't have everything on her list. I've conceded more than I should have. She already has the upper hand because even though she doesn't say it, she knows I haven't a clue as to what I am doing. But once again, her ability to take the lead gives me the breath I've not been able to catch since the accident.

"Fine. No vacation," she mumbles, but she doesn't seem convinced.

"Speaking of budgets." I pull an envelope out of my inside suit pocket. "I was going to give this to you tonight. This is a credit card in your name for you to use for anything the girls need. You will also be given an envelope with cash in it at the beginning of each week. You will use this money to handle school functions, field trips, lunch money, etcetera. Please make an attempt to budget appropriately. If you need more, you are to let me know. You will be meeting with John tomorrow. He will make sure you are up to speed on the girls' security."

"Why are you smiling?" I ask Finn, who has been quietly watching our conversation.

"I'd rather think it was obvious, my brother and my girl getting along."

"I hate to tell you brother, Samantha's not your girl anymore. She works for me now. She's mine." I point out to get a rise out of him. When he looks to Sam for support, she simply shrugs her shoulders with a "he speaks the truth" expression on her lovely face.

Finn turns his shocked look from her to me then to his food, where he mumbles something unintelligible. Samantha smiles and winks at me, equally amused with our ability to tease my brother.

I like it. More than I should.

Samantha and Finn talk about what classes she is taking. Apparently, she was enrolled at NYU several years ago, so it was a natural selection when she decided she wanted to finish her courses.

"When is Camilla back from holiday?" Finn asks. He keeps the disdain for my fiancée out of his voice. Just barely.

"She's back tomorrow, after the last show in Paris."

"How much did this trip cost you?"

"None of your concern, and I would ask you not to use that tone."

"Fine," he mumbles.

"That reminds me, Samantha. I'll need you to take a different night off this week. Camilla will be back, and I would like to take her to dinner on Thursday."

"That's lovely. But no."

"I'm sorry?"

"No. I'm not changing my night off."

"May I have a coffee to enjoy the show with please?" Finn asks the waiter as he passes by.

"So, you can't change your night off?"

"I can't because I won't."

"Samantha, let me explain some—"

"Walt. You said yourself, no amendments. Thursday is my night off. I wanted Fridays, but you said, no, it had to be Thursdays."

I take a deep breath and try to calm the beast inside.

"Samantha, would you please change your night off with me this week? I promise not to make it a habit."

"Thank you for asking," she replies with a genuine smile. I do realize now that I didn't ask at first, and the decent thing would have been to give her the choice.

"Thank you for accommodating."

"Oh, I'm not. I'm just thanking you for asking. Take the girls with you."

"Pardon me?"

"Take the girls with you to dinner. Camilla's been gone a few weeks. I'm sure the girls will be excited to see her."

"That would be a no," Finn mumbles behind his coffee cup.

"Finn, shut it." But it's too late.

"Camilla and the girls need to spend time together," Samantha frowns.

"Enough!" I say louder than necessary based on the heads that turn and the protective stance Finn dawns in an instant.

"Enough. Forty-eight hours with these girls doesn't make you an expert."

"I know more than you realize."

"Jesus. What is it with you? You're a nanny for fuck's sake. And an annoying one at that. Be a nanny. Christ, I didn't hire you to rearrange our lives. You know nothing about how we make it day to day."

"I do. And like it or not, I have come to know you while I worked with your brother. Which is how I know that you are trying to divert me into an argument by referring to me as 'just a nanny'. Only a fool would look around your life and think this is all fine. And you're no one's fool."

"Finn, I'll see you back at the office." I stand to leave.

"You need to be the one to tell the girls tonight they don't have to finish summer school." Fuck me, she never quits.

"You can tell them," I answer, dropping cash on the table.

"No. This is good news; it needs to come from you."

chapter four

I didn't see Finn again after we returned to the office. And maybe it makes me an arse, but I purposefully skipped a couple of meetings, so I wouldn't have to. I didn't have the stomach for a lecture on what a dick I was to Samantha. I already know that I was, but she's just so…right. And it's annoying as fuck.

What's more is she's not even saying it in a condescending or condemnatory way. It's more like she understands the path we are traveling. And maybe she does. She's the first person to talk to me about what is best for the girls. The guys just want to support me, but she's right, I can handle the business side of things. With the girls, I'm drowning.

The door dings and I step off the lift and into my apartment, exhaling from exhaustion. I'm hit by a cacophony of music and laughter coming from the apartment. Rounding the corner to the living area, I see Samantha and Finn at the island laughing and cooking with the girls.

"There he is," Finn says, flashing his megawatt smile. "Just in time to show them how to flip the pancakes."

"Finn says you're the best," Poppy exclaims.

"He is, Pops. He taught me when I was your age." Finn glances over the bar at me and winks. The wink is my brother's apology, a sign that he's with me in this. And damn if I don't need that more than I even knew. "Go change, we'll wait."

On my way to the bedroom, I can't help but notice that my steps feel lighter than they've been in weeks.

"I'm sorry if I pushed too hard today," Samantha says from behind me as I drop my suitcoat on the bed.

"It's fine," I answer, loosening the tie from my neck.

"For the record, I think you're remarkable."

"What?" I turn toward her, confused by her words.

"I think you're remarkable. You have a ways to go and that is to be expected, but you suit up every day. You haven't left these girls. Not everyone would have done that. It also occurs to me that I haven't said I was sorry that you lost your friend. I know you haven't had time to process the grief, but I under-stand what it's like to lose someone you love."

"Thank you," I nod. That's nice to hear, especially, strange-ly, coming from her.

"But I'm still not changing my night," she smiles a shit eat-ing grin and leaves before she can gain the satisfaction of my laughter.

I emerge from the bedroom having taken a cue on my attire from the others. Finn is in shorts and a T-shirt, the girls are in pajamas, and Sam has on Finn's joggers again. Only they are no longer rolled up, but cut off.

"She cut off your lucky joggers." I look at Finn aghast.

"Ugh. Please tell me you don't call these your lucky jog-gers for the reason I think you do." Sam makes a fake gagging noise as she pours herself a glass of cranberry juice.

"Yes. My team always won when I wore them." He winks at her. Poppy is youthfully oblivious and an actual giggle es-capes Zinnie. Another first.

"And by team you aren't referring to your double-O-and-seven, are you?"

"Sam." Zinnie laughs and nudges her with an elbow. She's getting to sit at the adult's table for once and she's clearly en-joying it.

"What?" Sam feigns ignorance. "I'll have you know your Uncle Finn has quite the way with the boys."

"Mary Poppins speaks the truth," Finn says, handing the skillet to me before shifting away from the stove.

"You like boys?" Poppy suddenly looks up from her doll and zeros her big browns on Finn.

"I do."

"Like my daddy liked my mommy?"

"That's right."

She shrugs. "I like boys and I like girls."

"You can like anyone you want sweetheart," Finn says, kissing her on her head.

"Remind me again. What are we making?" I ask.

"Panacakes!" Poppy shouts.

"Yes, but what kind? Chocolate chip? Blueberry? Mickey Mouse?"

"You can do Mickey Mouse panacakes?" Poppy asks in a disbelieving whisper, suddenly very serious.

I lean over the island and flash her with a smile. "I can."

Sam laughs when Poppy looks to her to see if I am telling the truth. Poppy stands in her chair to peer over the island and while Finn holds her in place, we all decide blueberry Mickey Mouse pancakes are the menu tonight.

I make a large stack of what, for the most part, resemble Mickeys. There are one or two rogue pancakes that bear more of a resemblance to a blob than a Mickey, but I happily put those on my plate. Poppy pulls a chair around and helps me flip the last ones, eagerly watching as they fly in the air and land on the griddle.

"More serup please!"

"Syrup," Sam corrects. "And just a little more." She helps her pour an acceptable amount.

"These are better than Mommy's," Poppy says.

"That's because Mom couldn't cook. Remember when she would make lasagna, Pops?"

"Yuck." Poppy scrunches up her nose. "It was horrid."

"She uses the word horrid, but pancakes have an extra vowel?" Finn chuckles.

"Jenny couldn't cook?" I ask Zinnie. It's the first time I've said their mother's name.

"No. She tried. Even took lessons," she laughs.

"Why is that funny?"

"Because she got an F."

"She was that bad, huh?"

"No, you don't understand. This wasn't a class that gave grades, but the teacher told Mom her cooking was so bad, she had to give her an F in hopes it would keep her from ever cooking again."

"All these years, I never knew Jenny couldn't cook."

"Nope. So, if yours are edible, you're ahead of the curve," Zinnie says, picking up her phone to answer a text. Before she can, Samantha has removed it and placed it under her thigh, earning her an eye-roll.

I use the opportunity to tell the girls they have the option to stay home for the summer and not finish summer school. I scarcely have the words out of my mouth before they both choose to stay home and Poppy cheers in delight.

"Guess it's settled." I mumble through a mouthful of pancakes.

"Poppy, carry your dishes to the sink please," Samantha tells her. "Since you and Walt cooked, Finn and Zinn will help me clean."

Finn rolls his eyes at Zinnie who stands grabbing her plate.

"Let's go old-man. I've got chats to snap."

"Ugh. Less with the old man talk." Finn grabs his chest like he's in pain.

Sam turns to me and says, "I gave Poppy her bath when she got home from school. If you want to read her a book, I'll come in and say goodnight in a minute."

Read her a book? Is that something I should have been doing I wonder.

"Yes, Walt, read to me." Poppy grabs my hand, and I'm staggered by the genuine happiness I see on her sweet face.

"Alright, but I get to pick the book," I say.

She cuts her eyes at me, and nods her head. "Okaaay," she says cautiously and with a hint of suspicion.

"Say goodnight to your sister and Finn."

Poppy follows Samantha's orders and hugs Finn, giving him a kiss before hugging her sister goodnight. And just like that, we're off to her room to read.

I choose a book about a princess with pants from a box that we brought over from her old house. I've seen her with this one a lot, so I assume it's a favorite. I've just cracked the spine when Sam walks in.

"Goodnight, ladybug. I love you." Sam gives her a kiss and hug.

"Will you lay with me while Walt reads?" Poppy asks in a manner that I already know Sam can't refuse. I know because I wouldn't be able to. She looks to me and I shrug. "I can read to two as easily as I can read to one."

"Okay, but just for a minute," Sam whispers loudly and climbs over Poppy so she's behind her. Poppy thoughtfully shares her pillow before she wiggles into Sam and pulls her arm around her and Edward.

Fifteen minutes later, I have two sleeping beauties on my hands as I read the end of the book to myself. I watch their synchronized breathing. I haven't been very fair to Samantha. I seem to falsely judge her at every turn, but the woman can be infuriating. She never stops pushing when it comes to the girls. She's so vested and it's only been a couple of days. I don't understand.

I place my hands on each side of them and bend over and give Poppy a kiss on her cheek, close to her ear. The tip of my nose rubs Sam's jawline, and without thinking I leave a kiss on her temple. She smells divine, like syrup and soap. She has on no makeup. Her eyelashes are fanned across her cheeks and her lips are parted ever so slightly. I stand there longer than necessary, appreciating her features.

Pulling myself together, I head back to the kitchen where Finn is putting the last dish in the cabinet and Zinnie is wiping down the counter.

"So, what did she say after that?" Finn asks.

"She said she was just kidding, and tried to blow it off like she wasn't being serious."

"That's the worst," Finn says. "I hate it when people wrap an insult into a joke. Everyone knows they meant it."

"I know, right?" Zinnie agrees.

"Who are you talking about?" I ask, grabbing two beers out of the fridge, handing Finn one.

"Becky."

"Ugh." I feign disgust and an eye-roll. "It's always a Becky." I say, pretending I know what they're talking about. I'm rewarded with a laugh from my brother and from Zinnie.

"Still early. Anything you need to do?" I ask her.

"No. I think I'll go to my room and talk to some of my friends."

"Alright." *Just do it, for Christ's sake. You've battled giants in the financial world. Just fucking do it.* I walk to her, wrap her in a hug, and kiss the top of her head. "Good night. I'll be in my office if you need me."

"Okay," she says after a bit of a delay. I've weirded her out.

"See. That wasn't so hard," Finn says, clinking his beer to mine once she's left the room.

"Fuck off. Want to shoot some pool?" I ask.

The game room is on the opposite end of the apartment from the girls' bedrooms, so we can play without disturbing anyone. "I've missed you," he says, rolling a ball to the center of the table.

"Since when did you become soft? I've been here the whole time."

"Your wrapper," he points to my body, "has been here the whole time, but your insides haven't been. I can't remember the last time we played pool, or spent five minutes in a room together where the conversation wasn't centered around work."

"It hasn't been that bad," I scoff.

"It has really. I'm just saying tonight felt good. It felt… right. There was never a question in my mind as to why Everett chose you."

"Well that makes one of us, because I wonder every day what that bloke was thinking."

"You forget, I know what he was thinking. You're the best big brother anyone could ask for. I knew you had what it takes to make this work, but I was never more certain of it than tonight."

I have to give credit where credit is due. "That was all Samantha."

He stops gathering balls and gives me a strange look.

"What?" I ask. He doesn't say anything but just nods and rolls the last ball to the center.

"So, Camilla is back tomorrow?" he asks, but it sounds like more than a casual question.

"She is." If he's not going to speak his mind, I'm not going to offer anything either.

"How would you say she's getting on with the girls?"

"What's your point, Finn?"

"Do you think she understands that the girls are yours now?"

"No. I'm quite certain she thinks I ordered them out of a catalog and can send them back when I'm finished."

"You mock, but I'm not sure you are too far from the truth."

"Finn."

"I'm just saying, now that you have some real help with the girls, maybe you can concentrate on Camilla. Make sure you are on the same page."

"Cut her some slack will you? Neither of us wanted kids. We're both figuring this out."

A knock at the door draws our attention from the conversation at hand.

"I just checked on Zinnie. She's online with some friends.

Poppy's asleep. Are you in for the evening?" Samantha asks me.

"I am. I plan on working from the study tonight."

"Then I'm going to head home. I have some packing to do. My goal is to move in Thursday night."

"I thought you couldn't switch with me."

"Not couldn't, wouldn't."

I roll my eyes at Finn. She starts rattling off something about amendments.

"Fine. Fine. Fine. I get it." I break the balls with more force then necessary.

"Before I go..." She walks over to the side of the table, placing herself directly between Finn and me who are standing on opposite ends. She puts both hands on the table and leans forward as though she were an Army general about to negotiate a difficult treaty.

"This ought to be splendid," Finn snickers.

"Do I have a title?"

"Do you need a title?" I ask her.

"I'm just curious how you see my role here. If you have a title for me, it will give me, us, clearer boundaries, a way to manage expectations."

"Nanny."

"I don't think that fits." *Of course, she doesn't.* "No."

"Au pair?"

"No."

"Well, you can't be a governess. You don't have a degree from uni."

It's a pompous, dick move, and I want to retrieve the words as they come out of my mouth. Fuck. Have I always been such a snob?

"I think we've established that already," she says with a

hint of hurt she's clearly trying to hide.

"What about 'Family Manager'?" Finn offers. Sam smiles like he hung the moon and I hide my fake gagging reflex with a cough.

"Does that work for you?" I ask her.

"It does."

"Good. Now that that's settled." I bend to take my next shot.

"Now that that's settled," she says, straightening herself. "I believe we are all in agreement that the family consists of you, the girls, and Finn."

"Okaaaay," I say with the same caution Poppy exhibited earlier. I get the feeling I'm being baited into something.

"Here it comes," Finn grins, his hands wrapped around his cue.

"As Family Manager, I will be instituting some changes to the routine in this household."

"Really? Do tell." I stand from my shooting position.

"Starting Monday, Maria will be scheduling your work days to start an hour later."

"And why would she do that?"

"Because you need that time with the girls in the morning, and when school starts you will be alternating between taking Poppy and Zinnie to school."

"Isn't that what I hired you for?"

"No."

"Are you sure about that?"

"Yes."

"These one-word answers aren't really doing it for me."

"Fine. You hired me to manage the family not take your place."

"I also didn't hire you to manage me."

"Yes. You did."

"No. I didn't."

"You aren't managing yourself, and at this point in time, it's having a negative influence on the family. So, until you are in a position to manage yourself again, it falls under the purview of the Family Manager."

"And there it is," Finn smirks.

"Finn." Samantha and I both grumble at the same time.

"Let's get one thing straight—"

"Yes, let's." She leans against the table. "I take my job very seriously, as Finn can tell you, and you are in desperate need of managing. Maria has done her best, but she can only do so much since her priority is to manage your work agenda."

"Fine, but I don't need the extra hour. I already have the time built in to take the girls to school."

"True, but after you take the girls you will need the hour to come back here and work out."

"What?"

"You heard me. You've stopped working out since the accident. I know because I have access to your schedule. You have a high stress job, with no outlets. You are the girls only living guardian. I can't have you dropping dead at the age of forty from a stress-related heart attack."

I just stare at her like she's an alien creature that has landed in my game room. But she's not intimidated and has no qualms showing it.

"Also—"

"There's more?"

"You need to sit down with the lawyers and determine guardianship of the girls in the event something happens to you."

"Samantha..."

"It's time to start making decisions like these girls are staying. I had Maria schedule a meeting with Pierce for next week. That gives you enough time to decide, but not too much time to overthink it."

"Any other decisions you would like to make for me?" I seethe.

"I'd re-think the tie you wore today, but other than that, not at this moment."

"Go home, Samantha. Before I fire you."

"See you tomorrow, Finn," she says sweetly over her shoulder and leaves.

I survey the room expecting to find debris from the tornado that is Samantha Abbott.

chapter five

"Pivot! Pivot! PIVOT!" A girl with purple hair and tattoos down one arm is yelling over the top of a grass green couch when Quade and I exit the lift. Her attempt to rock the couch from its position, jammed against the door casing, is proving futile. It's Thursday night, and since Samantha is irritatingly off tonight—despite my attempts to coerce her into trading—Quade and I moved our meeting to the apartment, so I can keep an eye on the girls.

Zinnie would have begrudgingly watched her for me, but each time I have to ask, which is often, I feel slightly evaluated by her. I can almost hear the words in her head, "Well, I never had to watch her *before*."

I've been having this reoccurring nightmare that the girls and I are in a room that is filling with water. It reaches our ankles; the girls are watching me. It's to our necks in no time at all, and their eyes beg me to save them. But I'm motionless. I can't get my mind to search for a way out. So, I sit and pretend the water isn't rising, pretend we aren't about to drown. I convince myself that if I can get through one more day before the water is over our heads, I might find a way to safety.

There's some fairly intense laughter veiled from the other end of the couch. One person cackles, the other wheezes like a person in an emphysema commercial.

"You have to stop. I'm going to pee myself," gasps a familiar voice.

"Oh my God, stop before she pees on me!" says one less familiar.

"Pivot!" the purple girl yells with a bright smile on her face.

"I'm peeing!" The other end of the couch drops, and a blur runs into the other room.

"You have to stop," the unidentified voice directs from the dropped end. "You know she pees every time we carry something heavy."

"That's because someone always ends up hurt and you know that makes me laugh!" Sam says, coming out of the bathroom, still tugging her shorts up.

"Please on all that is holy, do not urinate on my rug," I say, unamused by the scene enfolding in front of me.

"Jesus Christ!" The purple haired girl drops her end. "Fuck!" she swears when it lands on her foot. She dramatically falls to the floor, pulling her toes as close to her body as she can get.

"See!" Sam giggles, laughing uncontrollably at her friend's demise, running back to the bathroom.

"You must be Walt." The tattooed arm shoots up from her prone position on the floor, offering me her hand. "I'm Zoe."

"Nice to meet you, Zoe. I hope your foot isn't injured."

"She's fine. I'm Grace." A red-headed beauty leans over the couch to reach for my hand.

"Ladies, I'd ask you to mind your language while in front

of the girls please."

"The girls aren't here," Sam says as she reenters the room.

"What?" I ask with more agitation than is probably warranted. I'm certain I didn't hear her correctly.

"Charlotte took them with her to pick up the pizza."

"I'm sorry, what?"

"Charlotte took—"

"I understood that part. What I'm perplexed about is why *you* are feeding the girls. *You* are off tonight. Wouldn't trade with me tonight because *you* are off tonight. I cancelled my plans because *you* were off tonight."

"By chance are *you* off tonight?" Zoe asks Sam.

"Slow your roll. I am off tonight. I promised my girls pizza as payment for helping me move. Zinnie and Pops were just hanging out, so they asked if they could go. I didn't think you would mind."

"You didn't think I would mind?"

"Is this a game you two play?" Zoe asks, her eyes darting between us.

"Move your sweet ass and let me in here," Quade says stepping up to the end of the couch, moving Zoe out of the way. "While I appreciate your 'Ross' routine, it appears you girls could use some help."

"Hey, Quade," Sam sings.

"You're Quade?" Zoe and Grace ask at the same time.

"Been telling the girls about me?" Quade's teeth stretch the width of his face.

"You know it," Sam winks. "Help me get this couch in here and I'll share my slice with you."

"How about a kiss instead?"

"Quade," Finn growls, walking up behind us.

"No? A slap on the ass?"

"Just go to the other end, arsehat." Finn shoves him out of the way and Quade crawls army style under the stuck sofa.

"Thanks, Finn."

"You're welcome, Grace. You guys are bringing it in at the wrong angle."

"Why are you even bringing this—" I motion to what appears to be a couch from an old 70's sitcom—"in here. There's a perfectly fine ten-thousand-dollar couch already in here."

"Not anymore. I had it moved to storage."

"You had it moved to storage?" I immediately hold my palm up to Zoe, when I see her about to speak.

"I had it moved to storage. I wanted Bessie."

"You named your couch Bessie?" Quade says as he and Finn slide it through the door.

"Bessie has seen a lot. I love Bessie." Sam plops down on the couch and affectionately runs her hand along the back. She's wearing jean cut-off shorts and a man's white undershirt. Her hair is held back by a polka dot headscarf that covers her blond hair. Quade plops down next to her and rests his hand on her thigh.

"She has good bones," he says as Finn slaps his hands away.

"Quade and I moved our meeting here, so I could look after the girls." I attempt to bring us back to my point. My point is that I have been inconvenienced when in fact she planned to be here all along.

"Samantha?" Grace says nodding her head in my direction.

"Right," Sam says looking up from two pictures she's holding in her hands. "I know Zinnie will be happy she doesn't have to look after Pops. There's plenty of pizza coming if you guys haven't eaten."

"Sweet." Quade stands and asks if there is anything else he can help move before the pizza gets here. Despite my protest for a delayed meeting, thirty minutes later he and Finn have moved a couple dozen boxes off the freight lift into the nanny's quarters.

"Pizza's here!" Poppy's voice rings down the hallway.

"We're coming," Sam yells back, dusting a lamp before finding a place for it on the side table.

"Could we please refrain from shouting? We're not barn animals."

"You should let me give you a massage. I could work on your chakras. Relax you. Help you see through your third eye," Zoe says, rubbing my shoulders.

"Samantha," I implore through gritted teeth.

"Zoe, stop touching Walt," she instructs, not even glancing this direction. "But you ought to let her. She's an awesome masseuse."

"Thank you, but I see just fine out of my regular two eyes."

"I got pepperoni for you," Poppy says, having materialized next to me and taking my hand. Her soft brown curls bounce as she pulls me to the kitchen, where there are five large pizzas spread out on the island.

"How many people are you expecting?" Finn asks, folding a slice of veggie in half and taking a bite.

"We'll snack on them all night while we unpack," a dark-haired girl answers. She's striking. Her skin is pale, her eyes are slate gray, and her hair is black as coal. "I'm Charlotte." She offers her hand before taking her place next to Zoe. The four girls are standing on the opposite side of the island next to each other, each as unique as the next.

"So, Zinnie," Zoe says, taking her plate to the table. "Tell me about this girl Becky."

"Ooh," Charlotte says with a bite of pizza in her mouth. "Does she have good hair?"

All the girls stop and look at her.

"What? That was perfect timing and you know it," she insists, popping open a Diet Coke.

Zinnie tells the story she told Finn the other night. Poppy sits in Grace's lap and listens intently, pretending she understands what's going on.

"So how did you handle it?" Grace asks.

"I told Becky we weren't friends anymore."

"What? Why?" Zoe asks.

"That's what Finn said I should do."

Four heads turn at once to Finn, who stops mid bite. "What?"

"Why would you tell her that?" Sam asks.

"Because she doesn't need friends like Becky. And she needs to know she can stand up for herself." He cautiously begins to chew, looking to the others for affirmation.

"Did you hear Becky say it?" Sam asks her.

"No, Jake told me."

"The same Jake that Becky also said hit on her? The same Jake that hit on you?"

"The problem isn't Becky. It's Jake," Zoe says.

"Finn's right that you should always stick up for yourself, but I agree with Zoe. It sounds like Jake is spreading rumors to cover his tracks."

"That little prick. If he spreads a rumor involving you, you come see me," Finn says. Zinnie seems genuinely pleased by his protectiveness.

"Language," Sam reminds Finn.

"Alright, chicas. We have a long night ahead of us." Zoe stretches before standing and looking to Zinnie and Poppy.

"I'll see you cats in the morning. You can show me some ideas for your rooms, so I can draw up some plans."

"That reminds me," Sam says, grabbing a slice of all-meat to take with her. "Zoe is the designer I hired to help me with the girls' rooms."

"I beg your pardon?"

All the heads in the room turn to see Camilla standing at the entrance.

"Camilla." I walk over to her, bending for a kiss. She tips her head slightly so that my lips fall to the side of hers.

"My lipstick hasn't set yet," she says quietly. She's fresh from the runway shows in Paris and looks stunning.

"You remember Finn's PA, Samantha. She was leaving him to go back to school, so I hired her to be the girls' nanny."

"Family Manager," Quade quips, going quiet when I glare at him.

"What happened to the governess from Willingham?"

"She left."

"I see," Camilla says. "I can call them in the morning and attempt to convince them to send someone else. Zinnia, darling, you must give this next one a chance. I don't know how many more opportunities they will afford us, but I have some connections I can work on."

"Actually, Samantha is full-time. We're going to try her for a while," I say cautiously, trying to get a read on my fiancée. She doesn't seem pleased.

"Lovely," Camilla says.

"Alright ladies, let's go," Samantha says to her group.

"Can I help?" Poppy asks.

"Pops, it's Samantha's night off. Give me a few minutes to meet with Quade and then we can read a book, alright?"

"Alright," she says, looking like someone stole her Edward.

"I thought we were having dinner tonight? The Steins are meeting us there," Camilla reminds me.

"I can't. I have the girls tonight. I rang you this morning and left you a message."

"Go. The girls can hang with me and Quade," Finn says, and there's an unexpected oddness that settles in my chest. Disappointment.

"It's settled then," Camilla smiles, but it doesn't reach her eyes.

"Cheers," Finn answers the foyer phone. "Thank you," he says before hanging up. I raise a brow in his direction.

"Oh, the front desk is sending—" The lift dings and a man I don't recognize steps into the foyer, stopping in mid-stride when he notices a growing number of people are observing him.

"Hello?" he says with apprehension.

"Jake!" Sam's face lights up as she bounces across the room, leaping onto the man. He catches her with ease, lifting her a few inches off the floor to plant a swift kiss firmly on her lips.

"Hey, baby." He smiles and kisses the tip of her nose before setting her back on her feet.

"Hey, man." Finn shakes his hand.

"Finn," Jake says, then looks back to Sam. "I thought your last day was yesterday? I was surprised when you said to meet you here."

"It was. I'm working for Walt now." She makes the introductions, and when I shake his hand, I immediately know I don't like this guy. Reading people is an integral tool to my success. Quade's, too, and he's clearly on the same page as I am.

"Working for Walt?" Jake asks.

"Come help us unpack and Sam can fill you in," Grace

says, breaking the uncomfortable tension billowing in the room.

"Let's go, girls," Finn says to Poppy and Zinnie. "There's some gelato at Eataly calling our names."

Quade, Finn, and the girls catch the lift down, while Samantha and her group move to the nanny's quarters leaving Camilla and me alone.

"How do you expect the girls to get into the best schools if they don't have the proper upbringing?" Camilla asks.

"They will have the proper upbringing."

"With an American girl who hasn't finished courses? I thought we agreed the goal was to prepare the girls for St. Mary's?"

"Camilla, I don't know that a boarding school is what's best for them. They've already lost their parents. With their age difference, they will be on different campuses. I don't think separating the girls is the wisest decision."

"A few years apart is a small price to pay to ensure they are socialized in the best circles. Just think about it darling," she says on our way down to the car. "Besides, they make it fine through the day currently and they are in different schools."

I know this is going to be a fight, and I really don't feel like fighting.

"What?" she asks, sensing there is more to be said.

"I'm allowing the girls to stay home the remainder of the summer."

"Why would you do that?"

"Sam and Finn both felt like—"

"Samantha and Finn are not their guardians. You are. A good guardian can see what's best for them, even when it's difficult."

"That's what I'm trying to do, Camilla. I'm doing the

best I can," I say, hoping for a little encouragement. A little understanding.

"I'm not sure you are. If you were doing your best, the girls would be in boarding schools in London. Not in the States being looked after by a girl whose parents thought it was appropriate to give her a boy's name. They must have been friends with Everett's Jenny. Lord knows that woman had no upbringing. Who names their children after flowers?"

I sense this isn't the time to point out Camellia is pretty fucking close to Camilla, so I don't.

"Camilla, please tell me you never speak about their mother in that manner in front of the girls."

"Of course not, dear. What's done is done. We can't change their names at this age."

Her comment stops me dead in my tracks. She's not suggesting…

"Oh, there they are." She smiles for the Steins, and I pray to any god who will answer that dinner goes by quickly. But the gods are pissed at me and dinner is as boring as I anticipated. By the time we are back in the car, I couldn't be more ready to be home.

"I have an appointment to get fitted for my dress in the morning," she says when the car comes to a stop, "so I can't stay, but I thought I would come up since I've been away a few weeks."

"That sounds perfect." I open the door and hold my hand out for her. She slides out of the car as if exiting a stage, and people near on the street take notice. She nods and smiles as if she is the most approachable person they might encounter. The porter greets her, and she gives a polite nod in his direction, calling him a name that isn't his. I'm just pushing the button to the lift when the doors open and Quade and Sam's friends step off.

"Leaving?" I ask with an arched brow. Leave it to Quade.

"We're going to pick up a few supplies for Sam. We'll be back in about thirty minutes," he says happier than a lark. "Finn took the girls to his place to watch a movie. Pops fell asleep about an hour ago, so they are spending the night with him. Need anything?"

"No. Thank you," I say from inside the car.

The lift doors close and I move to kiss Camilla.

"We're almost home. Just wait, darling," she says, scrolling through a society page on her mobile.

"His name is Vinnie," I say with exhaustion in my voice.

"What?"

"The porter you greeted as Ralph, his name is Vinnie."

"What does it matter? He's the help."

The lift opens, and the apartment is quiet. Quiet enough that I can hear music coming from Sam's quarters.

"I trust you will let her know that is not acceptable?" Camilla says over her shoulder. I follow her down the hallway to my master wing.

"Certainly," I placate. I really could give a rat's arse about a little music.

"I need about twenty minutes," she says, entering my room.

I sit on the edge of the bed and remove my tie and suit-coat. "I'll just pop down to Finn's and see about the girls."

"Fine," Camilla says from the closet.

I decide to stop into Sam's room to ask her to lower the music and to remind her guests are allowed in her quarters, but not about the house as they please. Unbuttoning my shirt cuffs, I come to a stop just outside her door when I hear her. Jake is still here, and from this angle I can see his arms around

Sam. She's laughing as he kisses his way down her throat.

"They'll be back in ten minutes," she moans.

"Good. I only need three. I haven't seen you in forever."

"It's only been four days."

"Like I said, forever."

"We have to be fast," Sam says breathlessly as Jake turns her to the wall. He pins her wrists in his hand while his free hand pushes her shorts down her thighs.

"Fuck me, you're ready," he says when his hand finds its prize.

"God, yes."

He lifts his shirt and his dick is already sheathed. Sam's T-shirt hangs over her body, but he raises it slightly, so he can guide his way inside her. I'm out of their line of sight, but I can see the curve of her backside. Her moans confirm that he's found what he was looking for. There's no foreplay. No preparation. Just fucking against the wall, and even though it's wrong, I can't pull myself away from watching her face—cheek pressed against the plaster—as he pleasures himself by way of her body.

"You like this, don't you?" His hand snakes under her hair wrap and pulls her head back, allowing him better access to her jaw. "I asked you a question."

"Yes," she answers breathlessly, her arms still pinned above her.

"Yes, what?"

"Yes, I like it."

"I like it, too," he says before running his tongue along her jaw.

His body slaps against hers, the sound echoing off the bare walls and his free hand moves from her hip to her wrists. He pounds hard into her several times before releasing one of her arms.

"Get there Sam, we're on the clock. Touch yourself."

She does as she's told, her fingers moving down her body. I can't see them, but I'm aware the minute she touches herself by the look of pleasure on her face.

"Fuck yes." He releases her other arm, so he can grip her hips with both hands.

"Get there, dammit," he says between clenched teeth.

"I'm almost, almost..." she cries out in pleasure, shuddering as her release flows through her. Jake picks up his pace and slams into her one last time before unleashing a string of expletives, his body falling against hers.

"Talk about wham-bam-thank-you-ma'am," Sam giggles, and it pulls me out of my reverie. My hand is massaging my trousers-covered cock. I back out of there as quietly as I came and close my bedroom door behind me.

"I was thinking," Camilla says, removing an earring before I lift her against the wall, plunging my tongue into her mouth. She whimpers and when I let her up for air she demands to know what I'm doing.

"I missed you," I answer, but even as I say it, I realize it's not true, but she's grinding her sex against mine, so I store that thought away for a later day when I have time to evaluate what that might mean.

Setting her on her feet I turn her to the wall and pull her nightgown up her body exposing her arse. Her body is tight and flawless with no curves to be found. I palm her breasts and she shimmies her slender backside against me.

"Bed," she hums.

"Here," I tell her, rolling a condom down my length.

"No." She maneuvers to face me. "I'm not some whore you picked up on the street. We're not fucking against a wall.

Especially not when you're still dressed."

I bristle irrationally when she unknowingly refers to Sam as a whore. My breathing deflates, along with my dick, as my forehead thumps against the wall.

"Walt?" Camilla calls from the other room. I don't answer but take the time to remove my clothes, willing my dick to harden again. I don't want to have this conversation right now.

By the time I'm on the bed, my libido is napping like it just had a margarita under a palm tree. I kiss down her body hoping it will ignite the fire, but it's no use. By the time my mouth closes over her pussy, I know. It's not happening.

Another twenty minutes passes before Camilla finally comes on my tongue, and when I move up to kiss her, she wraps her hand around me. I know there is no chance she is going to blow me. Her lips haven't touched around my cock since she had that extra glass of wine a week after we started dating.

"Come on, darling. You can do it." Camilla's inert tone threatens to keep my orgasm at bay. My displeasure at the inevitable conversation if I don't come shamefully propels me to close my eyes and remember Samantha's moans, the curve of her back, the way her body shook when she came. And just like that I'm hard. A minute later, I come.

chapter six

I close my eyes to it all. The late hours I've been keeping every night to take care of work and the girls. All this change Samantha has created with her moving and rearranging my life. My rising irritation with my fiancée, especially since it's not her fault. She is nothing if not transparent about how she feels. She isn't the one who's changed. I am.

"I'll call you after my fitting tomorrow. We can make plans for the weekend. The girls are still going to their grandparents for the gala?"

"They are," I answer, eyes still closed.

"Don't be lazy, darling. Walk me to the elevator." She waits at the door while I wash up and throw on a pair of joggers that sit low on my hips. Her eyes see nothing. No glances at my body. No finger that lightly caresses the low crevice on my hips. I open the door and a moment later the lift stops on Finn's floor. I exit, she stays, the door closes behind me.

Finn and Zinnie are playing a card game in the living room.

"Poppy?"

"Blue room," Zinnie answers without looking up from her game. Her hand slaps at the stack of cards on the table and she declares "war".

A sliver of light shines onto Poppy's face when I open the door. She's sleeping on her back, Edward given the prime real estate next to her heart.

Squatting down, I push curls off her face and my hand slides down to cup her cheek. In an unaware sleep, she nuzzles my hand. My heart feels like it's going to explode. This child. She's had so much heartache at such a young age. I wonder what she makes of it all. Her breath has a slight rasp to it, the remnants of her cold.

This is the first time I've touched her like this and I wonder why that is. I've spent many nights staring at the girls from their doorways while they slept, trying to burrow my way into their heads to figure out what it is that I'm not giving them. A peek into how to do this better. Maybe Camilla is right. Maybe the girls would be better off in a place where there are other girls their age, and they have people looking out for them that know more than I do. Just as quickly as the voices come, they leave when Poppy rolls on her side and pulls my hand to her chest where Edward once was.

And I feel it. Her heartbeat. I move to my knees to get into a comfortable position and sit there until mine syncs with hers. I kiss her forehead, thanking her for the encouragement.

"I was just about to send a search party out for you," Finn says, knocking the deck of cards against the table, evening them up before sliding them back in the box.

"I sat with Poppy for a while. Wanted to make sure she wasn't having any problems left over from her cold."

He nods; he knows I'm full of shit.

"Where's Zinnie?" I ask.

"She went to bed. Had a call to take." He adds air quotes to the last part. "Camilla coming down?"

"She left. Had an early appointment."

"Are you sure…"

"Don't." I cut him off. "I can't right now."

"Okay," he says with kindness in his eyes that frustrates me.

"I'm going upstairs. Call if the girls need anything."

"They won't. Quade says he and the rest of the Ox Five were going out for a drink. You should go. Meet up with them."

"I'm rather exhausted."

"It would be good for you. I've got the girls. You can go without worry." He studies me. I know he wants to say more, but he's holding back.

"Thanks, but no."

I take the stairs up to my place, entering through the back entrance. The door to Sam's room is closed and there's no light coming from underneath. I groan at the thought of what she might be doing in there.

"Fuck it," I say to no one as I stand in an empty apartment. Alone.

Fifteen minutes later, I'm dressed in jeans and a black T-shirt headed out to meet my boys. Pierce responded within a minute, letting me know they were at Hush, the hottest club in town. I'm a bit underdressed, but I don't give a fuck.

The night is warm and seeing as I am in an unusual mood, I lower the car window and watch the city and people around me fly by. I love London, it will always be my first love, but this city has something, too. It pulls at me. The excitement. The hardness. I watch tourists stopping to take their picture in front of the New York Public Library. People frustrated trying to get around them. People running to catch the bus. Storefronts still open. This city is alive no matter what time you step out your door.

My driver drops me off and, as expected, the bouncers open the roped entrance before I've even stepped onto the sidewalk.

A gentleman in an expensive suit greets me. "Mr. Nelson, your party is in the Penthouse." I nod and the security men around him clear a path, guaranteeing me access to our roped off area with ease.

The music thumps around me and the day melts off. This is what I need, drinks with my boys. I'd find someone to dance and blow off some steam, but I know a picture would end up in the paper tomorrow and Camilla would flip her shit.

"Tell me it's true. Are you really here?" Colin stands, pulling me into a hug that comes close to cracking my ribs. "Missed you," he says in my ear over the music.

I return the hug and give a handshake to the others. The last time the four of us were together in a club was the night Everett was killed.

"I understand we have a meeting," Pierce says. When it's clear I don't understand, he reminds me Samantha set it up to discuss the girls.

"Don't remind me. I'll probably cancel."

"No, you won't," he says, suddenly serious. "You should have done this the day you found out. We will meet and get this taken care of." And that's it. No more discussion. When Pierce speaks, everyone listens.

"I thought you would be helping the girls unpack," I say to

Quade who downs the last of his beer.

"Nope. I talked them into coming."

"What? Tell me you're joking."

"No. I'm not joking." He attempts a bad English accent.

"Quade, I don't want my work life and my personal life mixed up with each other."

"What the fuck are you talking about? We all work to-gether and we all play together. You've never cared before."

"I mean with Samantha. The waters are already muddied, and I don't need you inviting her to the things we do."

"Pshaw," he says, blowing me off as he finishes the last of his beer and makes his way to the dance floor. I watch after him, hoping the daggers I'm shooting at him will spear him in the back. But I'm not that fortunate. Not anymore anyways.

From our elevated platform, aka the Penthouse, I can see his destination. Samantha and her…squad, posse, whatever the fuck it is, have commandeered the dance floor. And I say commandeered because they are owning it. Every man and, apparently, a few women are watching them. The girls are clus-tered together, oblivious to the onlookers eye-fucking them as their hips swivel and dip, smiling like this is the best time of their lives. Quade muscles his way to them and easily turns his groove on when the girls encircle him, making him their dance bitch. Quade. He's loving life hard and has no qualms about being used. In fact, he looks seconds away from blowing a wad. He tries grinding against Sam's ass, but she laughs and slaps his hands away. She offers him a kiss on his cheek to soft-en the blow of rejection.

I get my first real look at her. She's splendid, and she's not even trying. Her hair is in a ponytail. If she's wearing make-up, it's not visible from this distance. She's wearing a black T-shirt dress that hits just at the top of her thighs. To boot, she's wearing a pair of killer heels.

A blur moves in front of my face. Peirce is waving his hand in an attempt to draw my attention.

"I'm sorry, what?"

"I asked," then he smirks, "how Camilla is."

"She's fine. We're fine. Everything is fine."

"You said that." He laughs then raises a hand to our server for another round.

"I was happy to hear you hired Sam." He waits, but I'm sure as shit not going to make this easy for him. I already know it's going to be painful for me. When he realizes I'm not to be baited, he gives his opinion anyways. That is why he is Pierce.

"I was a week away from stepping in," he says. I think he's watching me for a reaction.

"Be my guest. I completely concede that you would have been the better choice." I raise my drink in a toast to him. The lights move around us, the air cloudy from the mixture of body heat and the cool air from the air conditioning.

"But I wasn't their choice. You were. And you did the best you could for the first few months. Now it's time to do what's right."

"And what would that be exactly?" I raise a brow in defiance, looking for a fight.

"Don't." His voice is low but easily audible over the music. He slides forward in his seat, and locks me in a stare. I'm a tough son-of-a-bitch, but Pierce can be ruthless and we both know I lose when matched against him.

"Don't fucking fuck with me. We all know you are doing your best. Hell, you haven't even grieved the loss of your best friend. You went straight into guardian mode. You did the best you could at the time, but the shock wears off more and more each day and your best is different today than it was four months ago. As it should be. You don't need me to tell you that. So, man the fuck up."

"If everyone knew Sam was the fucking answer, why didn't anyone tell me?"

He closes his eyes for a minute and releases a breath like he's lost all his patience. Colin steps in, sensing he's moments away from pummeling my arse.

"Sam is not the answer. She's just proof that you are starting to make the right decisions."

We both smartly choose to ignore the standoff of silence, neither of us wanting to give into the other, and divert our attention to the scene folding out on the dance floor.

A wall of three very pissed off women stand between Sam and Jake. Sam still visible, but slightly offset, guarded behind their shoulders. She must have said his name, because it's clear the minute he realizes she's here. And instead of remorse or a deer in the headlights guise, he raises his arm and puts it around the girl he was tongue fucking and groping just a moment ago. That stupid fucker.

I stand and watch the scene unfold. It all happens in the matter of seconds, but it plays itself out in slow motion.

Sam nudges herself in front of her girls; they make room and stand shoulder to shoulder with her. It's clear Zoe is giving him a piece of her mind, and he's made the mistake of engaging her. I don't know what he's said, but Pierce has summoned one of his security men when Quade catches his death glare. He turns over his shoulder, murmurs something with the word fuck in it and darts to the girls. But it's too late. In all my days of anticipating an opponent's move, I never would have thought it would be Charlotte. My money was on Zoe. Jake must have made the same mistake, because he never sees the small fist jabbing towards him. The little dark-haired pixie can throw a punch, and, based on her stance, she's been trained to fight.

That's when all hell breaks loose. Jake lunges for her and the girls are on him like ants on sugar. Quade seizes Sam and Grace—one in each arm, their feet flailing about—and it's clear they weren't finished with their quest. Charlotte has been hoisted over Pierce's security guy's shoulder and Zoe is standing, arms crossed, glaring at Jake. Her posture begging him to try something. The bar's security escorts Jake out, who seems none too happy to be the one leaving.

"Put me down!" Charlotte yells over the music before she is righted on her feet. She's a second away from unleashing a piece of her mind on the guard that carried her up here when Pierce yanks her onto the bench, telling her to sit her ass down. Quade has Grace around the waist with Sam following behind who takes a seat next to Colin. I count the girls and look around for the fourth. Zoe is on the dance floor bumping with a woman whose mouth is locked over hers.

"I get dumped and she gets the girl," Sam huffs.

"That girl has been hot for her since we got here. Once Zoe went all badass on Jake, her fate was sealed."

"Zoe is a…" Quade starts.

"Lovely lady licker?" Grace supplies. "Yes," all three girls answer.

"Really?" Quade watches with apt fascination. "That is so fucking hot."

"Quade, no," Sam says, like someone scolding a dog.

"What a dick," Charlotte says, still simmering.

"Forget it." Sam waves her hand and grabs a shot from the tray of a passing waiter. The girls stop and watch her with unsure shock. Sam throws two more back and then stands, shifting her dress into place.

"You girls get some water and cool off. I'll meet you back down there." Sam reaches for a beer to take with her, but Charlotte pulls it back with a glare.

"I think we should go home."

"And I think we should dance," Sam challenges, already on her way to the steps leading down.

Charlotte mumbles to Pierce, "I might need to borrow your security. Let's go get our girl, Gracie." She sets the beer down and stands.

"Let her dance. Might do her some good to blow off some steam," Quade says, tipping his beer back.

"You don't understand. Sam hasn't been drunk since the—"

"Grace." It's a warning and Charlotte's glare shuts her up.

"Thanks for the night fellas," Grace says, extending a fake smile while standing. She and Charlotte trot down the stairs, and Pierce gives a nod to his security to follow them down. We watch men levitate their attention as the girls near the bottom step. Zoe has abandoned her admirer and is focused solely on Sam. By the time the other two arrive, Zoe appears grateful for the backup. The three women surround Sam, who is dancing without a care in the world, but it's clear an argument is brewing. The majority wins and I watch them escort Sam off the floor.

"Is your car out front?" Pierce asks.

"Yep." I already know where he's headed.

"I'll give the women a ride home," I concede, sounding more put out than I am.

I text my driver that I'm ready as I'm ushered out of the club into the night air. Hush's security has Jake on his stomach flat on the ground.

"What happened?" I ask the floor manager escorting me.

He has a wire attached to an earpiece coming out of his collar.

"The gentleman apparently hit a woman."

My eyes immediately jump up looking for Sam, wavering slightly when I see her. She's alright.

"You'll take care of him?" I ask.

"We won't kill him, but he won't raise his hand to a woman again," he growls. Jake is being lifted off the ground, his shirt splotched red from the blood running out of his nose.

"I think he's learned his lesson. Turn him loose." He nods and opens my door. I turn and call for Samantha.

"In. Now," I direct when her sweet face falls on mine.

I expect some pushback for my terseness, but she doesn't give any, nor does she meet my eyes. She makes sure her friends are all safely inside the limo before sliding onto the back seat. I climb in next to her and close the door. No one speaks for several minutes. I take an inventory, and no one appears injured.

"Who did he hit?" I ask, not seeing any physical evidence on the women.

"No one," Sam rolls her eyes. "He's an asshole, but he wasn't going to hit anyone. He just lunged out of anger."

"Don't you fucking defend that asswipe," Zoe bites.

"I'm not. Just stating the facts," Sam responds, never shifting her gaze from the window. Her legs are crossed, and sliding across the seat has caused her dress to slip up her legs. Lacy boy shorts peek out from under her hem. "There was no reason to leave. I'm fine."

"If you were fine, you wouldn't have downed three shots like they were water before reaching for a beer."

"She did what?" Zoe asks Grace. "You haven't done that since—"

"Zoe," Grace interrupts softly.

Traffic is heavy but the air in the limo is heavier. None of the women speak, but they each watch Sam like she might jump out at any minute. Her phone dings and by the time she fishes it out of her purse, it sounds like a pinball machine. She thumbs through the text messages before sliding her phone into her purse.

"Please tell me you are not going to respond to those," Zoe says rather harshly.

Sam doesn't answer, but she momentarily glances in her direction before turning her attention back to the window.

"Sam?"

"She was pretty. Did you get her number?" Sam asks instead.

"She was hot, and no, I didn't. I was out with my girls, not trolling for pussy."

"Could you be anymore vile?" Charlotte pushes Zoe's shoulder.

"Yes. She could be, and please don't say things like that in front of my boss," Sam motions towards me. We pull up to the curb and I climb out first followed by Sam and the group.

Zoe flirts with my porter pulling his tie out of his waist-coat and winking at him. I make apologies for her, and, once we're inside the lift, ask them to behave in a manner befitting of the building. There are a couple of giggles and a comment I'm not able to make out before laughter spreads through the car. I'm the only one not in on the joke.

The door pings open, and by the time they file out of the car, shoes are in their hands, and a couple of them have begun to unfasten their attire.

Twenty minutes later, after I've showered the club off of me, I'm in the kitchen grabbing a slice of pizza when Charlotte appears beside me with a bottle of tequila in her hand.

"Mind if we borrow some glasses? We still need to unpack."

I hand her three glasses.

"One more, please." She reaches out and I hand her one more.

"I thought you said Sam doesn't drink?" I hear myself asking despite my mind telling my mouth to shut it. It's none of my business. Or concern.

"I said she doesn't drink out. She'll drink if she's home or at one of our homes for the night. Goodnight." She effectively ends the conversation.

I watch as she leaves the kitchen. It's weird being in the house without the girls. This is the first night they've slept away since they moved in. I would love to fall into bed and sleep into oblivion, but I have a shit ton of work to catch up on.

The apartment is set up like a starburst. The foyer is the center. Half of the star is the living areas. The other half is a series of wings all branching off of the center. One is the master wing. The other is the kids' wing with a guest suite. The last is the nanny's quarters, home gym, and my office.

The main door to Sam's area is still open when I walk past. The girls are in their pajamas, pouring healthy glasses of tequila, when Sam walks out of her bedroom. She's wearing a shirt that's longer than the dress she had on earlier.

"You're welcome to use the guestrooms if you need to," I offer on the way to my office.

"Thanks, but we're used to sharing a bed. If we get too loud, please let me know." I don't acknowledge that I heard her, instead closing my office door behind me.

I work until exhaustion takes over, and I know if I don't sleep I'll regret it tomorrow. My day is slammed with meetings

that will be difficult enough to stay awake in without the added effect of tiredness.

The lights in Sam's place are still on when I look at my
watch. Three a.m. I reach in to close the door when I see the
bottle of tequila is now nearly empty. I step into her quarters.
Shit. Apparently, all that's needed is a little pent up anger and
some tequila and these girls can get it done.

The nanny's quarters are quaint: a living area, small kitch-
en with an island, and a bedroom with an en-suite bath. Like
the rest of the apartment, there are floor to ceiling windows in
every room.

Sam and her girls have all the boxes unpacked and everything is already in its place. For the first time, this space feels
lived in.

The green couch I didn't approve is against the wall to the
bedroom with a large colorful painting over it. There's something comforting and intriguing about the movement in the
painting. Everywhere you look there's color. But instead of
looking like a crayon box threw up in here, it's tasteful and
looks like it could be a shoot for a magazine. There's a stack of
frames in the corner that no doubt still need a home.

The door to her bedroom is open, with all four inter-
twined and passed out on her queen mattress. Each with a
hand on Sam in some fashion or another, as if to comfort her
in her sleep. I observe each of them. They look like the kind of
girls we would have wanted to hang with when we were in uni.
The kind of girls other guys would have envied you for.

I hit the switch, sending the rooms into darkness before
closing the main door behind me.

The sun rises before I'm ready. I swear the daylight comes sooner and sooner. I stretch my long body under the covers, begrudgingly pulling myself out of bed. You would think I was the one that drank a fifth of tequila.

A shower does nothing to calm my surly attitude and I'm not the best to be around by the time I make it to the kitchen for coffee. Finn and the girls have made their way back up to my apartment, and even though Sam's crew are all in sunnies, they appear to be functioning. The only thing that keeps me from kicking out these women surrounding my kitchen bar is the fact that coffee and breakfast are waiting for me.

"Don't you all have jobs, or do you live off the common people?" I snap.

"We're on our way home, boss man. Don't get your knickers in a wad," Zoe says, picking up a bagel as she stands to leave. "Zinnie and Poppy, I'll be back next week to talk designs. Can't wait to see what you all have in mind." Zinnie and Poppy beam back at her with excitement. "I told Mark to expect your call. He has a couple of guys who have an opening in their schedule to help with minor construction."

"Thanks Zoe," Sam says, picking up her dish and taking it to the kitchen. "Girls, get dressed. We have some shopping to do. Big girls, get to work." She kisses the top of their heads and they say their good-byes on the way to collect their things.

"If you must have overnight guests, I would appreciate it if you feed them in your own space."

"I'm sorry. I haven't had a chance to go to the grocery store. I won't let it happen again," Sam answers, taking it all in stride. Nothing gets under her skin apparently. Even being passed over for a pin-up Barbie that was probably more plastic than human.

"I would also appreciate you keeping nights like last night

to a minimum. This isn't a dormitory." God, I'm a daft prick, but I must infuse some space between us. I need my life with the girls to be separate from my work life and my life with the fellas. "Also, the girls will be with their grandparents this weekend. It was scheduled before you were on staff."

"Alright. That will allow me to get situated before having the girls full time next week. Anything else?" There's an edge to the question, but, still, she doesn't push back as one would expect.

"Not at the moment, you're dismissed," I reply, not looking up. I don't want to see that scowl that is almost certain to be on Finn's face. I'm met with silence and when I do finally glance up, Finn is standing to leave.

"We have a meeting in ten minutes," he says with his back to me, making his way to the stairs. He leaves without waiting for me. Something he never does.

As expected, the morning meetings are difficult at best on the amount of sleep I've had, but for once, I am caught up. Maria rings to tell me my lunch meeting is being held in our private conference room. The guys are here for our monthly meeting. Part of being in charge of Everett's estate is managing the business he owned.

"Are we sure this is what is best for the girls?" Colin asks, looking at stats in front of him before taking a bite of his lunch.

"No, I'm not. But it's an option that needs to be explored," I answer.

"When are you going to be sure?" Quade asks, closing his folder, his steak still untouched.

"Quade," Pierce says.

"Don't 'Quade' me. It needs to be said. Business is business. It's not personal. We all know that. Once you make it personal, mistakes happen. We need to look at this like it's a business we own and take the girls out of the equation."

"It's not that simple," Colin says.

"But it is. Financially, the girls are set for life, with or without Everett's business. So, remove them from the equation. Four of the best business minds are sitting around this table, and you mean to tell me that we don't know if this business is viable nearly five months after we've taken over?"

"I think the girls aren't what's mucking up your equation," Finn offers gently. He doesn't have a say in the business but he's joined us for lunch nonetheless. "It's Everett. He's the one you need to remove."

The weight of his statement sucks the oxygen out of the room, and the air sits heavy around us.

"Meet with Reid Beckett," Pierce says. "He buys businesses that are in jeopardy. He will have a perspective we can leverage right now."

Colin sorts through a few more stats. "The business I'm looking at is not in jeopardy."

"No, but it will be," I answer. "We don't have the time to give it the attention it needs. As far as I know, none of us have the interest to own it. The girls are too young to know if they would want to when they graduate from uni, which is six years for Zinnia, sixteen for Poppy. We either need to fill the CEO position or look at selling."

"Fine. Talk to Beckett. Anything else?"

"No. I'm meeting with Pierce to set up guardianship of the girls if anything were to happen to me."

"It won't, but that's smart," Colin says.

"I think we've all learned that none of us are guaranteed a tomorrow."

"It won't," he says firmer. "I can't lose another brother."

"Who are you making the guardian?" Quade asks. "Please tell me it's not Jenny's parents."

"What is wrong with her parents? They love the girls."

"I just think they are getting older, and I don't know if they are the wisest choice."

"What would you have me do, Quade? Do you want the girls?"

"I'd take them if it meant they wouldn't have to go through another change again. I just think they are too old."

"Noted."

"Anything else?" Pierce asks, gauging the temperatures in the room.

"One more thing." I look around. "Samantha is their nanny. Not your uni date or someone to go clubbing with. I'd ask that you don't blur the lines. It's hard enough to keep the girls separate from everything else without you all bringing Sam into our day to day."

"Have you ever thought that keeping the girls separate isn't working?" Quade pushes.

"Quade," Finn warns. He might agree with Quade, but he's too protective to hear the edge in Quade's voice and not bristle.

"I'm just saying, that sounds more like Camilla talking than you."

"Lay off Camilla. She's adjusting the best she can. This has turned her life upside down."

"You don't say?"

"Quade, just stop. I appreciate you caring, but you need to stop."

"Fine."

"I already asked Sam to be my date this weekend to the charity event, and she's my friend, but I will try to understand the boundaries you are setting," Finn replies. He doesn't mean it, but he's here to be on my side.

"Good. We're all in agreement then," I say, closing my folder and picking up my fork.

"Not even close," Quade, Colin, and Pierce pledge in unison.

chapter seven

The girls made it to their grandparents without incident and were delighted to see them. There's no chance I would admit it to anyone, but each time I watch them run into a big hug from Jenny's parents, it crushes me a little. It's another chink in the armor that has already been severely compromised by self-doubt.

Sam has been scarce all weekend, and I have seen very little of her other than the charity ball. The fact that that bothers me chaps my arse a little. Seeing as how Finn's sexuality has never been a secret in the crowd we run with, there was no confusion when Sam escorted him to the event that they were there as friends only. Thankfully, he views Sam in the same manner a big brother would and easily thwarted the wayward advances thrown her way. And let me tell you, they were plentiful. I blame the bronze-colored dress that melted to her figure like she was a statue dipped in the molten metal.

I've never felt jealousy before. It didn't matter who I was dating or what the situation was. I don't like it. Graham Taylor of Taylor Enterprises and I are engaged in a stealthy conversation, and while I have his focus, his arm is firmly planted around his wife. His hand splayed on her hip in a show of proprietary. When was the last time I felt possessive of Camilla? I do however understand what that feels like. And it has nothing to do with Camilla. Who, I might add, looks like she just stepped off the runway in a navy Dior dress. But she has a commercialized beauty; Sam's beauty is more natural. And fuck me, everyone seems to be appreciating it tonight.

It is fortuitous that the Taylors are here tonight, so I took the opportunity to talk with him and his brother Adam about a venture Adam wants to propose to The Foundation, the Taylor's philanthropic organization. Finn and I are on the board.

As Graham and Adam debate about some issue with the proposal, Finn walks up to introduce Samantha to Emme and Adam's wife, Jules. I had forgotten—Jules is a fashion designer and Emme is her business partner. Apparently, I glean, they are the ones to blame for the leers Sam has been receiving. It appears the dress Finn purchased for her is a Redden James.

"Our maiden names," Jules explains to Samantha who is gushing over Jules' designs.

They chat about the upcoming Fashion Week in New York and the grueling schedule. Jules talks about her show and Samantha says she would love to bring the girls. For them to see women doing powerful things. She also mentions Zinnie has an interest in fashion design.

"Would it be too much to ask that we swing by sometime so Zinnie can get a glimpse of what really goes on behind the scenes?" she asks Jules.

"Since when has Zinnie been interested in fashion?" I bark louder than even I thought was necessary. Six pairs of eyes take me in and I hate that I see pity in them. Samantha smiles politely in an attempt to sidestep the awkwardness I've thrown like a wet blanket onto the conversation. But still, how does she know this after not even a total of forty-eight hours with Zinnie? I've been with her for five months and couldn't tell you a single thing she is interested in other than her mobile.

Ever the consummate facilitator, Emme doesn't miss a beat and shifts the conversation to a funny story about Olivia, her eldest daughter.

The night spiraled from there, and by the time Camilla and I left, I was in a foul mood. Camilla was less than accommodating and asked to be taken home instead of going back to my place, but I needed to fuck. The kind of fuck you feel in your toes. It took some convincing, but she let me come up. She's not oblivious. She can feel that we are slipping just as I can. Both of us attempting to hold on until we have some normalcy back in our lives. The only problem is our definition of normal seems to mean two different things, where previously it was the same.

I want to let loose and be rough with her but it's not how we do things, so I hold back. My hands around her slender waist, the tips of my fingers touching. I get us both there, barely, before collapsing onto the bed next to her. Our breath weighted and winded. Neither of us speaking.

A time later, I leave her place.

Sam's door is closed and the lights are off when I get home. I stand outside of it. The temptation to pound on it and yell at her for no legitimate reason is heavy. I spend the rest of the night alone in my bed.

The following day is consumed by meetings with Brad and IT. There was another hacking attempt. They are happening closer together, each one more aggressive than the last. It's only a matter of time before we're unable to stop one that will cause irreparable damage to our company and the ones we partner with.

I schedule a meeting with Reid Beckett to discuss Everett's business and a second meeting with Elise Donovan. Everywhere I turn her name is mentioned. It's time to revisit.

Seeing as they are no longer in summer school and don't have to be in classes on Monday, the girls decided to stay another night at their grandparents. Saying no was on the tip of my tongue when they rang to ask, but I know it's important for them to spend time together. It's their tether to Jenny, and I want them to have that for as long as they can.

I've narrowly managed to avoid Sam for the remainder of the weekend until late into Sunday evening. Camilla wasn't up for coming over and I didn't feel like going to her place. I carried in from the Italian restaurant on the corner. Sam's door is closed but her light is visible and I could hear her music playing softly from the other side. I stand knuckles to the door, poised to invite her to eat and to apologize for my behavior the night before, but I can't. I have set this hierarchy in place for a reason and I need to stick with it. In a few days' time, the lines have become too blurred as it is.

Problem is, the girls seem happy for the first time since they came to stay. A desire for their happiness to be due to me and not Sam keeps my knuckles from tapping out an invitation.

I am slurping up pasta noodles when she comes into the dining area, drawing up short when she sees me eating alone. With enough food for three people. God, I'm a heel.

"I'm sorry, I didn't realize you were eating," she says. A pretty blush colors her cheeks but I don't know why. "Will you let me know when you have a minute?"

"Now's as good a time as any," I respond, picking up my

dinner plate and walking it to the kitchen counter where even more food is leftover. Normally I would toss what I didn't eat, but for some reason it seems wasteful tonight. Instead, I put it back in the containers and place them in the refrigerator. I'll have Maria heat it for lunch tomorrow.

"What can I do for you, Samantha?" I ask with my hip against the marble counter, my arms folded over my chest. She's barefoot, not even coming up to my shoulder. Her hair is piled into a large knot on the top of her head and, as usual, her face is natural. She's in Finn's joggers and a tank top that makes it clear she is slightly chilled. The thought makes me hard.

We each start a conversation at the same time.

"I think we need to discuss a uniform."

"You mentioned there was an envelope with cash?"

"Sorry?" she says, unsure she's heard me right.

"You first," I insist.

"You mentioned there was an envelope with cash."

"Yes." I don't offer more, curious to see where this is going. Does it make me an arse that I like for her to be uncomfortable? It certainly gives me an edge. A much-needed edge, because as sure as I'm standing here, this woman is going to be a problem. This is a classic example of why I should always go with my gut. I should have called the agency. Now it's too late. The girls are invested and that makes this dicey.

"How do I access it?" she asks.

Without answering, I turn and make my way to the study. She follows and I guide her over to a pad on the wall. I lift her hand in mine—ignoring the electricity from just her touch—and place her middle finger against the lighted pane, holding it in place. It turns green and the paneled wall pops open. I pull out a cigar shaped box, open the top, count out a thousand dollars, and hand it to her. "Take this. There's more here if you need it."

She frowns before counting out a variety of bills equaling sixty dollars and handing me the rest with a soft "Thank you." Nothing else. I wanted silence, but not... *silence*.

I follow her to the butler's closet by the lift. There's a row of cubbies along the right, and she's turned the space on the left into some sort of command center. There's a desk calendar affixed to the wall and she has pinned up a string with pegs. Attached to each peg is a card with a task and money clipped to it.

"What's this?" I ask. She jumps slightly not realizing I followed her. "I have the agency sending a new maid out next week. They get paid a weekly wage."

"That's great."

"These are chores for the girls so they can earn spending money," she explains.

"You understand these girls have a trust fund in the millions, and I can more than afford to care for them until they are of age?"

"That's not the point."

"And having them clean the loo is?"

"I don't think Jenny would want them to be spoiled. The maid will have charge of the house, but the girls will be expected to clean their rooms and bathrooms."

"And you think a five-year-old can do that?" I challenge mostly because like I said, I'm an arsehole tonight.

"Not on her own," she agrees, her back to me as she populates the calendar, "which is why I will have to help her."

"I can't think of anything worse." I really can't.

"Then you my friend," she turns toward me, "are living a sweet life."

She's right. And this is something I have lost sight of

recently. Unexpected, her statement triggers the feeling of utter grief at the loss of my best friend. Out of the blue, without
warning, it slams into me. My breath hiccups and suddenly the
room feels small and confining. I search out the exit in hopes
of making it out of here before the emotions I've been holding
back since the accident show themselves. I would have made
it, too, but I must have tripped her Spidey senses because before I reach the door, her cheek presses against my back and
her arms wrap around my chest. And...she hugs me. A real
hold-me-until-I'm-ready-to-be-let-go hug. Jesus Christ, how
long has it been since I've had that.

"I'm sorry you lost your friend," she says delicately. It's the
most I've allowed myself to be comforted since the accident,
and I have to will my body to step out of her embrace and walk
away.

chapter eight

The week goes by more smoothly than any since the girls came to stay. Begrudgingly, I admit that Samantha was right to take the girls out of school. They're opening up in ways I haven't seen before. In ways I never thought were attainable.

I attribute it to some of the changes Sam has made around here. The girls understand they have mandatory chores for their weekly allowance and chores they can do for extra money. A comment my mum once made plays in my head: "Boundaries give kids security."

Zinnie pushed back as I'm sure most teenagers would and went on an hour-long tirade about how her parents left her money and she wasn't cleaning a bathroom even if it was hers. Sam didn't budge and I sat in awe of her.

Ten minutes in, Zinnie gave me the pup eyes and clung to me like she knew I would save her. But I stayed strong, even though every part of me wants Zinnie to like me. But I was more scared of the look Sam shot me when she noticed I was starting to cave.

Twenty minutes in, I was ready to throw Zinnie over the outside railing.

Thirty minutes in, I attempted to leave the area, but Sam wouldn't allow it.

Forty minutes in, Sam put her foot down and said it was enough, taking away one week of allowance. It was clear that Zinnie was going to stay the course, but Sam threated to take away another week and she finally caved, storming off to her room.

"I need a strong bevvy after that," I moan on my way to the bar, where I pour myself a strong drink.

"You did good." It's a simple and rather unnecessary praise, but it spreads warmly through my chest. But that could also be the scotch.

"Today I brokered a deal for a little over 30 billion dollars. Tonight, I listened to a girl have a hissy fit for forty minutes and I'm told I did good. Consider my standards lowered."

"She'll even out, but I suspect it will get worse before it gets better. She's not sure how to handle days where she enjoys herself. It feels wrong to her right now, but it will get easier. She just needs an outlet."

I did good, I think, realizing how insanely proud I am to have earned that statement. Sam pats me on the shoulder before heading to Poppy's room to put her down for the night, and I'm left feeling like I've got this.

chapter nine

I don't have this. In fact, I'm beginning to wonder if Sam has this.

I took Camilla away the following weekend in an attempt to find our way back to who we once were as a couple. What I came to realize is that I didn't like who we were. I don't even recognize those people anymore. Camilla made it clear that I had not been taking her into consideration in all this, so I made a pact to try harder for the new us. I was rewarded with a stack of brochures for boarding schools she had contacted.

When I entered the apartment after dropping Camilla at her place, Zinnie was in a full-blown melt down, and she and Sam were close to coming to blows. Best I could make out was Zinnie had slapped her sister in frustration and later accused Sam of liking Poppy more than her.

I tried to help Zinnie calm down, but she quickly turned on me, and soon I was losing my temper, threatening to ground her for a month. She promptly yelled that she hated me for moving her here, and why couldn't I understand she just wanted to live with her grandparents.

I was seconds away from saying something I would have regretted but, thankfully, was never given the chance. Zinnie had run to her room and slammed her door, vibrating the walls around her.

I watch Sam close her eyes, take a deep breath, and count. She hits ten, her eyes open, she takes another breath and picks up Poppy, who is softly crying into a pillow on the couch.

"She's mean," Poppy says sullenly, laying her head on Sam's shoulder.

"She's sad. She doesn't mean it. I'm sorry she hurt your feelings and I know she is, too. Try to be patient with her. Do you understand what that means?"

Poppy shakes her head and Sam hands her over to me. "Walt will explain it to you while I run your bath."

And that's it. She leaves me here.

I fumble it, but eventually I get Poppy to understand what it means to have patience. A feeling of accomplishment matched by none other trickles through me.

Sam calls when the tub is ready. In no time, Poppy is swimming in bubbles, my sleeves are rolled up to my elbows and I'm washing her hair. I think she would have played longer, but it is late. She has already stifled three yawns, so I pull the plug and we watch the suds swirl down the drain.

She wobbles as she steps into her favorite pajamas, pink with white bunnies. She hands me a comb and I comb the excess water out of her wet curls.

"Brush your teeth."

She gives a feeble effort, and I make her redo.

"It's late. We'll read a story tomorrow," I assure her, making sure Edward the Elephant is in his proper place against her chest. Her eyes droop and she fights to keep them open. I run my fingers through her damp hair and caress her earlobe, stunned to hear myself say, "I missed you." Stunned even more to find it's true.

She hugs my hand to her heart, a move that's becoming familiar the last couple of weeks. The tips of my fingers tickling just under her chin.

"I love you," she says before sleep carries her away. My hand freezes and I stomp down the panic attack raising in my throat at her sweet words. Her genuine words.

"Good night." I kiss her forehead and reach to turn off a lamp that wasn't there before I left for the weekend. A nightlight is projecting stars on her ceiling, and I see for the first time her room is different. Sam and the girls have been out shopping every day for the last two weeks. I forgot they were going to outfit the room this weekend with all the items they bought.

I've been watching Sam's spending on the card I provided and it's been minimal. I really dreaded seeing the end result, expecting the room to look like a box store and not the designer caliber I'm accustomed to. But the room I'm in now looks like a little girl's dream.

The room is a generous size to start. They've sectioned it into a place for her to sleep and a place for her to spend her time. Simple strands of ribbon garland mix with strands of twinkle lights in the shapes of hearts and diamonds over her headboard. Understated but impactful. Her bedding is a plush pink linen with little pink hearts on the sheets.

What's really eye-catching is her play area. There are cushions and fabrics spread throughout, bookcases filled with books and baskets of things for her to do. In the corner is a swing you would expect to see under a large tree with soft rope handles.

The space is filled with memories, new and old. There are

pictures of her with Everett and Jenny. Pictures of them as a family. There's a picture of Sam and her squad covered in paint with her and Zinnie. And there's a picture of me laughing at something. It was from a week ago. Finn said something funny and I remember thinking how good it felt to laugh. I don't know who took the picture.

I pull her door closed and walk to the other end of the hall to check on Zinnie in the hopes she has calmed down.

Sam's voice is steady, but it's clear she hasn't made much headway.

"Fine. I'm sorry. But I'm not saying sorry to him," Zinnie spews without a hint of remorse.

"Don't say sorry unless you mean it. That's not an apology, and you were disrespectful."

"But I didn't disrespect you," Zinnie challenges.

"To disrespect Walt is to disrespect me. When you're truly ready to apologize, you know where to find me," Sam says without raising her voice or a change in her infliction. I have men on my team who would cower against less attitude than Zinnie is heaving her way.

Fifteen-year olds. They're terrifying.

Sam steps into the hall. She doesn't say it, but I can tell she's frustrated.

"Poppy is down."

"Great. Thank you. Good night." She turns to walk down the hall, and I hate the unspoken precedence I've put into motion, of keeping her in her place. Otherwise, I would ask her what I really want to know, but am too chicken shit to ask: *Will Zinnie always hate me?*

chapter ten

A yellow taxi narrowly misses me crossing against the light at 5th and 35th. I'm catching the chaps for lunch to discuss my meeting with Reid Beckett this morning regarding Everett's business. It's a Monday, which means they had to re-work their schedules to accommodate me and I'm running a few minutes late.

Christ. Pierce is going to be in a mood, I mumble inwardly as I'm shown to our table. They're all waiting for me, but instead of the agitation I expected to be met with, they are smiling and talking about something they are all apparently seeing on their phones.

"Sorry I'm late. Aren't you blokes a little old to look at nudies?"

"Get your mind out of the slums," Colin says.

"What possibly has the three of you enamored then? Porterhouse, medium, and a glass of burgundy, whatever your sommelier recommends," I tell the waiter, running my hand down my tie then turning back to the table.

"We're looking at Sam's Instagram," Quade says, turning

his phone my direction.

"You follow Sam's Instagram?"

"We all do."

I reach for his phone and glance through the photos. There's picture after picture of Sam with the girls. Painting their rooms. Decorating their rooms. Eating a hotdog with Gray's Papaya in the background. A picture of them at the zoo with their heads popped up in the prairie dog holes.

Christ, she's only had the girls at home for a couple of weeks and it's clear she's had them out and about, showing them the city. My thumb slides the feed upward, stopping on a picture of Quade with Sam and the girls. It's a selfie from a Yankees game.

"You took the girls to a Yankees game?" I ask with a bit more force than called for.

"Sure. Saturday night. You were out of town with Camilla, and Sam asked if I would like to spend some time with the girls." He pulls his phone back, not sure where my combative tone is coming from.

"You follow Sam, too?" I ask Pierce, surprised when he's nodding in the affirmative.

"It's been great," he says. "It gives us a way to keep up with the girls on the days we don't get to see them."

"I've decided to sell the business," I say out of context before taking a long sip of the wine the waiter brought.

"*You decided*," Colin says tartly.

"Yes."

"And did you plan on discussing this with us?" Quade asks.

"I am. We're discussing it now."

"Fuck you, Walt. 'I've decided to sell the business' is not a discussion."

"I told you all I was meeting with Reid Beckett. We met

this morning. Neither of the girls have a desire to run the business, we all have more than we can handle as it is. It makes sense to sell. Reid knows someone interested. I have a meeting with them next week."

"What the fuck do you mean you have—"

"It's done, Quade. With this off your plate you'll have more time for Yankees games." I glare at him in provocation. My jaw ticks. My stance belies a coolness that I'm far from feeling.

He doesn't say a word, but he looks like I've ripped his fucking heart out of his chest. Or off his sleeve, where he's always worn it. He shakes his head as if he doesn't understand, then stands, opening his wallet and throwing four one hundred-dollar bills on the table before turning to leave.

He makes it a couple of tables before Colin is following him to the door.

I down a large gulp of my wine and sit, looking at the table setting in front of me.

"Friday," Pierce speaks.

"What about it?"

"You have until Friday to read the letter Everett wrote you."

"Or?"

Pierce doesn't move, doesn't change his expression. His chest rises and falls with the same breath pattern. I'm vaguely aware that he's Sam and I'm Zinnie in this scenario. His posture mirrors mine, legs crossed, sitting back in his chair. The only tell is his fingers picking at an invisible thread on his knee. His eyes fly up and lock on mine.

"I love you. But it would be a mistake for you to underestimate me because of it."

He pauses then finishes with, "Friday. And fix this." He nods to the now vacant places at the table.

chapter eleven

"It's not fair." Zinnie stands over Samantha who is seated on the couch.

"How do you figure?" Sam looks up to her with a crook of her brow.

"WiFi is a basic human right. This is child abuse." Zinnie's voice climbs in volume.

"I don't mind having a conversation with you about it, but you will not stand here and yell at me like you have the right to."

"You make me crazy!"

"What is the problem? Why are you yelling?" I ask with my eyes closed, rubbing my temples. This has been a shit day. Like step in it, smear it on your pant leg, and walk around smelling of it shit day. "And please, for the love of all that is holy, don't scream. I have a splitting headache."

Samantha stands and leaves us in the living room.

"Sam changed the WiFi password and won't share it."

"Sa—" I stop mid-sentence when a couple of Tylenols are placed in my hand along with a glass of water. The kindness of it is almost enough to make me lose my train of thought. To make matters more confusing, she takes a seat back in her spot without even a glance my way. Like she didn't just do something for me that no one else does: take care of me.

"Sam did what?" I ask, greedily swallowing the pills.

"She changed the WiFi password and won't share the new one." Zinnie crosses her arms like, *Can you believe this shit* and *I know you'll fix it.*

"Samantha?" I turn to her for her version of the story.

"She wouldn't do her chores, she yelled at Poppy, and she slammed her door. Multiple times." She turns to Zinnie. "I told you, you want it, do your chores, apologize to your sister, and stop acting like you're the only person whose life has been turned upside down."

"Sam," I say in a surprised whisper. Surely, if anyone has earned the right to be pissed at the world, it's Zinnie.

"Don't you dare stand there and tell me about my life. You have no idea what my life is like. I want the password and I want it now."

"Have you done the three things I said you had to do to get it?" Sam asks her again with a calmness that only comes with knowing you're right.

Zinnia's face turns beet red and she stomps out of the room. A minute later we hear a door slam.

"If she slams that door one more time, I'm taking it off its hinges," Sam says before putting a pillow to her face and screaming into it. Finally, the hard shell cracks a little.

"If this isn't a good fit for you..."

"Don't," she snaps. "Don't you dare make excuses for her or make this easy for her."

"She lost her parents. Her everything."

"No, she didn't. She still has Poppy and she has you. She's

not alone. She's allowed to grieve and be upset about that, but she isn't allowed to behave in a way that disrupts everyone around her. Poppy is grieving, too. So are you. She can't hold this family hostage until she's ready to behave the way she is expected to."

Family? Are we a family? The thought rattles around in my head like dice in a cup. Bouncing off the sides, but not lodging anywhere.

"She gets the password when it's done. Until then, no."

"I agree she needs structure."

"She gets the password when she's done." Sam stands and leaves the living room area.

And that's how the rest of the evening went. Just...*ugh*. No one was happy. I did move up a level with Poppy. I went from her hugging my hand to a kiss on my eyelid before she went to bed. I think she was attempting to kiss me on my forehead like I do her, but her lips landed on my left eye instead.

I attempt to check on Zinnie, but her door is locked and she's not answering.

I'm too exhausted to go another round with Samantha over the best way to move forward with Zinnie. Instead, I pour a strong drink and shuffle to my home office to take inventory of the long list of things that need to be addressed: Quade, Colin, Pierce, Camilla, Everett's business, the hacking, the girls. They've always been on the list, but its escalating. Zinnie is escalating.

When the accident first happened, I put the girls into counseling to help them deal with their grief. They begged me to stop going, and I acquiesced. I'm beginning to rethink that decision. It's clear Zinnie is not handling this as well as I thought. In the beginning, she really seemed to take to Sam, but once Sam started putting rules in place, Zinnie has been pushing back.

I bypass my desk, opting instead for the leather chair nearest the fireplace. I rest the tumbler on the armchair between my fingers, the taste of smooth brandy on my tongue. My head is leaned back, and it's the most at peace I've been all day.

Pierce's stern words echo, and I find myself replaying our conversation from lunch. Pierce is right, it would be a mistake to underestimate him, but we both know what happened today. I felt…jealous. Yep. Jealous. I didn't like seeing Quade with the girls. They all looked happy. Like a family. I've been busting my arse to keep the girls' heads above water, and he swoops in and makes them happy with a fucking baseball game. It's my life that's been turned the fuck upside down, can't there be at least one benefit to it?

I load the Instagram app on my phone and establish a profile. I've always thought social media was a bit of a bore and for, well, commoners. God, I sound like an elitist.

It takes me a minute, but I finally figure out which account is Sam's. I'm not sure how I feel about the girls' pictures being on social media, but am slightly placated when I see the account is locked. I ask to follow and a minute later my phone dings with permission.

I scan through the pictures, studying ones I saw only for a moment today. Her pictures go back quite a bit, but these appear to be pictures of Sam and her squad doing things out and about. There's one from several months ago at the trapeze place on the Pier. A video of Sam flying from one bar and missing the guy hanging upside down by his legs. She falls and my heart momentarily stutters until she is caught by the net below. Charlotte is next in line. That's it. Pictures of her girls only. No family. No pictures of Jake or any other dates. There are pictures of her and Finn, older ones. I'm reminded again of how close they are.

I thumb back up to the Yankees picture. Sam and the girls are all sporting ball caps with their hair plaited. The girls are sitting between Quade and Sam. There's another picture that I hadn't noticed before. This one is of Zinnie and Quade biting into a hotdog and Zinnie looks…happy. Like she did when Everett was here. It's a reminder that I'm fucking this up and it's more than I can stomach at the moment, so I close my phone and toss it on the ottoman. Maybe Camilla's right.

Sometime later, I startle awake. My body is stiff from sleeping in the chair. My brandy is still on the arm where I left it. A tilt of the glass to my lips empties its remains and I find myself in search of more. My mind hasn't cleared of the day's happenings.

Two glasses later, I call it a night. Sam's door is open when I pass. She's on her laptop, hair piled high on her head, legs curled under her while she flips pages in the book next to her. Her teeth bite into the pencil between her plump lips.

"Everything okay?" she asks, my shadow giving me away as I walk past. I stop and turn back.

"Fine. Why?"

She looks at her phone.

"It's almost four in the morning. You have an early day tomorrow. Is your head still hurting?" She seems genuinely concerned.

"I was catching up on some work." I lean against the doorframe. "I could ask you the same."

"Oh. Well, I have a paper due tomorrow and it needed some work."

"I don't know how I feel about the girls being on your Instagram account. I don't like them having the exposure."

She looks confused by the change in topic, but has the good manners to appease me. Like she would if she were speaking to one of the girls. Like I'm a child.

"The only people who follow me are my girls, your guys, Finn, your parents, and the girls' grandparents. I wouldn't accept a request from anyone else. It's just a way for everyone to keep up with them."

"The girls aren't their responsibility," I snap.

"What's going on, Walt?"

"I don't want you putting the girls in danger."

"I wouldn't do that."

"You don't know that. You don't know what can happen online."

"I don't live in a bubble. That is why it's a locked account. If you're looking to pick a fight, this is a good way to start one. Do you want to talk about what's really going on?" She studies me like she can see inside me.

I don't like it.

I walk away without engaging her further.

I'm gone before the girls are up. I have a slammed day that will require all my focus as it is. It's becoming more difficult with each passing day to turn off the life around me and focus on business only.

Quade doesn't show for two of the meetings he was scheduled for, and I'm not surprised. He isn't one to make light of his feelings. When he's hurt, he doesn't hide it. I know I hurt him, but tough shit. I don't have the capacity to worry about that right now.

"You ready?"

"For what?" I look up from my computer to see my brother standing in my doorway.

"It's Tuesday. At six."

"And?" I ask, my fingers tapping on my keyboard. I've only made it through a few hundred emails today. I have a few hundred more to go.

"And it's five after. We're already late. Let's go."

"I don't even know what you are talking about. What's 'Tuesday at six'?"

"You didn't talk to Samantha today?"

"No. I've been busy."

"She's starting a new tradition. Well, an old one with a new twist."

"Finn, I swear to God I don't have time for this beat around the bush shit. Just get to it. I have work to do."

"Sam heard about the dinners the Oxford Five always had on Tuesdays. She is starting it back again. It's being held at her place."

"It's *my* place," I growl. Finn rolls his eyes.

"Are you coming with me or not?" He turns and leaves me in my office. He knows I'll follow him. I can't not.

Maria has our lift waiting and a few floors later, I exit to the sounds of…well, everyone. They're all here. Pierce, Colin, and Quade. Along with Sam and her group. The only ones missing are Zinnie and Poppy.

Dishes are being placed on the table and people are milling about. The doors to the veranda are open and the sounds of the city are just audible below. Stevie Wonder is playing in the background and Charlotte is telling Colin that Stevie is Sam's favorite. They look happy, like they've all known each other for years.

"You're late," Sam says to Finn and me disapprovingly but with a smile on her face nonetheless. She places a bowl on the table.

"I wasn't aware I needed to be here," I counter.

"I knew Finn would bring you." She shrugs a shoulder and then turns her back on me. If we were alone I would push her against the wall, hands pinned above her, grinding my cock hard against the crease of her arse. Right before I lifted the hem of her dress and deep-dicked her in one swift, solid stroke, I would remind her that you never turn your back on your opponent.

Holy fuck what is wrong with me! I shove Camilla to the front of my mind, forcing myself to remember that Sam isn't mine to do with as I please. For some reason, that frustrates me. Almost as much as everyone being in my house.

Sam's mobile rings and I hear her giving Zinnie a time to be home.

"Where are they?" I ask.

"Poppy is with her grandmother. Zinnie is out with Darren."

"Who's Darren?"

"Her boyfriend." That halts the chatter. All the men in the room stop and gape at her like she has lost her mind.

"Since when?" I ask, so shocked that I sound nearly calm.

"At least three months."

"You allow Zinnie to have a boyfriend?" Colin accuses me.

"Does this look like a face that knew she had a boyfriend?" I bark back.

"Sit," Zoe says loudly, pointing to the chairs around the table. Sam and I each take a place at opposite ends of the table. Boys on one side and girls on the other. Finn is to my right. "Grace." Zoe looks to her friend and the girls all join hands.

"The fuck?" Quade says.

Grace raises a brow. "It's called prayer. You could use some," she says before gesturing the blokes should hold hands.

They do, but not without mumbles.

Grace prays. I was raised Anglican, like most of England, but my family rarely practiced. There is something sweet, almost comforting, about the prayer Grace gives. It's clear it means something to her, that she trusts in it. And I can't help but wonder if some of her words might sprinkle over those of us that need it most.

"Oh, for heaven's sake. You can start passing the food." Charlotte rolls her eyes at my boys who are sitting stock-still.

No one says anything for several minutes. All more interested in our plates than we should be. I must admit whoever cooked did an ace job.

Sam is the first to break the silence. "I asked you all here for a reason," she says putting her fork down and taking a sip of wine. "I spoke with all of your assistants today and scheduled your weekly dinners back onto your calendars."

"Our weekly dinner?" I ask in disbelief, but she mistakes it for ignorance.

"Yes, I understand you guys had a weekly dinner with Everett before he died. I'm starting it back up."

"Don't talk about him like you knew him," I spit.

"Then start acting like someone who did. All of you. I understand grief—"

"No, you don't," Quade says softly. "You have no idea what this feels like."

Zoe starts to say something, but Sam cuts her off with little more than a glance.

"I'm not here to argue. My heart breaks for each of you. I am truly sorry for your loss." She pauses. "The fact remains, he left his children in your care. All of you. The girls need you all to heal so they can heal. I'm thinking the weekly dinner is the best place to start. Tuesdays at six. I expect all of you to be here. Unless you are out of town, this will be your number one priority. The girls will know they can rely on this consistency, no matter what you boys are arguing about."

"My assistant told me about it today. I'm in," Pierce says. One by one, the others agree.

"You need to stop," Sam says to me, suddenly.

"Stop what?"

"Stop doing this all on your own when you don't have to. You have a family." She points to the guys. "The girls need that. These women are stepping up. The girls need strong female role models in their lives, too."

"Can I speak to you for a minute, please?" I stand, motioning to the other room.

"No, anything you need to say can be said here. In front of family."

Holy fucking hell, if I could put my hands on her right now. "You're fired."

There's an audible gasp from the table. The ones who know me know I'm not fucking around.

"I'm not fired. You don't intimidate me and I could never be scared of you. I am, however, getting pissed," she says, standing at her end of the table, glaring at me. "And you don't want that."

"True," Finn validates.

Traitor. He moves his hand when I make to stab him with my fork.

"You will do right by these girls, which means putting them before yourself. It means making sure they are surrounded by friends and family. It means making sure they know there are boundaries. It takes a village, *this* is yours, so stop pissing all over it like a spineless…" she turns to Charlotte and asks out of the corner of her mouth, "what's something that's spineless?"

"Fire urchin," Charlotte blurts.

"Fire urchin?" Zoe whispers.

"They have no spine," Charlotte says matter-of-factly.

"Obviously, you understand my point," Sam says to me.

"Can't say that I do actually."

"Why? Why are you being this way? It's clear you love the girls. It's clear these men would have your back no matter what. Everett believed in you. What you're doing isn't fair to the girls. You're taking it out on the people you need the most. Get it together!" She raises her hand as though she wants to hit the table to emphasize her point, but thinks the better of it.

When I don't answer, she turns to my guys.

"You have to tell him."

"We tried to tell him," Colin says, "but he was too blinkered to listen."

"You speak about me like I'm not sitting right here," I say.

"Would you rather us talk behind your back?" Sam asks before turning her attention back to the guys, like something has just occurred to her. "When did he start getting snippy with you guys?"

"Yesterday. Lunch," Quade says. "After he saw the Instagram account."

"Is that what this is about?" Sam asks me. "He started in on me about that account this morning." She mumbles, and I can see the wheels turning. When she zeroes in on me, I have a feeling I'm not going to like it. I mentally brace myself.

"All of this could have been avoided if you had just said what was bothering you, but you had to choose the difficult path." Then her eyes and tone soften. "No one expects you to get this right all the time you know. Any of you." She points to me and my lads. "None of you have kids in your life other than

Zinnie and Poppy. You four are a team. Act like it."

"That's your big revelation?" I ask. Part of me really had hoped she would have the answer.

She releases a deep sigh. "Walt, you are their parent now. You can't be their uncle."

"I'm their guardian."

"For all intents and purposes, you are their parent. That means you get the real thing. You get the girls no matter what mood they are in. No matter what is going on in their lives. No matter how they are feeling. The guys are their uncles. That means there are going to be times they get to be the fun ones, while you get to be the one they hate, the disciplinarian, the rule maker. But it won't always be like this. You are a visual reminder of the person who took their dad's place. A dad they didn't want to give up. As they work through their grief, they will see you for Walt, more and more, little by little. You know it's true. You see it already in Poppy. She's younger. Her grief is very different than Zinnie's. She's already come around in ways Zinnie isn't even close to. You can't be the fun uncle right now. They need a father."

"I'm not looking to be the fun uncle."

"The sooner you understand your role, the easier it will be. Until then, it's not fair to take it out on the guys. They have roles, too. Pierce will always be the one they go to when they're in trouble, because he will help them work through it. Quade will always be a soft place for them to land. Colin will always be the one they need when they want to just forget the world for a while, because they know he will keep them safe. Finn gives them a true uncle experience."

"So, I get all the crappy leftovers is what you are saying."

"You don't mean that," she says, leveling me with a glance like she knows it to be fact. I wish I had her conviction.

"And what if I did? I'm not sure this is what I signed up for."

"If you really mean it, then now is when you need to rely on us even more," Quade says. "But I need you to get there soon, because I really want to nut-punch you right now. *The crappy leftovers.* What about bath time? Reading time? What about midnight cereal? You didn't think I knew, eh? The girls told me that night I took them to the game. You get to see the real girls. That's not crappy leftovers. Jesus. All this because I took them to a fucking game?" Quade asks.

"No. He's been simmering for a while. We've all seen it. Now we know how we can fix it," Pierce says.

"I don't need fixing."

"Oh, you need fixing," Colin says, and a cacophony of agreement rises from the table.

"So, Tuesdays at six," Charlotte says. "Will there be dessert?"

The lift dings and Zinnie steps off. Everyone greets her, and she comes to stand at the end next to me.

"Did you have a good time?" Sam asks her.

"I did. We watched a movie."

"That's sweet." Uh oh. My eyes dart to Zinnie when I detect Sam's sarcasm. "What time did I tell you to be home?"

"Seven."

"And what time is it now?" We all watch the exchange between Zinnie and Sam like spectators at a tennis match.

"Almost eight."

"I hope it was worth giving up the movie tomorrow night."

"What? You can't do that!" Zinnie's voice raises three octaves.

"A simple call to tell me you were running late. To ask my permission. That's all it takes. I've told you this before. No movie tomorrow night."

Zinnie doesn't say anything, instead stomping off in the direction of her room.

"She's about to scream. She's fine. No one get up," Sam says, taking a sip of her wine.

As if she choreographed it, Zinnie lets out a scream that is pure rage and frustration and stomps her way back to the table.

"I want my door and I want it now," she screeches.

"No," Sam says.

"I want my door and I want it *now*."

"Repeating it isn't going to make it so. I told you last night to stop slamming your door. You continued to slam your door. You locked it when I told you to stop locking it. I let you go out in spite of your behavior. You still didn't hold up your end of the bargain. When you can start treating the people in this family with the respect everyone deserves, then you can have certain privileges back."

"I hate—"

"Ah-ah-ah, careful. Your phone is next."

"You are not my mom."

"No. But I am charged with making sure you are safe and cared for. Something your mom would have seen to. I know this is difficult—"

"Don't." Zinnie cuts her off. "We were fine without you. It wasn't perfect, but at least the other nannies were oblivious and just let us be."

"Well, I love you, so that is not going to happen."

"I don't want or need your love or you for that matter." Zinnie's words are filled with complete disdain. "You're just the hired help."

"Zinnie that is enough," I insist. Sam has a great poker

face, because she doesn't even flinch at those words, but I see it in her eyes. That hurt her.

"No," Sam says. "Get it out of your system if that is what it's going to take. I may be the hired help, but I take my job seriously."

"Stop." Zinnie's voice sputters, and I can hear the control she is trying to exert over her emotions. "Stop acting like you know what we are going through." I cringe when Zinnie echoes a comment I made to Sam not even thirty minutes ago. But Zinnie is on a roll and Sam seems set on letting her speak her piece. "You sit around here like you belong. You don't belong. *You*, don't know what this feels like. *You* didn't lose your parents. *You* didn't lose your best friend. So, stop trying to be something in our lives." Zinnie wrangles her emotions in and then with every bit of anger, resentment, and sadness she adds, "You're nothing."

Before I can take a breath, much less respond, three chairs scrape against the floor. Samantha's squad stands. Their mien is a mixture of empathy and anger.

"Girls," Sam says, clearing her throat of her own emotions. I don't know what's going through her head, but I would give anything to make it where she never has that look on her face again. "Don't," she instructs them.

"She doesn't get to say that. Not to you. Not after—"

"Don't." Sam cuts Zoe off and turns back to Zinnie. "When you start behaving the way you are expected to, you will get your door back." Sam stands. "Until then, no movie tomorrow night. Now, if you fellas don't mind taking clean-up duty tonight. My girls and I will do it next week. I think we're going to take a walk and get some ice cream." Sam excuses herself. Three friends following behind.

Zinnie immediately breaks, flinging herself into my lap,

throws her arms around my neck, and sobs. I don't move other than to wrap my arms around her, holding her while she releases emotions that have been on the brink since the night of her parent's accident. Finn places a hand on her knee. Pierce kisses the top of her head before clearing the table. Quade and Colin quietly assist.

The sobs wracking her body eventually settle, until hiccups are all that's left.

"I'm sorry," she whimpers softly.

"I know." I kiss her forehead and the tenderness sets her off again. Fifteen minutes later she's asleep against my chest.

"I'm sorry, too," Quade says.

"Nah. I'm the one that's been acting like a prized idiot. This has been harder than I think I even realized. I should have asked for help already."

"You shouldn't have to," Colin says. "We've been giving you space to deal with this. We should have been in this sooner. I just didn't see how hard things were with the girls."

"I think Sam pegged our roles," says Pierce. "Now it's up to us to make sure the girls know they can count on us. And you, too."

"For what it's worth," Quade says, "there are five other people in this room and you're the one holding her. I'd take that over a baseball game any day."

chapter twelve

Finn stays after dinner and we shoot some hoops in the gym we share on the floor above my apartment. After Zinnie passed out from the exhaustion, I carried her to her bed where she woke up and cried some more. I sat with her until I was certain she was sound asleep.

Eventually, I left her and went back to hash out the business details with the guys, which I should have done from the beginning. I went over all the items Reid Beckett had advised me on and together we made the decision to share a secondary trust for the girls. Then we discussed the best way to protect the girls from someone later in their life using them only to access their wealth. It's not something the girls need to worry about now, but it's something we need to consider when setting a trust's parameters.

Without question, we are on track to making better decisions for the girls. I feel considerably lighter than I did earlier today but still weighted from the hard things to come.

I miss my shot and Finn makes a comment about my lack of focus.

"Although, you didn't appear to have a problem focusing at the gala the other night," he says, sinking his shot. He checks it to me and I work my way toward the basket.

"Come on, little brother. You know I rarely lose focus. But what specifically are you speaking of?" I fake past him, shoot, make it, and grab my own rebound.

I move back to the top of the key and we both catch our breaths. Finn wipes a bit of sweat off his brow before I charge the board again.

"I've never seen you possessive about anything in your whole life, but one guy just glanced in Sam's direction, whom you never took your eyes off of, and you were ready to throttle someone."

I stumble and miss my shot. Finn makes a show of looking at the floor to see what imaginary bump I stumbled over.

"I need her focused on the girls. She can't do that if some arsehole has her distracted."

"If you say so," Finn chuckles, stealing the ball for a layup.

I take a seat on the floor, breathing heavily.

"Need a break old man?" Finn squats down in front of me.

"I can't even tell you how much I've aged over the last five months," I admit, laying back, greedily sucking in air.

"Let me ask you something. Do you feel like you have a little more balance after this evening?"

"I don't know, man. I just wish that life gave you a map, you know? Made you an outline. Explained which chapters were hard. Showed you where the accidents were. Where the streets aren't finished. Which way to turn. I have an app on my phone that can get me from here to bumblefuck, but I can't figure out what the hell is around the next corner."

"It'll come soon enough." He seems a little surprised that I so readily admitted that I'm not sure what the hell I'm doing.

But I'm too tired to not pretend it's not how I'm feeling.

"I was looking for the Seleske file the other day. The one you said you left on your desk."

"Yeah. I saw it was gone. I figured you had it."

"I saw the brochures for boarding schools. Please tell me you are not going to ship those girls off."

I release an animalistic noise as I pull myself up into a sitting position.

"I don't know yet."

"I'm your brother and I will always love you, but if you send those girls away, I don't know if that is something I can forgive."

Ouch. Hearing that hurts more than I thought it would.

"What if it's what is best for them?"

"It's not."

"How can you be so sure?"

"Because I am. I have eyes. I can see."

"Camilla—"

"Is a bitch for even suggesting it."

"That's not fair. This has been an adjustment for her, too."

"Please. You and Camilla have always had a relationship of convenience and comfort. You were both selfish when you decided to get engaged. The relationship was a fit for both of you at the time."

"I'm not sure it fits me anymore. To be honest I don't recognize that person anymore." I admit.

"Good. He was a daft prick."

"If you felt that way, why didn't you say something? You would let me marry someone you don't like or respect?" I ask indignantly.

"I like and respect Camilla. I just think she's a very different person than you are now, and if she tries to send my nieces to a boarding school, I don't know if I can be responsible for my actions. But that would be on you, bro. Because you hold the power to make sure that doesn't happen."

"Speaking of Camilla, can you keep the girls Thursday night? It's Sam's night off and I swear it always seems to be the only night I can't change my plans."

"Sure. Maybe I'll take them to a Yankees game."

"You're such a motherfucker," I laugh. "Now, help an old man up."

Finn and I part ways in the stairwell when I stop at my floor and he heads down one more flight to his.

I swing by my office to grab a few reports to read before checking on Zinnie. Her room is empty. I look in all the places I think she might be, but can't find her. I ring her mobile, but it just leads me to her bedside table. I call Sam's. No answer. I call Finn. He hasn't seen her either. By the time I have Zoe on the phone learning Sam came back a couple of hours ago, Finn is standing in the apartment ringing security, who is in the apartment seconds later.

The security on the door confirms they didn't leave through the lobby and moments later the security feed shows them on the deck outside.

"Fuck. I think it's their goal to give me a fucking heart attack." I breathe a sigh of agitation and relief, and in that moment I'm hit with a hundred percent clarity that I don't want to be separated from the girls. Boarding school is not an option.

"Jesus. Me, too. Remind me to teach Sam how to leave a damn note," Finn grumbles before heading back to his place. I slide open the door leading to the terrace, a space that has gone virtually unused until recently.

Around the corner on the west side of the terrace, I find them on a double-wide chaise lounge outside of Sam's room.

Zinnie has entwined herself around Sam, who is wrapped around her in a way that makes it seem like she's helping to protect Zinnie. Something I reason she needs right now. They are both sound asleep, the remnants of tears streak Zinnie's face.

I enter into Sam's apartment to search out a blanket, and I notice she has unpacked some more boxes. There are pictures I haven't seen before. These must be her parents. I'm not sure two people could look more in love than they do in this picture. A family picture: her, her parents, and those must be her siblings. Then there's a picture of her and a little boy. Her and her squad. A graduation picture. Setting the frame down, I grab the quilt off of Sam's couch and cover them both, leaving them each with a kiss to the forehead and to sleep in the great outdoors.

The next morning, they're up before I am, making breakfast. Finn is at the bar drinking coffee and reading a paper.

"What are your plans for today?" I ask, pouring my tea.

"I forgot to look at the calendar?" Zinnie says, looking over her shoulder to Sam. "What are we doing today?"

"Well, I talked to your grandparents and Poppy is having fun with the little girl who lives next door, so I thought we would wait and get her this afternoon." She turns, handing me and Finn each a plate of breakfast before carrying hers and Zinnie's to the table. "And since you are on lockdown from the movies..." Sam glances up to see Zinnie frowning at her, pepper shaker in hand halted mid shake. "Too soon?" Sam asks, chomping on a piece of bacon, she and Finn laughing. I see a hint of a twitch to Zinnie's lip but she looks determined not to let her snicker out. Seeing that's all she gets, Sam moves on.

"As I was saying, I thought we might spend the day together. There's an exhibit at The Met on the history of fashion

I thought you might enjoy. Also, I texted a friend and she can meet us for lunch today. I thought you might be interested to see her studio."

"That sounds okay."

"Yeah?" Sam says with a bit of hopefulness.

"Yeah. I'd really like that," Zinnie confirms thoughtfully.

The lift pings, and Quade saunters into the room.

"Yes. Bacon." He gives a fist pump of excitement for pork and piles it on a plate. "This always reminds me of uni." He points to his plate of eggs, bacon, tomatoes and toast. "The only thing missing is…"

"Baked beans," Finn, Quade, and I finish in unison.

"Yuck," Zinnie says, scrunching up her nose. "Baked beans for breakfast?" Zinnie shudders like she might just gag.

"What are you doing here?" I ask Quade.

"Early for our meeting. Thought I would come see what was going on. I wanted to ask if you needed me to take the girls tomorrow night since you are going to that benefit. I know it's Sam's night off."

"Oh, are you and Jason still going to that art opening you were telling me about?" Zinnie eagerly asks with round eyes like she is dying to know more.

"We are," Sam answers coolly.

"This is what? Date five?"

"Six," Sam corrects her.

"Wow. That's exciting. So, you won't be coming home then?"

"Why wouldn't she be?" I ask Zinnie.

"It's the sixth date," she says, like I am ridiculous for even asking. "The date you have sex on."

Everyone at the table either chokes on their food or looks like they just ate something sour.

"Who told you that?" Samantha asks. She's the only one slightly amused.

"Kimmie. She read it in *Cosmo.*"

"Don't believe everything you read. There's more to it than the number of dates. Like love, maturity, preparedness."

"How many dates have you been on with Darren?" Quade asks looking green.

"Like a hundred," she rolls her eyes, "but don't worry. I promised my dad I wouldn't have sex before I was twenty. I plan on honoring that promise. And even then, he has to check all the boxes my dad and I agreed upon. But I'm a girl and Sam is a woman and sometimes women just want to have down and dirty sex. She's old enough to decide for herself." Zinnie shrugs like this is the most natural conversation.

"I appreciate the girl power," Sam says, raising a fist in unity, "but I'm not sleeping with him on date six."

"What's your number then?" Quade asks.

"I don't have a number."

"Bullshi...hockey," Finn says.

"It's true. Just depends on the guy."

"I hardly think this conversation is appropriate for a fifteen-year-old," I chastise.

"You already slept with him," Zinnie sings, proud of herself for figuring it out.

"Oh my God." Sam rolls her eyes. "Clean up. We need to get going. I'd rather her talk to us than Kimmie who gets her information from *Cosmo.*"

She has a point.

"If you don't do it with Jason, you should go out with Colin."

"Colin?" Quade and I yelp together.

"Yes, Colin," Zinnie says dreamily.

"It's the man bun and beard, isn't it?" Samantha winks at her in solidarity.

"And the Scottish accent."

"I have a British accent. I don't see you wanting to go out with me," Finn says.

"You're gay, Finn."

"Thank you, Zinnie. I didn't know that." He winks at her.

"Colin. Colin is…whew. Just…whew. You should totally sixth date, Colin," Zinnie says.

"Go get dressed," Samantha laughs.

"Jason. What, is she working her way through the J's?" I ask under my breath while Sam loads the dishwasher.

"A long way to go till she gets to the W's," Quade snickers.

After lunch, Quade, Finn, and I attend our meeting about the project we are working on with the company in China. Right now our project lead is presenting via video conference, so I steal another look at my phone to see if Sam has posted any new pics of her outing with Zinnie yet.

Finally. It's of Zinnie studying a beautiful ball gown that looks to be from the late 18th century. The sunlight is at such an angle that Zinnie's face looks angelic. The caption simply reads "Beauty". And it is. My mom has commented with several faces that have heart eyes, which I take to mean she likes the picture.

There's a selfie of the two of them eating a large pretzel with the Plaza in the background, with the caption "Twisted up in knots over spending the day together".

A selfie of Zinnie with Emme and Jules Taylor in their

design studio, and another of Zinnie, Sam, Jules, and Emme at a donut shop with an empty box on the table in front of them. The caption reads: Emme wanted donuts.

"For someone who didn't think the girls should be on Instagram, you sure have checked it all day," Finn whispers.

"I love it," Quade whispers back.

"You can stop whispering," the project lead laughs. "The call ended."

"Thank Christ," Colin says, entering the conference room. "I didn't think it would ever be over." He plops in the chair next to Finn.

"What?" he asks when Quade and I greet him with a scowl.

Zinnie's door is still missing when I find her in her room Thursday night.

"Quade and Finn are here," I tell her, straightening my shirt collar. At least I don't have to wear a tie and jacket to this thing tonight. I would rather just give the money and stay home with the girls, but Camilla insists we need to be seen.

"I'll be right there." She types something into her laptop before slapping the top closed and then follows me to the main room where Camilla has arrived.

"Darling." She smiles at me. "Lipstick," she adds when I move to kiss her. My cheek brushes hers, my kiss falling to the air. She's dressed in jeans that fall just short of her ankles, heels and a simple short sleeve navy jumper, or sweater as Americans call it.

"Mila!" Poppy screeches and runs to her for a hug. Camilla

hasn't seen the girls in a few weeks.

"Ca-milla." She sounds out the correction for Poppy, stopping her before she hugs her legs. "Sorry dear. We have a party we're going to." Her hand is wrapped around Poppy's wrist, holding her at arm's length.

"Quade and Finn are going to take you out to have some fun tonight," I remind Poppy.

"Yay!" She jumps up and down clapping.

If only life were always as easy as this.

Sam glides into the main room obliterating that thought. She's wearing a white dress that falls just above her knees. It has a simple crew-neck collar and her arms are completely covered. Is it wrong that I'm happy she is completely covered? Because she is stunning in white. Fucking glowing.

"Sam!" Poppy shrieks and runs towards her. Sam squats, balancing on her six-inch heels, and when Poppy reaches her, she throws her arms around Sam's neck.

Sam stands, lifting Poppy with her.

"I'm going with Finn and Quade," Poppy whispers loudly and gleefully.

"I heard," Sam whispers gleefully back, and Poppy plants a loud wet kiss on her lips.

"Thank you for your sweet kiss. But you are a sticky mess. Zinnie, would you mind taking her to change?"

"Sure. Let's go, Pops." Zinnie holds out her hand, and when Sam sets Poppy down she runs into it.

The lift dings and a man I've never seen before enters the living area. Sam clicks her way over to him and stands on the tips of her toes to let him kiss her. Her entire fucking back is exposed. Fuck me, dammit. There's a slight sound of lips touching and when he pulls back he smiles.

"Strawberry?"

"Poppy just gave me a kiss."

"Aww," he says and plants one more on her.

She introduces Jason to everyone and then politely excuses herself. "I'm just gonna change," she laughs, pointing to her dress. There's a sticky, pink, glittery hand print on the sleeve and what looks like a red smudge of lipstick near her hip.

She leaves everyone in an awkward silence. After a moment, I say to Finn, "Text me when you're back here with the girls."

"I'm ready." Samantha says brightly. She's just as quickly changed into a pair of black leather shorts with gold buttons on the hip and a black shirt that is opened lower than necessary. She has a small, rectangle clutch balanced between her teeth, and she's pulling her hair into a ponytail.

Camilla offers to share our lift with her and Jason. "Talk about a one-eighty," Jason says on our way down. His hand lands on the curve of her behind as his other takes her purse for her. She puts in gold hoop earrings before taking it back. "You look amazing." He kisses her temple, and I fucking want to rip those lips off his face.

"Where are you kids off to tonight?" Camilla asks with a fake smile. Kids? This tallywhacker can't be more than a year or two younger than me.

"A new art exhibit is opening at the Lichterman Gallery," Jason answers.

I say a litany of gratitude to all that is holy when the doors open and we go our separate ways. Outside, I hold the car door open and watch Jason's arm skate around Samantha's waist as they walk in the opposite direction. Camilla calling my name snaps me back into the present and I slide in behind her.

"Thank Christ this event is at least causal. Let's get out of here as soon as possible," I mumble.

"Stop your whining. We need at least an hour to mingle, and it would be rude if we left before ten."

It's seven now. "I am not staying three hours at some benefit I don't even care about."

"Harriet and Charles are our friends," she says from her side of the car. We're not even touching. If it were Sam in her seat, I'd already have her back against the door, knickers slid to her ankles, eating her out like a man having his last meal…and now my dick could be used for batting practice.

"I can't do this anymore," I blurt out.

"Fine. Two hours, but we'll need an excuse," she huffs.

"No, this. Us."

"What are you saying?" For the first time in a long time I have her full attention.

"I'm saying…I'm not happy. This is not what I want."

"Since when? We've always wanted the same things."

"Since the girls." It's a truthful answer. This is more than just Sam and what I've been feeling for her lately.

"Oh, well. Just be patient, darling. It will be better once we have them enrolled at St. Mary's."

"I'm not enrolling the girls in a boarding school."

"But we decided that was what was best for them." She seems genuinely shocked by my announcement.

"No, you decided that was what was best. For you. For us. And maybe it was at first, but not anymore. I'm not the same person I was five months ago. I don't want the same things. I'm sorry. I truly am. You haven't changed. I have."

"You're giving me the 'it's not you it's me' speech?" Her expression is stoic, but her tone is incredulous.

"Appears so, but only because it applies. It really isn't you. It really is me." It's true. Camilla has never misled me about what she wanted. But over these past few months, it seems I've been misleading her.

Our car pulls to the curb in front of the townhouse, and we sit idle for a moment while Camilla opens a compact and checks her makeup. There's a slight tremor in her fingers. It's the only sign she gives that this is emotional for her.

"We'll be ready by ten," she tells my driver then opens the door. "We're going in here. We'll put on the air of a couple in love, then we'll part ways after. Remind me to give you the ring."

Does it make me a bastard to have expected a little resistance? I mean we were, after all, engaged to be married. Okay, yes, that makes me a dick, because even though I'm not ending this because of Sam and I haven't acted on my feelings for her, they're still there. But I've barely admitted them to myself, I'm not ready to admit them to Camilla. And I get the feeling they wouldn't be appreciated. Camilla and I won't be that couple you read about who broke up and remained friends. No. We will part ways after this and that will be it.

"I don't want the ring back," I tell her.

"Let's go."

"Camilla," I sigh. "I really don't—"

"You will do this, Walt."

And I do.

chapter thirteen

ossing the nine-carat diamond into the safe, it occurs to me that I never felt a connection to this ring. Telling, isn't it? Something so beautiful, but not a feeling at all. To say the ring is ostentatious like Camilla wouldn't be fair. I chose it because Camilla told me it was the one she wanted. In hindsight, I suppose that means I didn't really choose it. Also telling.

I have only myself to blame. Not once did Camilla misrepresent herself nor did she make any attempt to make me believe she was someone she wasn't. I meant it when I told her that she didn't change, I did. What made me think I could have a marriage like the one Camilla and I would have had and been happy? If I had remained that same selfish bastard, then maybe. But I'm not the same man I was almost six months ago. Zinnie and Poppy changed that. And I would be lying if I said the change was unwelcomed.

A thousand pounds lighter, I change into joggers and grab a beer. Just as I enter into the living area, the elevator dings and Quade and Zinnie file out laughing about who knows what. Finn carries a passed out Poppy against his shoulder.

"I can take her." I make to get off the couch.

"I got her. This is my favorite part," Finn says, moving in the direction of her room. There's an oversized foam hand with one pointed finger that says, "We're #1" resting against his back, still attached to Pop's hand. I have to give it to her, she can sleep anywhere.

"We didn't expect you home this early." Zinnie says, plopping down on the couch next to me. She types something in her phone then giggles before setting it on the cushion and looking my direction.

"I wasn't in the mood for an outing. How was the game?"

"Rad. We had great seats and we won. Think I'll head to my room," she says, phone in hand again, responding to a beep.

"Thought you were waiting for Sam?" Finn asks her, walking into the room with two beers in his hand. He drops one into Quade's waiting hand. "Pops is down," he tells me.

"I was, but when I texted her she said she wouldn't be back until morning. So, I'm going to talk to Claire. Good night."

"What do you say?" I lean my head back against the couch and prompt her. She changes direction, coming back to the sitting area.

"Thank you. I had a great time." She kisses Quade and Finn on the cheek, then starts back towards her room. A beat later there's a kiss to the top of my head from behind me. "Good night," she says, almost bashfully.

"Progress." Quade tips his beer to me after Zinnie has rounded the corner.

"What is this?" I ask, nose scrunched up, surveying the food being plated. I refrain from using colorful expletives because the girls are in the room.

"Green eggs and ham!" Poppy exclaims in the kind of delight that I'm pretty sure she only reserves for glitter cannons or seeing a real-life unicorn.

"Green eggs and ham?" I glance up to see that she's wearing a tall red-and-white-striped hat.

"Relax. It's food coloring," Sam whispers. She has on cutoff shorts and a T-shirt that's not tight but fitted in just the right way to showcase her gorgeous tits, which I may or may not have jerked off to last night. "Sam I Am. I am Sam." is printed in large red letters across her chest.

"Do you like green eggs and ham?" Poppy asks me.

"I do not like them, Sam-I-am. I do not like green eggs and ham," I reply, snagging a scone off the counter.

She giggles out loud and I swear it's connected to strings wrapped around my heart. How did it happen? When did it happen? I've asked myself this a hundred times recently. Sam laughs at something Finn said and it reminds me, once again, how much I misjudged her before she became the girls' nanny—er, our family manager. I'm a hundred and eighty days in, and more times than not that this still feels like complete chaos. She's got one month behind her and already life feels like it's balanced again. Like we've all been brought back to center.

Poppy gets a mischievous look on her face, like she is about to test me. It's clear she wants to see how far this can go. Her eyes narrow in challenge.

"Would you like them here or there?" Her lips slowly spread into a sly smile.

"Oh no you don't." I pick her up and swing her around. Her delight washes over the room. "We are not traveling down this street."

"Not even for a beat? Come on, Walt. It's just meat," Zinnie says with a raised brow and a grin and it knocks the breath out of me. Fuck it. In for a penny, in for a pound. I close the distance of the few steps between us and kiss her on her temple.

"Good morning, sweetheart. You look like your mom today."

She gives me a quick but heartfelt smile and her eyes glisten before she clears her throat and finishes setting the silverware on the table. Sam squeezes my arm in approval as I pass her on the way to the refrigerator. If I were the peacock type, I swear my tail feathers would be on full display.

Finn is theatrically recollecting a story from our childhood when Sam halts the conversation in the room with her reproachful tone. "*What* did you just do?" she asks.

I glance over my shoulder to see who has garnered her attention and am surprised to learn it's me. I'm not the only one. We are all taken aback by her sudden seriousness.

"Um...got the milk out of the fridge? I was going to pour everyone a glass," I offer as atonement for whatever sin I committed.

"You smelled it." She accuses.

"And?"

"And now I can't drink it."

"Are we in a different Dr. Seuss book I haven't read yet?"

"No. But it's a rule. If you have to smell it, then I don't eat or drink it."

There is a look of utter seriousness on her adorable face. Hair piled high on her head with a yellow ribbon tied into a bow around it.

"I apologize," I drawl like I'm addressing a cornered animal. The others are working to keep the smirks off their faces.

And they're not managing well, I might add. "I was taught you smell milk before you drink it."

"That's what the date is for." She reaches past me for the cranberry juice instead.

"The date doesn't...fine," I relent when I register her frown. I put the milk back, letting the refrigerator door hide my grin. You know, I once, in the days of yore, was a feared hard arse. Now, I can be brought down by a tiny woman and a jug of milk.

"You're eating this," Sam threatens, setting my plate in front of me. We've each taken our seats at the bar.

"Sam, if you will let me be. I will try them. You will see." I pick up my fork, encouraged by the laughter in the room.

"So, tomorrow is movie Monday?" Finn asks on his second helping of green eggs and ham. I have to admit, there's no difference in the taste, and the scones Finn baked made it even better.

"It is," Zinnie says. "Which one is tomorrow?" she asks Sam.

"Movie Monday?" I interrupt.

"Sam's been taking us to movie spots on Mondays. We already had a *Home Alone* Monday, a *Ghostbusters* Monday. What else? Oh, *An Affair to Remember* Monday. That one was my favorite."

"*Home Alone* was mine," Poppy says, licking strawberry jelly off the side of her hand.

"Tomorrow is *Breakfast at Tiffany's*," Sam says. "We are going to have Danishes and coffee," Poppy crinkles her nose. "Or hot chocolate," Sam corrects, "outside of Tiffany's and stare longingly into the window at the millions of dollars of jewels," she says with the raise of a shoulder like it will absolutely be a glamorous experience.

Breakfast out of a paper bag, standing on the street. Yep. Glamourous.

Zinnie is saving for a new pair of boots she wants for the fall, so she elects to do the dishes for the extra cash. Finn helps. Any opportunity to spend time with her.

"You know, I love how much time you've been spending with the girls lately. I feel like I see you more now than I ever did before," I tell him while the girls are all outside on the terrace. They gave in to Poppy's begging and are now in Wellies, jumping in puddles. I see legs spinning through the air. Zinnie and Sam are teaching Pops how to do cartwheels.

"It's because you do. See me more," he clarifies.

"So, West isn't going to work out?" I ask him about the man he was weak in the knees for a few weeks ago.

"No, he is hopelessly in love with Blake."

"Are you seeing anyone?"

"Not at the moment, no."

"What about just to get off?"

"Romantic, but no. Just me and my dick."

"Could we not."

"You started it."

"You can't hide out here with the girls. You need to get out more."

"I'm not hiding out."

"You are. And you can for a while longer because I rather enjoy having my little brother around, but don't wait too long. I don't want to have to kick your arse into gear."

"What are we doing today?" Zinnie asks, coming through the terrace door. Sam and Poppy are still hopping from one puddle to the next.

"What would you like to do?" Finn asks her.

"You said the headstones were delivered this week? I

would like to put flowers on Mom and Dad's grave." Her voice is a mixture of nervousness and resolve.

"Sure, we can do that," I nod.

"We can go dressed like this. Mom and Dad would want it that way."

"Alright. Let me get my shoes and we'll go."

"Will you go with us?" Zinnie asks Finn, and I know there is no way he could possibly say no to her.

"Of course." He kisses her forehead.

Everett and Jenny were buried in a plot Jenny's family has owned for years. Her parents will be buried here when they pass. Her grandparents are laid to rest on the same section of land, two plots over. I had to grease some hands because, evidently, it's illegal to bury two people in the same casket. I had one special made to fit the two of them together, then paid the family that runs the cemetery to look the other way. I just knew Everett would want to be with Jenny. So, next to Jenny, holding hands, was how they were laid to rest.

It's a gray day and a long quiet drive to the small town in Connecticut where Jenny's family is from. It's about an hour from Greenwich where Everett and Jenny lived, a blue-collar town. No pomp and circumstance here like you'd see in a cemetery in Greenwich. This one is pretty and well maintained, but has no flash. We pull up to a curve in the road inside the stone walls that stand guard over the loved ones buried here.

Slowly, almost cautiously, we exit the car. Sam pops the boot handing me and Finn each an oversized umbrella in case the dull mist turns into rain. She tried to insist on staying behind, but the girls weren't having any of it. I can still sense some apprehension in her body language.

Leaning back into the boot, Sam hands each of the girls a bouquet of zinnias and poppies she grabbed from the open aired flower shop on the corner next to Eatly. I recognize them, because they are the same flowers she has placed on a weekly basis around the apartment and next to the girls' beds. A small touch I've never thought to tell her I'd noticed.

She piles her arms with six bouquets of red roses.

"I want to carry some roses, too," Poppy says.

"Actually, honey, you have your mommy's favorite flowers for her grave." Sam points to the blooms clasped in her small hands.

"Then what are those?" Poppy asks.

"For my family," Sam explains quietly. "These are *my* mom's favorite."

"You have family sleeping here, too?" Poppy asks wide-eyed.

"Yes," Sam answers almost inaudibly before clearing her throat. "My family is resting on the hill there." Sam points to our right. "Under that tree. While you visit your parents. I'm going to go visit mine."

chapter fourteen

"You're not going with us?" Zinnia asks.

"No, babe. This is something to do with Walt. I'll be right over there if you really need me."

"I'll go with Sam." Finn thumbs in the direction Sam pointed, and I think his announcement startles her. She appears unsure, but eventually nods her head and hands him half the bundle of roses resting against the crook of her elbow. The girls and I watch as Sam and Finn turn towards the hill.

"This way girls," I coax gently. Poppy takes my hand in her little one; Zinnie follows suit not even a step later. This is the first time Zinnie has ever reached for my hand, and it awakens a clarity that I have never experienced before. It's not just about me anymore, but the three of us. I know in an instant that their well-being and security are my top priority.

Finn has always been the life that I valued more than my own. In a life and death situation, I would sacrifice my own for Finn's. I never thought anyone would supersede, not even Camilla.

The crunch of leaves and acorns under our feet,

announcing fall, give way to the soft green grass that is laid out like a carpet around the gravestones. None of us have been here since the day of the funeral. A day that is a complete blur but yet so clear to me. It was sunny. The girls were walking zombies. Quiet from the shock that had yet to wear off. And, if I'm honest, didn't actually wear off until Sam came into our lives.

Zinnie was surrounded by her friends. Poppy was passed around from one of Jenny's friends to the other, all shocked to learn Jenny chose me to take care of her most cherished possessions.

I'm not naïve. I knew people assumed Everett and Jenny chose me because I could give their daughters the financial security that less than one percent of the world experience. They didn't have the privilege of knowing that Everett was a better businessman than I am, and it's only by the luck of the draw that I was born into this wealth. They didn't know that Everett didn't need to pick someone with money because he has already ensured his girls and at least two more generations after them could be cared for on the wealth he has earned.

All of these misconceptions were underscored by their choice to be laid to rest in a working-class town, in a nondescript cemetery. But they didn't know the real Jenny. She appreciated the financial comfort Everett awarded her, but she was just as comfortable in this town as she was in Greenwich.

"Will I sleep here one day?" Poppy asks as we come to a stop at their shared headstone.

I was not in favor of letting Poppy think her parents were just asleep; I wanted her to learn early what death means, I was afraid it would confuse her as to what was really happening. Also I didn't want her to think her father just decided to go to sleep and leave her behind. But Zinnie was the one to settle

Poppy during the first few days, and it was either because of the trust she has in her sister or because Zinnie just knew it's what Poppy needed, but it clicked. Asleep or not, Poppy understood they weren't coming back.

Zinnie squats before the headstone and her fingers trace the names of her parents, pressing hard into the etching. Poppy joins her, kneeling just like her sister. The headstone is unique and stands out from the ones around it. It's large with a beautiful carved tree that stretches the length of the stone, and etched into the space below the canopy are two girls on tree swings. Under that are Jenny and Everett's names with the days they were born and the day they died.

Poppy stands up and walks back to me. Her arms shoot into the air and I lift her into my arms. She snuggles against me and we stand there together, while Zinnie silently finishes a conversation with her parents. I hear a sniffle, and when she stands and takes my hand again, her eyes are red-rimmed and watery.

"Ready?" I ask gently, and she nods.

When we near the car, Zinnie tugs on my hand, guiding me to where Sam and Finn have been this whole time. This area isn't as cared for as the others. Pierce handled Everett and Jenny's tombstone and has someone care for the area weekly. Here, the grass is trimmed but the fallen leaves haven't been removed.

Finn and Sam are clearing off the last of the debris. There are four gravestones. All simple and modest, embedded into the ground. None of them stand at attention like the one we just left. One is slightly larger; Samuel and Jeanette Abbott, her parents I assume. There are three smaller stones: Rory Abbott, Jonathan Abbott, Frank Abbott.

There's a soft gasp next to me when Zinnie realizes what

I've already noticed. They all died on the same day. I do the math. Rory would have been 15 at the time; Jonathan, 12; and Frank, 7.

Samantha lays the last bundle of roses against the last stone, and when she stands, Zinnie asks, "Your family all died on the same day?"

"Yes." Her voice is shaky. It's alarming. Since I've known her, her voice has never wavered.

"Sam," Zinnie says. Samantha draws Zinnie to her, holding her in an embrace as Zinnie weeps, apologizing for their fight the other night and for telling Sam she couldn't understand what this feels like. Sam rocks her gently, reassuring her everything will be okay. They stand there, two people connected in ways others never will be.

Poppy reaches for Finn who boosts her out of my arms and carries her back to the car. I observe each headstone. They died nine years ago this coming Wednesday, September 1st.

"I wouldn't have asked you to come today if I had known," Zinnie says, wiping her nose with the back of her hand. I pull a hankie from my pocket and give it to her.

"I'm a big girl. I could have refused."

"Do you come see them often?" Zinnie asks.

"No." Sam shakes her head. "This is my first time since their funeral." Neither speaks but Zinnie tugs on Sam to move her in the direction of the car.

"I have one more place I need to stop," Sam says, tilting her chin, motioning to the car. "Go ahead. I'll just be a minute." Zinnie gives her one last embrace before heading to the car. Sam walks in the opposite direction, and I surprise myself when I follow behind her, quickly matching her pace.

About fifty yards from her family is a headstone that reads, "Daughter, Sister, and Friend, Kathryn Michelle Yates".

Her date of birth puts her at the same age as Sam. She also died on September 1st. The same year as her family. This grave has fresh flowers already on it and has been cared for.

"Hey Kitkat," Sam whispers as she lays the roses on the grave. She closes her eyes for what must be a short prayer, and when they open, they're glossy and heartbreakingly sad. It's like someone sucked the life out of the woman in front of me.

"Ready to go home?" she asks. Something about the way she calls my apartment "home" makes my heart soar to a level that feels quite dangerous.

I want to say "no". Demand that she unzips that protective shell and let it fall to her feet so I can see what is really underneath. I want to know so that I can protect her from whatever is hurting her.

Instead I tell her "yes", and we make our way back to the car.

The drive home is somber and quiet. Finn retires to his apartment and I decide to work in the office for a while, making a few phone calls. Not long after we get home, the heavy rains that were expected this afternoon are here. In search of Pops to see if she has more puddle jumps in her day, I find the three girls passed out in Poppy's room. Three sets of socks-covered feet pressed around each other. Their chests rise and fall to the same tempo. Today was difficult. For all three of them. I observe them while they sleep trying to imagine what each must feel when they think about their parents. I lost a friend, a best friend, but what they've endured goes deeper. The room is already a muted gray from the weather, but still I hit the button to close the blinds to the large window, soundlessly closing the door behind me.

The weather doesn't let up, and when dinner rolls around, Finn shows up with enough Chinese food to feed a small army while I wake the girls.

After multiple servings of fried rice and Moo Goo Gai Pan, we settle into the TV room, lights dimmed, blankets and pillows everywhere as we watch Audrey Hepburn in *Breakfast at Tiffany's*. Zinnie, Pops, and I share one oversized couch. Finn and Sam share the other, her head resting on a pillow against his thigh. I love my couch mates, but I admit I'm a little jealous of my brother.

"Have you always been with men, or have you dated women before?" Zinnie asks, looking up from her phone.

"It's always been boys for me," he answers cautiously.

Zinnie shrugs. "You and Sam would make a cute couple."

Finn has been absently playing with Sam's hair while she has been dozing off and on. Even though she slept this afternoon, I get the feeling she is still exhausted.

"Sam and I are really good friends. I would go as far as to say she's one of my closest, but she's missing a key element."

"What?" Zinnie asks.

"Do not answer that question," I warn.

Sam giggles and turns to her other side. "Trust me, Zinnie, if it was in the cards, I'd be the luckiest girl there is."

Finn's ministrations falter momentarily as he gently massages the back of her neck.

"Thank you, Sam," Finn says with a knot in his throat. My brother. He's a fucking catch. For a guy or a girl. He's got a heart of gold. I don't understand why he struggles to believe it.

"Aren't you the one that started Movie Monday? Shouldn't you be watching?" I ask Sam's back.

"I'm listening. I know this movie by heart. It's one of my favorites." She burrows in.

"I can't believe I missed the week you guys watched Ghostbusters," I mumble.

chapter fifteen

The girls are still asleep when the buzzer sounds alerting me that my packages have arrived. I must remember to write a letter of gratitude to the personal shopper at Bergdorf's. To pull this together after hours on a Sunday goes above and beyond.

The doorman brings in the last of the packages and I set about following the directions the personal shopper provided.

Dear Mr. Nelson,

Thank you for entrusting Bergdorf's with your needs. If there is ever a time we can be of service, please do not hesitate to contact us. I have included a business card with exclusive 24-hour access to our team.

Attached is a detailed description of your purchases, organized by gift recipient. I have numbered them for your convenience.

Sincerely,

Jessica Smith

Vice President of Private Services

Dandy. If only everything I did came color-coded and

numbered for me.

I grab a pen and check off the inventory as I hang the garment bags on the backs of the barstools around the island. I want them to see these first thing in the morning.

Twice checking the list to make certain I have each item set out accordingly, I stand back and admire my hard work. Tomorrow morning, they will walk into all the goodies I just organized, each pile with its own colored-coded silk ribbon. Ms. Smith included a single white envelope and card as I instructed, and I jot a note to my girls telling them to enjoy their day, whom each ribbon color belongs to, and request they meet me for lunch at Pierre's.

I've never taken pleasure in giving. I give endlessly. Finn and I both do, but it's always been an expectation. I would expect anyone with my wealth to give back. This is a different kind of giving and there's something about it. Something I like.

"Care to clue me in?" my brother asks while we wait for our next meeting. It's only seven in the morning; we've been in meetings since five. When more than half your clients are on the other side of the globe, you make adjustments with your time.

"What do you mean?" I ask, turning the page on the financial section of the newspaper, a bagel from this morning's breakfast cart dangles from my mouth.

"You are almost giddy."

"You make me sound like a little girl."

"If the shoe fits…"

I roll my eyes, fold the paper back to its original size, and take a large swig of black coffee.

"Would it have anything to do with checking your phone every five minutes?"

My smart-arse answer is interrupted by a buzz on my phone. Finally.

Sam: The girls are gonna flip! When did you do all this?
Me: Some of us were working while others were slumbering
Sam: Some of us work hard and were tired.
Me: Are you implying I don't work hard?
Sam: Seriously, the girls are going to love this. This is so special. ❤

My fingers hover over the keypad. Fuck it. In for a penny, in for a pound, right.

Me: And you?

The little dots seem to pulse forever.

Sam: I love anything with my name on it tied in a satin bow ;)

Holy Shit. Someone get me some ribbon to tie a bow around my dick, because it has "Sam" written all over it.

Sam: But I haven't opened the gifts yet… waiting for the girls to wake up.

More dots.

Sam: Thank you.
Me: You don't even know what it is.
Sam: I know I'll love it.
Me: Is that so?
Sam: Yes.
Me: What makes you so certain?

My question goes unanswered. No more dots pulsing in and out. I almost growl in frustration.

"I love the idea. I fucking do. But be damn sure you know what you're doing," Finn says when I finally look up from my phone.

"What are you talking about?"

"Sam. You need to be sure, because if you hurt her…" He doesn't need to finish. The threat is implied.

"I don't know what you're tal…" Hell, even I know that this is fake indignation. I know it. He knows it. "Fine. But it's really new—" He clears his throat. "Fuck you! Fine! I've been feeling this way for a while."

"See," Finn says with a shit-eating grin. "That wasn't so hard, was it?"

"Trust me, things are harder than they've ever been," I grumble.

"You need to end it with Camilla before you start something up with Sam."

"Camilla and I ended it weeks ago," I tell him, picking up my phone to view a notification I just received. Sam has sent a video. "I'll be back in a minute. Start without me if necessary."

In the privacy of my office I tap my screen and watch a video of Zinnie and Poppy coming into the kitchen to find their garment bags and ribboned boxes. There are loud shrieks, followed by laughter and unadulterated joy.

Poppy puts on her tiara and gloves. Zinnie goes straight for the shoes. Her shriek when she realizes they are Louboutin's is only audible to canines. The only difference between hers and Sam's are two inches. Zinnie's are three inch and Sam's are five. Poppy and Zinnie both clutch their dresses and wave into the camera with a smile that makes me feel like the Grinch when his heart grows three sizes.

I watch and re-watch the video, each time taking in something new. The curve of a smile, a previously missed dimple. I'm on my third—okay, fine, fifth, I'm on my *fifth* view when a text pops up from Zinnie. There's a video attached. I push play and watch as Sam opens her boxes unaware she is being videoed. She takes her time opening each one. She pulls the Valentino from the garment bag and holds it against her. She runs her fingers over the fabric. The next are her shoes. She's wearing nothing but an oversized T-shirt. The hem sits just beneath her rump. She never walks around in this state of undress when I'm home. She smiles and gives a little clap before bending over to slide her foot into the soft leather, a hint of green knickers poking out. Zinnie focuses on Sam's legs as she balances into one shoe then the next.

She walks across the room and her legs look fucking fantastic. Skipping back to her packages, she lets Poppy open the gloves and the tiara before she opens her box with the sunglasses. She slides them in place on her face. She props her chin on her shoulder as she gives Poppy a coy little smile before opening the last box. There's an audible gasp as she opens her Tiffany pearls. Her fingers caress the smooth beads. I got the girls a single strand, but for Sam I got a three-strand necklace, all perfectly sized and curated.

Sam sits in stunned silence. Zinnie zooms in onto her face and a tear falls from under her dark glasses. Sam's fingers quickly slide under the rim to remove the evidence. She clears her throat and tells the girls to get dressed. They have a breakfast to get to.

Thirty minutes later, I check my phone and there is a selfie on Instagram of the three of them in their sunglasses, smiling in the back of a cab. The caption reads, 'Three Audreys on their way'.

Comments from the guys start to appear. One from my mom commenting on how beautiful they look.

Finn kicks me under the table and I quickly fall into step with the meeting.

The morning crawls by until it's finally time to meet the girls for lunch. I invited them to our usual meeting place with the guys. I might not want to share the video with the guys, but I knew they would love seeing the girls dressed up. I couldn't leave them out of *all* the fun.

"Is it just me or does Sam appear to have a proclivity for themes?" Pierce asks. "Movie Mondays, Tuesdays at Six."

"Not just you," Colin confirms.

"I, for one, dig it," Quade says, ordering two fingers of scotch.

We hear a bit of ruckus as Poppy charges through the restaurant and straight into Finn's arms. Her delight draws a chuckle from the on-lookers before all eyes turn to Sam. Her dress accentuates every curve, and even though the dress in the movie was longer, the personal shopper and I took some liberties. Sam's dress pinches in right above her knees, and the image of her legs wrapped around my waist as I rut into her over and over is in the forefront of my mind. The men stand as Zinnie and Sam take their seats, Poppy giving everyone a play-by-play of their morning adventures. Sam is seated between Colin and Pierce, who leans toward her and whispers that she looks stunning. When she blushes, I nearly turn the table over and throw Sam over my shoulder in a sign of ownership.

But I don't own her. So, I stay put. Poppy's frenetic story-telling is an excellent distraction.

"And then this manger man—"

"Manager," Sam says.

"Manager man," Poppy tries adding extra letters, "came and got us after we finished our breakfast and told us we were expected inside, then he let us choose from a whole big glass box."

"You don't say?" Finn responds with the look of utter surprise.

"We were given the option to choose something else," Zinnie explains, "but there was a glass display case that had three items in them waiting for us." She shows them a picture of the case.

Three felt bust displays surrounded by shards of ribbon matching the girls' morning presents each displayed necklaces: one, a gold necklace with a tiara charm for Poppy; another, a rose-gold necklace with a camera charm for Zinnie. The third is a white-gold necklace with two modest round cut emeralds, one bezel-set in rose gold, the other in yellow gold.

Zinnie and Poppy show off their pearl necklaces after the guys respond to the pictures of the other presents with the appropriate amount of oohs and aahs. Sam doesn't. This doesn't surprise me. I had already received a call from the manager telling me Sam was reluctant to accept the gift and only did so when he explained he would be fired if she didn't. Of course, that was not true, but you don't get to his position without understanding whose side to play in a business transaction.

Pierce toasts our lunch guests before the waiter takes our orders. "Only a real lady can pull off a tiara in the middle of the day."

Lunch is a weaving of conversations, a minimum of four at any given time. There are several business acquaintances who stop by to say hello, but they only have eyes for Samantha. A few glance toward Zinnie, but Quade shuts it down before I even have an opportunity to respond. Good thing, too. The looks to Sam had me boiling, but the glances to Zinnie made me fucking murderous.

"You learn quickly they don't have to be your blood for the parental protectiveness to take over," Graham Taylor says as we leave. He and his brother, Adam, are having lunch at a table near ours, so I stop to say hello as we leave. If anyone has experience in this area, it would be Graham. He has one adopted child and they are in the process of adopting a second. Graham and Emme also have a biological child.

"It's hard to explain. Your biological children are a gift, but your adopted children are a choice. You find your heart has the ability to love all your children with everything you have for what is uniquely theirs. To tell a child they were chosen is an amazing gift to give them."

"I swear you sound more and more like dad every day," Adam ribs.

Graham shrugs unapologetically. "You're a good man for taking in Everett's girls. I can see the difference in you. Just wanted to let you know it's clear you're finding your footing."

"With the girls, yes, with the woman he was eye-fucking over lunch..." Adam smirks.

"Yes, well, let's let the man figure some things out for

himself."

I think about Graham's comments on my way back to the office. My steps lighter than they have been for months. But the feeling is short lived when I find Brad waiting for me in my office.

"It's not good," he twitches nervously. It's like he needs a fix because there is a puzzle he can't solve, and it's making him crazy.

"It never is when you leave the thirteenth floor to pay me a visit," I mumble and hit the intercom for Maria to locate Finn.

"He's back," Brad says.

"Who's back?" Finn asks, entering my office.

"The hacker. And this time he did some damage."

"What kind of damage?"

"He's frozen five of our largest accounts and I can't figure out how."

"Fucking figure it out or I'll get someone in here who can. Christ. Maybe that's what I should have done already," I threaten, aggravated by the knowledge that our systems are still vulnerable.

"We're doing our best," Brad bites back before slamming the door behind him.

"You know he's on our side," Finn reminds me.

"I know. But Jesus, we've been three steps behind this fucker for too fucking long."

"Yes, well, dropping the f-bomb over and over will certainly make everything better," Finn quips, leaving me to stew. I know zero about coding, even less about IT systems, and I absolutely loathe being at the mercy of anyone else when there is a problem to be handled.

My sour mood continues through the evening. My plans to get home at a decent time were waylaid by this predicament we are in. We have a tight window to report to the SEC if we feel we have been breached to the point that investors should be worried. It's now nine the next morning, I'm on my third meeting, and we're on the clock. We have four hours to report.

The doors open to the conference room we have been using for ground zero. Finn and I haven't left since we both arrived in at five. There's a low murmur of voices and I look up to see Samantha. I know Finn kept her on for some IT projects, but she wasn't scheduled to be in the office until the girls are back in school next week.

She's wearing high-waisted dress trousers with a silk white shirt that shows lace underneath. Her hair is lifted high into a bun on the top of her head. She's wearing glasses and a simple gold band on her middle ring finger. Brad rolls out some blueprints on the table, and when Sam leans over to jot some notes on the paper, the dangle at her throat glitters. The necklace with the bezel-set emeralds sways softly as she moves. It highlights her neck, which is beautiful, and even in the chaos and frustration of this day I can't help but imagine how it would look with my come pooled at the base of her throat, spilling onto the sheets beneath us.

"What's the verdict?" Finn asks. Sam stands from her bent position.

"This code makes Brad's team look archaic. I was able to break some of the code, but I can't see how they froze the accounts. The money is there, but it's not—for all the sense that makes."

"So, we need to make a call to the SEC?" Finn asks.

Sam looks at her watch. "Clock started when?"

"Yesterday at noon," Brad says.

"Give me an hour, but keep your team on it."

"Where are you going?" Finn asks.

"To see Elise Donovan," Samantha says.

"We met with her," I remind her.

"But you didn't hire her. She can fix this," Sam says over her shoulder as she exits the conference room.

"Who is Elise Donovan?" Brad asks.

"She's a little bit of everything. Political Operative, Publicist, Marketing Consultant," Finn says.

"She a fixer," I grumble, a tad bit angry with myself. I purposely haven't been back to Elise after we first met with her several weeks ago. I inadvertently accused her fiancé of hiring the hackers so that we'd be forced to go to the SEC and take a hit to our stock. My stubbornness may have caused more frustration than necessary.

An hour later the conference room doors swing open, and Sam walks in with Elise.

"I need three million dollars wired to this account in thirty minutes," Elise says with no preamble, dropping a piece of paper in front of Finn. "Your accounts will be unfrozen, and you can report a repaired glitch to the SEC instead of the breach. Then tomorrow, I need two million transmitted to the second account listed. This will serve as a deposit. Three days tops your system will no longer be susceptible to these attacks. Once the rebuild is complete, you will need to send a remaining five million dollars to the third account."

"Let me get this straight. You want me to spend ten million dollars because you tell me to," I say slowly. I'm being a dick, but it grates mine that she is waltzing in here on her white horse like she's fixing this.

"Yes. That sums it up," Elise says, not remotely bothered by my surliness.

"And I would do that because?"

"I'm Elise Donovan."

"Ten million is nothing," Sam says. "Pay it and this all goes away. The patch we build after each hack is costing more than ten million. Ten million is a steal."

"What's to say they won't come back?" I ask. "We haven't been able to keep them away as of yet."

"Can we have the room please?" Samantha asks, nodding to the various people situated around the conference room. They follow her command and my dick thickens behind the zipper of my trousers.

"I found a signature in the code," Samantha says. "It's Waldo."

"Who the fuck is Waldo?" Finn asks.

I'm a tenth of a second away from commenting on his f-bomb but think better of it.

"You remember the airline system failure last June? The one that grounded flights for four days?" Elise asks. "That was Waldo. He cost the airlines about 150 million dollars in lost revenue and all he did was break the code in one place."

"It's his signature. It's so simple it's hard. Most hackers have to re-write the code extensively. It's hard to correct, but at least you know what you are correcting because it's easy to spot. With Waldo, you don't. It's literally one break in the code and a virus is hidden behind that break."

"So, he's called Waldo because?"

"It's like looking for a needle in a haystack. Like looking for Waldo, or Wally as you Brits call him," Elise says. "He also claimed responsibility for the electrical grid hacks that kept L.A. in the dark for two days this summer. The list goes on and on."

"What does he want?" I ask.

Elise shrugs. "It could be anything or nothing. It probably has something to do with the fact that you have more money than God. At one-point Waldo was like Robin Hood. Hitting greedy banks, government agencies, etc., but somewhere down the line started using his talent for evil instead and is more than likely doing this for fun."

"This is ridiculous," I bellow.

"It's ten million dollars. Do you know what it will cost you if you don't spend this? Hundreds of millions. Plus, your stock will plummet from the rumors of SEC investigations alone."

"I say pay it. It's a steal. What's your hesitation?" Finn asks.

"It feels like we're being held hostage and I don't like it," I answer. "I mean, who is more at fault? The person holding my accounts in peril or the person holding the repairs hostage until I agree to pay the ten million? What guarantee do I have that the person I let in to fix this won't create chaos himself?"

"Because I know the person who can fix this," Sam says. "And if you look at the accounts in front of you, you will see they are not personal or off shore bank accounts, they are charities. So, you get the credit for giving and you get Waldo out of your system."

Finn addresses Elise. "I thought Mask was the only person you said could get us out of this?"

"That's correct," Elise says.

"You know Mask?" Finn asks Samantha. "How?"

"I can't and won't answer that question. Elise represents Mask. The clock is ticking, we need an answer." Sam looks from Finn to me and back to Finn. He nods, and Elise exits the boardroom.

chapter sixteen

"You made it." Zinnie smiles when my guys enter the apartment. "I was worried you wouldn't," she easily admits with a smile on her face that is so genuine and candid, it's impossible not see what Tuesday dinners have come to mean to her.

"Of course, we're here." Pierce drapes an arm over her shoulders. "I changed my flight to Paris to be here."

Zinnie shrieks and starts throwing rapid-fire questions at him about the city and how she can't wait to go there one year for fashion week and the pictures she would love to get. Pierce sits with her on the couch and answers every question. He's always had a fondness for Paris and it's with ease that he promises her a trip on her sixteenth birthday.

Another shriek and she's pulling on my arm, begging me to let her go.

"Let's just see how you do this year in school," I offer without commitment, which brings about a slight pout, but when she plops back down, Pierce whispers something in her ear and she bursts out laughing. The fucker.

Colin is on the floor with Poppy. Her small hands are wrapped in his as he lifts her in the air above him with his feet like she is flying. Her giggles echo off the high ceilings.

When Finn and I came home, Zoe and Grace were already here. They hung out with the girls today while Sam worked on the security issues with us.

"Where's Sam?" Finn asks, popping a piece of pepperoni in his mouth. He snags two more before Zoe slaps his hand away.

"She went to pick up Charlotte," Grace says, sliding a tray into the oven.

I toss a beer to Quade, who's also getting his hand slapped from the mound of cheese Zoe is grating.

"How did she seem today?" Quade asks Finn before tilting his beer back.

"Better," Finn answers.

"How did who seem?" Grace asks.

"Sam," Finn replies.

"What's wrong with Sam?"

"Nothing is wrong, she just struggled to bounce back after Sunday. I think the Movie Monday outing helped."

"Kudos to you on the outfits." Zoe tilts her beer in my direction.

"I think today is what really did the trick," Finn adds. "We were so busy with the security issues, she didn't have time to worry about anything."

"I don't understand," Grace says. "What happened on Sunday? Did you get a call?" she asks Zoe, who shakes her head.

"Nothing happened," Finn says, "she just seemed…help me out here." He looks to me to describe her countenance the last couple of days.

"She just seemed a little stuck in her head. But I'm sure it has to do with tomorrow being September 1st."

"How do you know about September 1st?" Grace's tone is slightly accusatory. Her level of protectiveness goes up a notch.

"We took the girls to the cemetery Sunday, and while we were there, she put flowers on her family's graves," I answer.

"I had no idea she lost her family," Finn says.

After a long pause Zoe says, "She doesn't like to talk about it."

"Nine years ago," Finn says. "She would have been eighteen?"

"Nineteen," Zoe whispers.

"But she's only twenty-seven."

"Her birthday is September 1st," Grace explains. My heart sinks into my stomach so suddenly, I almost spit up my beer.

"Oh my fucking God," Quade says, his eyes are watering. "She seems so normal. How can anyone be normal after losing your entire family on your birthday?"

"She is normal, Quade." Grace says, even though it's clear that's not what he means. He means how does someone survive that. The four of us have barely survived losing Everett, and the girls their parents. I say a prayer of gratitude that the girls at least have each other.

"Did you know her back then?" Finn asks. I find myself torn. I want to know more about this woman I am certainly falling for, but it seems wrong for it to come from anyone but her.

"She was my roommate at NYU the semester before, but I had moved in with my girlfriend at the time," Zoe says. "And then after, Sam dropped out of school."

"I'm sure she needed the time," Quade says thoughtfully.

"She did, but she needed to work more," Grace says,

chopping peppers.

"Why?" he asks.

"They were poor. They didn't have burial insurance, they were upside down on their house. This was right when the housing market crashed. She had to pay hospital bills, so she couldn't afford that and school. After you took a chance on her," she nods to Finn, "she was able to make more money and pay off her debts. That's how she gets to go back to school now." Grace stops and looks to Finn. "If it wasn't for you it would be years at least before she could go back."

"The fuck?" Finn says with a mix of emotions. Anger appears to be winning out. "I would have taken care of anything she needed. Why didn't someone tell me?"

"You've met Sam, right?" Zoe shoots at him with a "don't act stupid" look.

I squeeze his shoulder in support. My brother has a heart larger than anyone. He sees someone in need and it's his natural reaction to want to take care of them.

"The girls are as good for Sam as she is for the girls. She would have never gone back to the gravesite if it wasn't for them. They're healing her. You're healing her," Grace adds looking at me. I glance over my shoulder to make sure she isn't talking to someone behind me. "Yes you," she smiles. "Now start chopping or out of the kitchen. Sam would not want us to stand around talking about her."

"That's our cue," Quade says, and Finn and I follow. We are not chopping menfolk.

The lift dings and laughter fills the room.

"Sam!" Poppy runs and jumps into her arms. Sam lifts her to her hip and gives her hugs and kisses. All in five-inch heels.

"I missed you today," Sam says, giving her a tight squeeze.

"I missed you, too," Pops attempts to whisper. One more

kiss and then Sam sets her on her feet before making her way to her room.

When she reenters a few minutes later, my gaze is drawn to her. Lately, I always know when she has entered the room. I'm falling for her. Hard. She's become as natural to me as my own skin.

She's wearing Finn's joggers low on her hips and the top she's wearing shows a small strip of skin between.

"Thanks for getting dinner started," she says to Zoe and Grace as she pulls her hair into a messy pile on her head. "Alright, everyone. Time to make your pizza," Sam shouts and the crew makes their way to the large island.

"You want to help Pops?" she asks me. She gently puts her hands on my hips to shift me to one side so she can reach the pizza crust sized for Poppy. I'm not even sure she's aware that she's touching me, but I have to press myself against the counter to keep my thoughts private because I'm in joggers having the control of a fucking teenager.

While Sam continues to direct traffic, I take a breath and make sure I'm decent before I lift Poppy up to the island, so she can build her pizza. Finn helps her with her sauce and she declares her pizza a masterpiece before following me to the pizza oven.

Fifteen minutes later, eleven pizzas are baking, and the girls are cleaning up the island remnants of any pizza making.

The buzz and flow of dinner has become a new normal. The only thing halting the multiple conversations is my telling the girls that Camilla and I are no longer engaged. It's not like I was putting off telling everyone, but the time never seemed right. I have to admit, no one seems surprised or upset by the announcement. Zinnie seems almost relieved, and Poppy only understands a little. It feels awkward for the focus to be solely on me and I'm more than a little grateful when Charlotte changes the subject.

A couple hours later, Quade is putting Poppy to bed and the men are cleaning the dishes. Which, to be fair, simply means we are loading a dishwasher.

"The Walt I know goes after what he wants," Pierce says, coming to stand beside me. His eyes land across the room on Sam.

"What are you talking about?" I bristle.

"You're playing house. Get off your ass and do something about it."

"She's dating Justin."

"Jason," Quade corrects, now on the other side of me.

"He knows it's Jason. He just doesn't give a fuck," Colin says with this Scottish twang. "And I agree. Pull your dick out of your own arse and put it to good use."

"She's not just a fuck, for Christ's sake," Finn says. "She's more than that to him. And she's not just any woman. You're going to have to pull out all the stops for her."

That night in bed, Finn's words play over and over in my head. What does pulling out all the stops look like? And how far is too far while this Jason bloke is in the picture?

I send a text to Finn letting him know not to expect me in the office tomorrow unless it's an emergency. I get a simple thumbs up in response and ring Charlotte. She's reluctant to tell me anything, but she does mention that Sam has not celebrated her birthday since the accident. She also agrees she thinks it's time she did and gave me a few hints about things Sam hasn't allowed herself to do in a while.

The next morning, I giddily pad my way to Zinnie's room and gently nudge her awake.

"Go away," she grumbles, pulling the covers over her head.

Can't say that I blame her. It's six-thirty in the morning, but we don't have much time before Sam wakes up.

"It's Sam's birthday. I'm going to make her a special breakfast. Want to help?" I ask.

"Can't we make her a special lunch?" she asks, throwing the covers back and sliding to the floor. "I'll meet you in the kitchen." She yawns and stretches. As she makes her way to her bathroom, I go in search of a curly-headed little girl.

"Good morning, sunshine," I say softly, sitting on the edge of her bed.

"Good morning sunbunny," she giggles and cuddles into my neck. This one always wakes up ready for anything, but lately it seems like her first order of the day is to be assured that I'm here, so I give her all the time she needs. "You smell clean," she says.

"Why thank you."

When I tell her about Sam's birthday, she jumps in excitement. I try to shush her, but she pushes me out of her room telling me she needs to find something.

I'm staring into the fridge when Zinnie walks up and stands next to me.

"Oh my God," she says in disbelief. "You don't know how, do you?" Her tone is one-part mocking and one-part relishing at my dilemma. I look at her and she rolls her eyes. "Fine. But you're helping *and* you're cleaning."

"Deal."

I spend the next thirty minutes playing sous chef. Poppy joins us with a picture she has colored for Sam and some paper board from her room.

"We have to make her the crown and stars," Poppy says to Zinnie who smiles and nods. She cuts the shape of a crown and stars out of the board and hands Poppy the tube of aluminum foil.

"Am I late?" Finn asks, coming in from the back stairwell.

"No. Can you help Poppy tape foil on these while Dad and I…" Zinnie freezes in her tracks then corrects herself. "While *Walt* and I finish breakfast." No one says anything. We just give her a minute to adjust.

When she comes back to her station to flip the flapjacks, I watch as her teeth worry her bottom lip. I kiss the top of her head before I wash the blueberries she assigned me to. I have no desire to replace Everett. But I would be lying if I didn't say there was a part of me that doesn't hope that one day they can see me as a father figure because somewhere, I'm not sure where or when, the lines blurred for me. All I see are two beautiful girls who I think of as mine. And they are. I used to begrudge my life being turned upside down. Now…well, now I'm grateful for it.

One of my security team enters discreetly into the room with the package I was expecting. The 24-hour service at Bergdorf's came in handy sooner than I anticipated.

Poppy places the three aluminum foil stars around her plate and the crown on top of the box, then shouts "Happy Birthday!" when Sam comes around the corner. Zinnie, Finn, and I follow suit in what is obviously a feeble and unrehearsed declaration of surprise.

To say Sam is shocked would be an understatement, and I'm about to second guess myself when Zinnie takes her hand and smiles at her. "We're celebrating you today. And that's okay." They share a moment between two people who have seen the same horrors. Sam nods tearfully and wraps her in an embrace and then gives Finn and Poppy a kiss and a thank you. I'm at the stove plating the last of the eggs when she gives my arm a squeeze and a peck to my cheek.

"Thank you," she says.

Like a complete moron, I don't respond. I don't tell her that I could give her the world if she would let me. I don't tell her that without her, my relationship with the girls would have never happened. I don't tell her that I see her for who she is. I don't tell her. I just nod my head in affirmation and hand her a plate of eggs. Fucking eggs.

We take our seats and Poppy proceeds to explain that the crown and stars are a tradition in their family. If it's your birthday, you wear the crown for breakfast, and you are given three stars to wish upon.

Sam pauses to think of her wishes and makes them without sharing. And in some ways I feel cheated that I don't know what they are, so I can make them happen.

"How did you know it was my birthday?"

"We have our ways," Zinnie says.

"Finn told you." Sam gives him a side-eye glance but none of us correct her. I don't want to rat out her friends. She picks up the box that Poppy has declared is from all of us and pulls the ribbon off. Inside is a bangle with five deep-blue sapphires. It's causal but stunning. Exactly as I described her to Ms. Smith, the personal shopper.

She gasps and makes a fuss over the gift. She slides it on and angles her wrist different ways catching the sunlight on the jewels. Her eyes are wet with emotion.

Breakfast is a success and when I announce they need to dress for fun and walking, they scatter off while Finn and I do the dishes.

"You really need to hire a maid," Finn moans. "I've washed more dishes in the last several weeks than I have in a lifetime."

"I don't think Sam wants one. She did hire a woman who performs deep cleaning every two weeks and I still have a laundry service, but she wants the girls to have normal chores."

"Her nobleness is giving me dishpan hands."

The girls are ready to go by the time I wipe the last counter and we bid farewell to Finn. He takes the stairs down and we take the elevator up to the roof where there's a helicopter waiting to take us to Coney Island.

Sam is fun. Vibrant. She likes to laugh. All things I love—I trip walking off the elevator, but catch myself. Wait. Love?

I don't have time to dissect my thoughts because Poppy is darting towards the open door and I have to scoop her up, explaining the seriousness of getting in and out of a helicopter thirty-three stories in the air. Once we are secured inside, she climbs into my lap and clasps a shared buckle around us both. From this vantage point she can see the buildings out the window while the pilot takes us on a tour of the city before flying us to Brooklyn.

I can't recall the last time I was at an amusement park, much less enjoyed myself. Maybe it was the company I enjoyed. Either way the day was a splendid success. The heaviness of the day before washed away in a never-ending supply of rides, games and cotton candy. The girls were the happiest I've ever seen them laughing and squealing. They didn't have a care in the world and I found myself praying all their days could be amusement park days.

"It's your turn to take her." Zinnie says nudging my shoulder when she falls onto the bench beside me.

"How is it my turn already?" I faux grumble as Sam pulls on my arm, lifting me into a standing position.

"I can't spin anymore, and Poppy is too short to ride with her." Zinnie says, pointing me in the direction of the ride Sam is anxiously awaiting.

"Let's go Walt. There's no line." Her fingers are wrapped

around mine and she doesn't let go even after my feet hit the pavement. I like the feel of her hand in mine. I'm addicted to her touch and it's not even sexual. We ride the cyclone and it's a whirlwind of rushing hills and plummeting valleys. As in all things, Sam is fearless in a challenge and leaves her hands in the air even when topping speeds of sixty miles an hour. She didn't feel the need hold on, but that didn't stop me from pushing her hips onto the seat every time I thought she was going to be propelled from the car. She cheers as we come to a stop and pops up as soon as the rail holding us in is released.

We wind our way back to the main path where Zinnie and Poppy are still seated, sharing a caramel apple. It's almost dusk. We have a short time until it's dark. We've been waiting to ride the Wonder Wheel at night to have the vantage point of seeing the park when it's lit. Sam stops and tries to convince the girls to go with her on the Spook-A-Rama while we wait, but they aren't biting. My hand is once again wrapped in hers as she steers the two of us to the added destination. The kid manning the ride, looks disinterested. The exact opposite of my riding partner who climbs into the crab shell shaped car that is ours for the duration of the ride. He gives us a spiel about keeping our arms in the car and sends us on our way. We push through some doors and it's pitch black. I literally could not see my hand if it was in front of my face. Sam shrieks when a puff of air is blown down our backs, she jumps and shifts herself against me. Her hand giving my thigh a squeeze when a scream pierces the silence. I wrap my arms around her and she willingly settles against me. She giggles when I jump slightly when animatronic rabid dogs jump against a cage directly next to me.

"You're rather enjoying this." I grumble teasingly.

"I am." She says seriously, and her hand finds my cheek

turning my face in her direction. A light flashes, illuminating her face and there's a look of pure appreciation on her features. She leans forward and with the gentlest touch of her lips to my cheek she says, "Thank you Walt."

"For what?" I ask trampling down every ounce of desire inside me trying to burst through to deepen the kiss.

"For giving me back my birthday."

"Sounds like a good time was had by all," Finn says in my office.

"It was a great time," I admit, grabbing the last of the files I need. After taking the day out of the office yesterday, I have a ton of work to catch up on after Poppy goes to bed.

"It's Thursday," Finn prompts as I slide the last note in my pocket and close the flap on my briefcase.

"That it is." Which means I should get to the apartment soon. It's Sam's night off and she has some concert she is going to with Jason. The squad was swooning over it at Tuesday's dinner. I tried to hide my disgusted eye roll. "You having dinner with us, or have you decided to actually have a life and get out of the house?"

"Have you decided to actually tell Sam you have feelings for her?" Finn fires back as we step into the lift.

"You've been hiding ever since you lost the fight for your boy." I ignore his comment and stay on my track. The one with street signs and directions. The other is a one-way street to who knows where.

"I didn't *lose* my boy. I just decided he was meant for *another* boy and bowed out like a gentleman should."

"Like you have any inkling of what a gentleman should and should not do."

"Well, I'm… learning," he chuckles, following me into the apartment.

"Perfect timing," Sam says, walking up to Finn. "Can you zip me in this? And full disclosure, you might need grease and fishing wire to get it closed." She takes a deep breath, her breast billowing high on her chest, and Finn reaches down to the middle of her arse and pulls her zipper up.

Fucking motherfucker. If he was off chasing dick, I would be the one zipping her up. I would know what—if anything— she has on under her dress. My finger would be guiding a path against her smooth skin for the zipper, ensuring it didn't snag on anything.

Instead, I watch a gay man with zero appreciation for this situation zip her into a dress that she looks like she was sewn into.

"Wow," Finn says, admiring her when he is done. "You look delicious." He says the last part like a cheesy character from a BBC show, eliciting an eye roll from Sam.

"I thought the festival was outside?" I frown at her attire. "Aren't you overdressed?"

"It's inside and I'm not overdressed. I'm just dressed."

"Like sex," Quade adds, entering the apartment. He struggles to take his gaze off Sam and focus on me. "Ready?"

"Ready for?" I ask.

"Meeting? Prospective client?" he says, like I'm supposed to have known this.

"I have the girls," I remind him.

"You're meeting is on the calendar. Zinnie is watching Poppy until you get home," Sam says, sliding into a pair of heels with Finn holding her elbow. She smooths her dress and the buzzer rings for the lift.

"Claire?" Sam says when a young girl with a soured expression walks out of the girls' wing. "I thought you were hanging out with Zinnie tonight?"

"Yes, ma'am, I was but Zinnie isn't up for it. She said we can hang next week after school."

"Is everything okay?" Sam asks. Claire answers despite appearing hesitant.

"She caught Darren kissing Lauren Myers."

"That little fu—" Sam's hand clasps over Quade's mouth before he can finish, then pats his cheek when she's sure he knows better than to continue.

"I tried to help take her mind off it, but she's just not ready."

"The doorman will make sure you get a cab," I tell her, showing her to the lift just as Jason is coming out. By the way Claire bats her eyes at him, I assume we could say he looks dreamy.

"You look unbelievable," he says, admiring Sam. Blarmy arsehole. I leave the two love birds and head towards my office with Quade, but when I hear her response, I can't help but pause as I round the corner and eavesdrop.

"So do you, but I'm sorry I can't go tonight," she says.

"What do you mean? You're dressed, you're ready to go."

"Something's come up with Zinnie. She needs me tonight." It surprises me when she doesn't offer him more of an explanation.

"You're really sharpening those creeper skills," Quade whispers behind me, causing me to jump. I shush him and he leans in, propping his chin on my shoulder to get into a better listening position.

"She can need you tomorrow. Let's go," Jason says with irritation.

"I can't. I'm sorry."

"But that's just it. You can. And if you don't, then that's it. I won't be with someone who isn't committed to putting us first."

I almost dance a jig. I know Sam, and this ultimatum won't fly.

"Then I'm doing you a favor," she says without an ounce of regret or question in her voice.

"These girls don't care about you. You're a damn nanny. The fucking hired help. I can't believe you are choosing them over me."

"Yeah. You should go."

I know that tone. I have come to speak "Sam" fluently. This man needs to get on the lift quickly before Sam tells him how she really feels.

We hear some shuffling of feet and a few mumbles. She must be walking Jason to the lift. Quade and I trip over each other to get to a spot where we can hear more of the conversation, but Finn catches us, so we pretend like we were just walking out of the office.

"Idiots," Finn mutters.

"So, I called them and said—" Quade pretends he was mid-sentence when Sam steps back into the room. "Oh," he says, feigning surprise, "I thought you were leaving?"

"I don't want to leave Zinnie when she's upset," she says stepping out of her shoes and yelling for Finn, who magically pops his head around the doorframe like he wasn't standing there listening. "Can you unzip me?"

"How the hell would you have gotten out of this tonight?" he asks her.

"I had hoped to have someone else to do it for me," Sam grunts on her way into her room.

"Another night maybe," Finn offers, and I hear Sam tell him there will be no more nights with Jason, before she closes her door.

"How bad do you wish you were Finn right now?" Quade jabs.

A minute later Finn opens the door and informs me Sam said to go to my meeting, and that she would be here with the girls.

"You guys go ahead," I tell them. "I'll be there in a minute."

I, regrettably, give Sam another minute to be presentable and knock on her door. I hear a muffled command to come in and when I open the door I hear her say, "I'm in here."

I wind my way into her bedroom. All of the other nannies had a few photos out, maybe a bag here or there. The room looks like she's been living here as long as I have. I feel a comfort wash over me just being around her things.

Her mobile rings when I enter her bathroom, and she puts it on speaker.

"Hello?" Sounds like Grace.

"Hey. Code Blue," Sam says with a hair tie in her mouth. She's combing her hair back with her fingers.

"What? Jason already?" Grace asks. I hear a muted shuffling on the other end.

"Actually, yes, but the Code Blue is Zinnie. Darren."

"That little shit. I'll cut his balls off and sew them to his face."

"Oh my God, Grace. Leave the tough talk to Zoe."

"I can totally pull off the trash talk."

"Sew his balls to his face?"

"Fine. I'll call the girls. Be there in twenty."

"Sorry. What's up?" Sam says, disconnecting her call before she begins washing the makeup off her face.

"You didn't have to cancel for Zinnie. I could have taken care of her." I pretend this is what my visit is about when clearly that's not why I'm in here. I actually don't know why I'm here. But instead of standing here with my dick in my hand like a total tool, I pretend this is about Zinnie.

"It's her first breakup. She sent her best friend away. Of course I'm staying." She runs a washcloth over her face one last time before turning off the water. She props her hip against the bathroom counter and looks at me. I can tell she knows I have something else to say. She's missed a couple beads of water and my eyes trail them as they trickle off her cheek and fall to the curve of her breast below.

"Yes. Well. I'll just be around the corner if you need me. Um, I mean if Zinnie needs me," I stammer and attempt an exit that hopefully is less awkward than I feel. Her hand on the crook of my arm stops me.

"You really are doing great with the girls. I can see the difference in them."

"Silly Sam. Don't you see?" I lean closer to her. "The difference is you."

I've stunned her into silence. This woman who has a response for everything. Before she can lessen my words with a quirky response I leave her room and freshen up in my own. The lift dings as soon as I press the call button, but it's not empty. It's carrying Grace and Charlotte.

"Zoe's on her way. She's picking up the pizzas. I brought ice cream," Grace says. Charlotte adds, "And I brought cookie dough and Kit Kats." She holds up a tub of raw chocolate chip cookie dough.

"Ooh, Kit Kats make everything better!" Sam says behind me.

chapter seventeen

Oomph. I grunt bumping into Quade's back when he comes to a complete stop just inside the door. It would be a lie to deny I manipulated our meeting to end early, and Quade insisted on coming back to the apartment to see how Zinnie was doing.

He holds a finger to his mouth and cocks his head to the side. Then he quietly sneaks us into the kitchen undetected, allowing us to eavesdrop on the scene in the living room. He hands Finn and I a beer before snagging one for himself. Sam and her crew, the two girls, and Claire, who apparently was invited back, are strewn about the living room. Alanis Morisette is playing in the background.

"And the whole time he was trying to make me think I was the crazy one. Like I was being emotional or irrational every time I said that he was hooking up with someone else," Zinnie says. "I am so over men. I'm going to be a lesbian like you." She points a spoonful of cookie dough towards Zoe. The area around them is filled with every comfort food you can fathom.

"Not all men cheat," Charlotte reminds her.

"Who came up with code blue?" Claire asks.

The women each furrow a brow in thought before Zoe declares it was Grace, to which they all nod in agreement.

"Because of Benji," she recalls.

"Ugh. He was a total dick...tator." Zoe catches herself, eyes darting to Poppy as Sam bounces a pillow off her head.

"Watch it. This Code Blue is G rated."

"Fine. Then let's dance some more. Dancing makes everything better," Zoe declares standing. "Zinnie. This is the last thing I'm going to say, then we're going to eat and dance—the prettiest thing a girl can wear is confidence."

And she's right because confidence looks damn good on Samantha.

"To Zinnie!" They raise their glasses and dancing commences.

"That's my cue, boys." Quade tosses his coat on the island, rolls up his sleeves, and kicks off his shoes. They shriek with surprise when Quade barges in and then swarm him as he throws himself at their mercy.

While Quade basks in the glory of feminine youth, I have spent the last few hours actually working on the issues that came up during our meeting. I'm spent. I lean back in my chair and stretch, checking the clock. I need a break, so I leave my office in search of a snack of some kind.

The music has been turned down but is playing softly. There are wrappers scattered everywhere, pillow and blankets strewn about. The guys have left, but there are still sleeping women strewn about the living room. Zinnie and Claire are bunking on the floor. Poppy is on a couch with Zoe and Grace. Charlotte is wrapped around Sam like a flag.

We grew up in a tidy, reserved house. In turn, I have always had a tidy, reserved house. It should feel unsettling to me to see a living room that cost more than these women make collectively in a year in shambles. Instead, it feels right. I dim the lights and turn off the music all together. Something calls at me, something powerful, and I head back to my room.

I place my watch on the top of the dresser in my closet, and I notice Everett's letter. The letter has been here all along. I always place my watch next to it at night when I prepare for bed, but I've always ignored it, pushed it away. But tonight, I can't ignore it. I pick it up and the weight it carried just weeks ago is no longer there. The thickness that was once overwhelming now boasts of information and guidance.

I carry the letter into the bedroom. Propping my back against a bank of pillows, I take a long drink of my bourbon. Then another. My thumb traces Everett's chicken scratch. *Walt.* A line drawn abstractly under my name. I slide my finger under the sealed lip of the envelope and pull the thick vanilla-cream paper from its confines.

Walt,

Yep. I'm dead.

That's the only reason you would be reading this. That and the girls haven't turned 21. I really didn't want to write this letter. Felt like it wasn't necessary. Needed. But if you're reading this, then Jenny was right. Better to be prepared than to have your arse blowing in the wind.

I know I should have asked you. Told you. Given you some kind of clue that if something happened to both of us, you would be raising two girls. But where does one start a conversation like that? How does one say to a man who never intends to have children, "Hey, by the way, you don't want to have kids, but there's a minute possibility you will be raising mine. And, oh yeah, they are ten years apart. And, oh yeah, they're girls."

God, when Jenny got pregnant with Zinnia, we were kids. We didn't have a clue what to expect or how to love something more than ourselves. How to be responsible for something that needs oxygen and nourishment to survive. Are you fucking kidding me?

So, I did what I always do. I researched. I went to the university library and read everything I could get my hands on. I talked to people who had paved the road before us. I crunched numbers and solved all the mathematical equations that told me just how much I was going to fuck this up. Anything to give me an inkling what I was getting into. This is what I learned: Nothing.

Nothing that taught me how to be a parent. Nothing that gave me the security I so desperately needed and craved at the time. Nothing. There are no guarantees when it comes to parenting. Sure, there are ways to hedge the odds, but nothing with any surety.

Once I realized there was no guarantee, I went in search of best practices.

I found it talking to Jenny's grandfather. He told me, "Son. The only thing you have to do is love. Love them more than yourself. The rest will fall into place. You'll make mistakes, then you'll correct them, and then you'll make more."

I remember looking at him like he was delusional. How does someone love something more than themselves? But I knew I could figure it out. I fell in love with their mom, right? I would eventually learn to love them. It was the only thing I had to hold on to.

Turns out the crazy bastard was right. What he failed to tell me is it would be instantaneous. One minute, I'm Everett. The next, I'm so head over hills in love with the tiny creature placed in my arms that I know there is nothing I wouldn't do to ensure her wellbeing. And then her sister's. Their happiness, their sense of security.

So, I wrote this letter, because I do love my girls. I do care about their wellbeing. I want them to be happy and secure. To feel loved and cared for. And when I had to choose who to give the most precious commodity I have to, it was easy to choose. You.

Jenny and I never hesistated. There was no discussion for either of us. We chose you from the beginning. So, don't fuck it up you fucking arsehole.

Sorry. A little beyond the grave humor.

You are going to fuck this up. I can't tell you how many times I did, because I lost count. And I will let you in on a little secret. Most of the time the girls don't know when you are.

Also, you're welcome. I had to figure out that little nugget all on my own.

I'm sure you're wondering why two people would choose a man who has said so many times that he never wanted children to be my children's guardian. One word: Finn.

September, first year at uni. We were surrounded by women and prospects. Every guy wanted to be us and every girl wanted us in her bed. We were on our way to having exactly what we wanted. Your phone rang. You could have ignored it, but it was Finn, so you answered it. He didn't say anything alarming. He just wanted to talk to his brother for a minute. The senior classmen were giving you shit about being on your phone. When you hung up you told them you had to leave. They threatened you with everything in the book. You wouldn't make it into any fraternity. You would be black-listed. You would be the one ev-eryone laughed at. I remember thinking, what the hell are you doing? And I said as much, but without an ounce of hesitation, you said he needed you and you were going. I asked you what he said, and you said, "Nothing. I just know he does." And you left with no regards to what it meant for your future.

To love our kids is programmed, hardwired into who we are. But the kind of man, husband, and sibling we are is a choice. And time and time again you chose Finn. Hundreds of times you put him before yourself.

So. You can blame Finn. Go ahead. I won't tell anyone the truth. That you love another more than yourself and that is why we chose you.

I know our girls will miss us. I know it will be difficult. But it will get better. You will get better. They can and will come to see you as their dad. And that, my friend, is how you honor me.

You were my greatest friend,

E

I read. And read again. It explains the whys, but the an-swers to how aren't in here. For some reason, that's comfort-ing. Everett didn't know them either and learned it as he went like I am. I trust he would not have left out anything of value. He wasn't the kind of guy to leave something to chance. He gave me the map. Love them more than myself. Which, I do. I didn't at the beginning. And I'm not sure I even did a month ago, but there is no debate about it now. I love those girls like they were my own.

chapter eighteen

The weekend is controlled chaos. The girls want for nothing, yet I still found myself with a list of items to purchase before school started. After hour three of Zinnie trying on no less than a hundred outfits, I found myself wishing I had hired a personal shopper to have everything delivered to the house. I'm quite sure I vetoed more outfits than I approved. Jesus, there was an outfit that I swear made her look like she could be Sam's age. I'm not going to get through these teenage years unscathed.

Every free minute Sam had this weekend was spent studying. She mentioned being behind, but I don't think I realized to what extent. I haven't been able to pinpoint if she is truly behind or if she is putting more pressure on herself than warranted. My hope is that, with the girls starting school, her time constrictions will open some. I make a mental note to talk to Finn about her work schedule. I don't want her pulled into so many directions. Every part of her adult life has been hard work. I want to make this chapter as easy for her as possible.

"Alright," Sam says, handing the girls their lunches. Today

is the first day of classes. Zinnie begged to go to school on her own. I finally relented, but only because she will have security discreetly following her. I don't want to alarm her, but she is never totally out on her own.

The four of us take the lift down, after stopping on Finn's floor to show off the new outfits and uniforms. Zinnie turns left to head to her school. Sam, Poppy, and I are driven to Poppy's school where we find a long line of kids being walked in. There are a couple of dads here, but mostly moms and nannies dropping off their kids. Sam and I meet Poppy's teacher, and before we can get a hug or even a pat on the arm telling us we will be okay, she's gone. Off to a brightly colored rug on the floor where already she is making a friend.

"Well that was like a knife to the gut," I grunt, closing the car door behind me. "You think she would at least have made sure we were alright before darting off to do her own thing."

Sam smiles and her hand lands on mine, squeezing it.

"You will be just fine," she assures me. "You would rather have that than tears and fits at being abandoned."

"I suppose. But a little something to acknowledge what I'm going through isn't too much to ask. Fancy some breakfast?"

"I would love to, but I have to get to class. I have to present a paper. It's half my grade for the semester, and I'm already behind."

I work to keep the disappointment off my face. "First the girls. Now you. Guess I'll have to find Finn for some companionship." She laughs, and my cock twitches at the delightful sound. It's hearty and airy with just the right melody.

The day moves by with ease. We haven't had any more hacking issues. The ten million appears to have been a sound investment. Elise held up her end of the bargain. After the threat was eliminated, Mask created a shield that has, so far, been impenetrable.

Because I got to drop off the kids today, I promised Finn he could pick up Poppy. I'm pretty sure he looked at his watch no less than a dozen times in our last meeting.

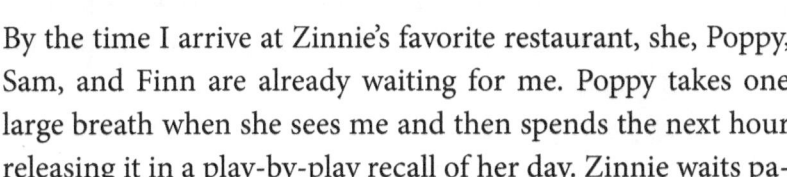

By the time I arrive at Zinnie's favorite restaurant, she, Poppy, Sam, and Finn are already waiting for me. Poppy takes one large breath when she sees me and then spends the next hour releasing it in a play-by-play recall of her day. Zinnie waits patiently for Pops to get all her stories out of the way, and as we walk back to our building, I finally hear how hers went.

Until today, I was never grateful for small things, like hearing your kids made friends, liked their school, hearing about every bit of the tedium of their day. I wonder if my parents felt this way? I doubt it. I'm pretty sure the nanny dropped me off on my first day of school.

"Sam?" A deep voice stops our advance.

"Professor Blume," she says with surprise.

"Zeke, please. I didn't know you had kids," he says with what sounds like disappointment.

"I'm Zinnie. She's our nanny," Zinnie offers with a deviant smile and nudges Sam closer to him with her shoulder.

"What kind of name is Zeke?" I ask from the corner of my mouth.

"The kind of name that fits a man like that," Finn says appreciatively. Am I missing something? He's about my age. I guess he is what some would call good-looking.

"Talk about wanting to stay after school. I'd like to beat his erasers," Finn says under his breath, warranting an elbow to the ribs from Zinnie.

"And this is my boss, Walt," Sam says.

He nods his head at me, and I level him with a glare that I hope conveys the depths to which I will fuck him up if he even thinks of acting on his lust for Sam. His eyes shine as if he is accepting a challenge. I take the bait.

I place my hand on the small of Sam's back and give her a slight nudge forward, letting her know we need to be going.

"Well, it was lovely seeing you. I'll see you in class on Wednesday," Sam offers with smile.

"I look forward to it. Make time to stop by my office. We can see how your paper is evolving."

"My times don't match your office hours. I planned to email a draft."

"You have my number. Text me a time you are free, and I'll work my schedule around yours. Want to make sure you take advantage of all available opportunities afforded to you. You're my keynote speaker, after all. Nice to meet you young ladies." He winks at the girls and I clench my fist to keep from poking him in the eye.

"Oh my God, Sam! He was hot," Zinnie says, tugging on her arm and walking backwards for a minute to catch a glimpse of him walking away.

"Zeke? Really?" I grumble aloud. Sam laughs, shushing me. Like you might do to a friend. Or worse, a brother. My head falls back in frustration before Finn squeezes my shoulder in solidarity.

When we get back home, we part ways. Finn and I head to the gym to shoot some hoops, while Sam and the girls work on homework and bedtime rituals. When I arrive back home a couple of hours later, Sam is helping Zinnie with her economics homework, explaining what it means to make a business plan.

"Do you think it's too ambitious?" Zinnie asks.

"I don't. Not all businesses succeed. At least you are try-ing. Finish writing your business plan and have Walt look at it before you have to turn it in. He'll give you his honest opinion. So far, it is a strong start, but I think you are being conserva-tive in your profit predictions. Now, bedtime," Sam adds, look-ing at her watch.

"Good night, sweetheart." I hug Zinnie when she plac-es a kiss to my cheek. After she leaves, I watch as Sam pulls out books and notebooks along with her laptop. I should have stayed to help the girls with bedtime and homework, so she could study. I'm such a jerk. But she doesn't complain or seem put out. Instead, she opens her music app and her fingers tap away on the computer.

When I get up at three in the morning to grab some water, Sam is still up. Hair is going in a hundred directions. Glasses I didn't know she wore rest on the bridge of her nose. The mu-sic is still playing, and she's oblivious that I'm creeping in the shadows.

I'm up at six to grab some breakfast before going to the office. Today is Sam's day to drop off Poppy at school. Only she's still at the table, music playing, her head is resting on her arms.

"Shh. She's asleep," Finn whispers from the bar. He's blow-ing on a hot cup of coffee.

"Do you ever eat at your place?" I ask.

"No," Sam says, sitting up and rubbing her eyes. "And I'm not asleep. I was just resting my head."

"You need sleep," I chastise. "You can't keep going at this pace."

"I'm going to shower," she mumbles dragging herself to

her wing.

Thirty minutes later, Zinnie goes to check on Sam. There's a small scream, followed by laughter, a thud, and more laughter.

"Sam fell asleep on the toilet," she giggles, running back into the kitchen. "I think she's going to need a minute. She's running late."

"Come on. I'll take you today," I tell Pops.

"Can someone push the elevator button for me?" Sam asks, jumping into one shoe, then the other. The lift dings just as I fasten the last button on Poppy's jumper.

Sam's arms are full when she jogs into the entry. The three of us stand in a row, watching in amusement at her bedlam as she distributes kisses, papers, and instructions to both girls and Finn. Without a thought, she does the same to me. Her soft, full lips touch the soft skin of my newly shaved cheek. Six steps later and she's in the lift, turning suddenly. She points as she counts each person just now realizing she gave one more kiss than usual. Mine. She blushes. And, fuck me, is it a sexy blush.

I laugh, attempting to make it less awkward for her. "Get going," I say, shooing her along. She chuckles again and issues a sorry with a backwards wave over her head.

As the door closes on the two of them, I can't help but think about that kiss. If it had just been two inches to the left...

A giggle and an elbow to my arm pulls me from my daydream and Zinnie hits me with a wink.

"Go on now. Grab your things. We need to go."

The week continues in much of the same fashion. Our mornings have become a well-choreographed movement of timelines and routines. By the time the weekend rolls around, the girls are thrilled to be out of school and quite frankly, I am exhausted. I honestly had no idea how much of a time suck kids can be. Though I wouldn't change it for anything.

Saturday is play dates, and time with friends. Sunday is family brunch and one more shopping trip to get the last of Zinnie's school clothes. Sam, Finn and I rock, paper, scissor our way out of going. I lost. Always choose rock. Always.

An hour later Zinnie and I were wandering through Bergdorf's looking for more clothes and items she insisted she needed for school.

On our way to yet another rack of clothes, we inadvertently passed the counter that carries the perfume Jenny always wore. The scent triggered Zinnie and the result was immediate. She burst into tears in the middle of the store, drawing the eyes of nearly every shopper around us. I tried everything I could think of to soothe her, but I finally had to give up and bring her home, my arms wrapped around her the whole way.

The minute she entered the apartment, she ran to Sam, fell onto her lap, and sobbed. I tried to offer a gentle explanation, but Sam, in her unique ability to offer comfort, gave Zinnie what she needed. Time to cry.

"Will it always be this way?" Zinnie sniffs.

"It gets easier, but it never totally goes away. You will always think of your mom when you smell her perfume. I always think of my mom when I smell her soap. But eventually, you get to where the tears aren't there. Just the memory."

"Don't get me wrong. I love living with you guys, but some days I miss my parents so much it feels like I can't breathe."

"I know, honey."

"Poppy?" I ask.

"With Finn," Sam answers, still rocking Zinnie back and forth.

"Might as well get this out now then while you're upset," I

sigh, sitting down across from them. I've been putting off this conversation. We've been on a stretch of good days lately and I just didn't have the heart to derail us. But she's upset now, so might as well get it over with.

"The District Attorney called me this week about your parent's accident. They want to offer a plea bargain to the man driving the other car."

"What? Why?" Zinnie asks.

"Well, he's young and they want him to go through rehab to get help for his drinking. He'll serve a reduced sentence in hopes they can rehabilitate him."

"So, give him a second chance?" Zinnie says, aghast. "That's what you're telling me? What about Mom and Dad's second chance? They didn't get one. Why should he? Our parents would be alive if it weren't for the choices he made. I hate him and wish they would kill him like he killed my parents."

"Zinnie," Sam chastises gently. "Don't say that. Accidents happen. Even when there are external factors like drinking and bad decisions involved. Hate is a horrible thing to walk around with. It will eat at you until you don't even recognize yourself. Trust me, I know."

"Did you hate the person who killed your parents?"

"I did. Still do sometimes. It's a work in progress. But forgiveness is forgiveness, and eventually I came to see that forgiveness is always for me, not for the other person. Because if you walk around with hate in your heart, it will destroy the person you are."

"I don't know if I can forgive. I don't know that I want to," Zinnie admits.

"Why don't you start talking to the therapist again. She can help you talk through these feelings. I wouldn't be here today without that kind of guidance and the love and support of my friends."

We sit in silence for a while before Zinnie agrees to give it another try.

I told Zinnie she didn't have to decide right away, but slowly, over the next couple of weeks, she made the decision to accept the plea bargain. She was thoughtful and smart and kind, and I couldn't have been more in awe of this child who took this on to decide.

Out of everyone, Pierce and her therapist were the most helpful. Her therapist helped her sort through her thoughts, and Peirce was honest and upfront. While the rest of us were giving her space to let her make her own decision, Pierce didn't hold back his opinion. In the end, it's what Zinnie needed—concrete guidance. So, when he told her he believed in rehabilitation over incarceration, I think it resonated with her in ways my opinion didn't.

I'm learning how important the people you surround your children with are. It really does take a village.

All of this weighted heavily on me all day, which made getting through work a bit more difficult than usual. And today was one for the books. I didn't think I would make it home for our Tuesday night dinner, and I would be lying to say that it doesn't still shock me that just the thought of having to entertain people tonight had me feeling a little out of sorts earlier.

"Where is everyone?" I ask Zinnie as I loosen my tie. She's sitting cross-legged on the couch with books scattered around her, laptop open on her lap. She removes an earbud and I repeat my question.

"Pierce texted that he would be late. Quade and Colin took Charlotte and Grace to pick up dinner. They didn't feel like cooking. Finn—I thought he was with you. Zoe wanted to pick Pops up from ballet. Dinner was moved back to seven. Sam is studying outside. Needed fresh air." She puts her earbud back in, her neck popping to the music.

Dinner at seven. That explains why I'm not late.

I change into jeans and a T-shirt before grabbing a scotch. I head outside to find Sam and enjoy the weather while it's still warm enough. Mother Nature led us to believe summer was over, but we've had an unusually warm week.

"Grabbing the last of the sun while you can?" I ask, taking the lounge chair next to Sam.

Silence. Correction, light snoring. Sam has been burning the candle at both ends. I've pushed her to slow down and to allow me to get her some help, but she insists she's the help and "help shouldn't need help". The decision to step in is an easy one. If Sam's not going to take care of herself on her own, then I have no problem being up to the task.

I lift her into my arms. Now that I'm actually counting, I think she has had three hours of sleep a night at the most. She mumbles an incoherent mixture of words about needing to study, but it's gone as quickly as it came.

"Sleep."

"Dinner."

"Next time."

She mumbles something about there are only fifty-two of these. I assume she means weekly dinners a year. And, yeah, in the scheme of a whole year that is not that many, but she will have to miss this one. I'm about to argue my point, but it's moot. She is passed out, her head propped against my shoulder.

Settling her under the covers in her bed, I curse the

heavens that she is dressed in something comfortable enough to sleep in, otherwise I would have helped her change. Just my dumb luck. Her hair fans across the pillow. No makeup. No adorning. Just Samantha in all her beauty. She has a mole behind her ear, and before I can talk myself out of it, I kiss it, drawing in her scent. My lips touch her forehead while my thumb skims her jawline, and without even thinking, I press my lips to hers in a kiss far gentler and controlled than I'm feeling capable of.

"Sleep," I order. But she is already completely under.

The main area is bustling when I enter. The gang is back with Italian and they are setting the table. Sometimes I like it casual, where we eat at the bar or we fix a plate and eat in the living room, but just as much I love to eat family style. Food being passed to and from, over conversations, tall tales, and clanging dishes. That is what it looks like we are getting to-night. Sam is right. We only get fifty-two of these a year. It's still not enough to make me wake her.

"Zoe is running a few minutes late. She and Poppy stayed to practice her pirouettes," Finn says, setting out the plates. Grace and Zinnie are discussing her latest changes to the blog she started. Pierce is laughing, and I watch him watching Charlotte. I'm not sure how I missed it. Possibly because he's closed off more than anyone. If it wasn't for the girls I'm not sure his heart would be recognizable. The women in this fami-ly aren't the only ones dealing with loss.

I'm around these people quite a bit, but there is more I can learn in sixty minutes of dinner than I can in a week of sporadic conversations. Like the fact that Poppy made her way onto some fashion website. Apparently, the way Sam and Zinnie are dressing her is catching the eye of fashion bloggers. Sam and Zinnie ran into her professor again yesterday. I could have gone without the play-by-play on that one. Zoe has a new girlfriend. Quade went out on a second date, which is unheard of. And a boy kissed Poppy in class today. That one stops all traffic.

"A boy kissed you?" Pierce says in a voice that sends a tinge of fear down the spines of everyone around the table. Except Poppy's.

"Yes. His name his Howie."

"And where pray-tell did this *Howie* kiss you?" Pierce asks.

"On the reading squares."

"No, dummy. He means where on your body did he kiss you?" Zinnie explains with a smile.

"Oh. On my cheek." She points to her cheek.

"You tell Howie to keep his lips to himself until you are 21."

"That's like a hundred years from now. I can't do that. I plan to kiss him tomorrow."

That little chunk of information was enough to hijack the rest of dinner.

chapter nineteen

"What are you doing?" I ask Sam as I leave my office. She's leaning against the wall at the end of the hallway, her cheek against the wall.

Sam and I have been dancing around each other for a week now. Okay, I've been dancing around for a week now. Sam has been completely normal and completely oblivious to the fact that we have already shared our first kiss. I suppose that is what happens when you kiss someone while they are sleeping.

It's been a lazy, stormy Sunday afternoon. Just what this group needed. The girls are a month into their school routines and they are ready for a break. Sam has been—I don't know how she does it, actually—juggling the girls, her classes, and working for Finn. Despite his and my objections.

I use to think she was stubborn and didn't like taking what she considers a handout. And while I do think she has a sense of needing to earn her way, lately it seems like more than that. Almost as if she believes all of this *should* be hard, and if it wasn't then it wouldn't feel fair. She hasn't communicated this, but she doesn't need to. I can read her so well now. More than I ever could with Camilla.

"Shh," she silences me when I walk up behind her.

"Why are you smiling?" I faux-whisper, my shoulder touching hers as I lean my back against the wall.

"I'm happy." And she is. I look at her beautiful smile, and it's a sight I pray I never take for granted.

"What makes you happy?" In this moment there is nothing I genuinely want to know more and find myself wanting to make sure she always is.

"Listen."

Laughter. The girls are laughing. I lean over Sam to peep around the corner, and as a result, the inches separating us disappear as my body aligns with hers. The girls are curled together on the couch watching an episode of *I Love Lucy*. It's the one where Lucy is in the chocolate factory. Once Poppy made the decision that she is going to be Lucy for Halloween, the redhead's antics have been gracing our telly every free chance there is.

"Our girls are happy," Sam says with a contented sigh.

I'm not too manly to admit my heart flutters when she says "our girls".

She stands there for a beat listening and peeking around the corner. She's taking it all in, but the only thing I'm taking in is her. I don't give myself time to think. I don't want to. I'm afraid I'll talk myself out of what I've wanted to do for weeks now.

My hands find a home in the curve of her waist and when my lips touch the shell of her ear, her body tenses.

"They are happy," I whisper. "You make them happy." It's true. I don't move my lips. I don't have my fingers on her pulse, but I know its accelerating.

"You make them happy, too," she says roughly. There is no doubt she can feel my erection pressing against her.

"Walt." The way she says my name has me at full arousal.

"I don't think this is a good idea," she says with a slight hitch in her breath.

"Then stop thinking," I say my teeth biting down her neck to the curve leading to her shoulder, access easily granted to me since her hair is pinned up. My heart wildly beats and skips when she finally gives me the permission I've been waiting for. She leans her head against my shoulder. If there was any question in my mind, it dispels when her hands reach behind us and pull my hips tighter to her.

I shift so my body is completely covering hers, enveloping her in me.

"What are we doing?" she breathes.

"If you have to ask, then I'm not doing it right," I whisper before my tongue dips inside her ear. Her hips push into mine, telling me she likes it. I skim my lips across the back of her neck to the other side, and she tilts her head slightly when I reach my destination. At the same time, my hands begin an exploration of their own. One slides under her shirt until it finds the hardened nipple at the edge of her breast. She is wearing two tank tops, but I'm thrilled she isn't wearing a bra. My hand massages her breast roughly. The thrill of finding her braless is nothing compared to the treat I find as my hands sink under the band of her joggers. She isn't wearing knickers.

"Fuck me. Is it your goal to kill me before I get started?"

"I didn't know you were going to have your hand in my pants," she chuckles, then shivers when my hand slides further down, my middle finger sliding between her folds, reaching my destination.

"Oh my God," she whimpers. And fuck me, it is a

destination that should have been top of my bucket list, because her sweet little pussy is everything I want it to be. Warm, wet, and waiting for my touch. I find her little nub and circle the pad of my finger in an easy repetitive motion that soon mirrors the one her hips are making.

"Oh my God."

"You said that already," I chuckle, quickening my pace, her wetness audible with each swipe I make.

"Please."

"Please what, Samantha?"

"I need more," she whimpers.

"What is more?" I wait for her to tell me. I need her to play an active role in what is about to happen next, because I'm minutes away from fucking her into tomorrow.

"I need your fingers inside me."

Not only do I not need to be told twice, but I also don't need it pointed out to me that she said fingers. More than one. Oh yeah, Sam and I are going to be good together.

My middle finger slides the rest of the way down, snaking its way inside of her. I want in there. Want it to be my dick more than I want air. Food. Water. This time I'm the one moaning my satisfaction. Sam raises on her tip toes so that I maneuver further inside of her. The knowledge of her desire elevates my dick into an iron spike in my trousers.

"More," she says, and I add another finger.

"God, yes." She inhales, her head falling to my shoulder, and her fingers tickle over my hand inside her. I realize I might come just from doing this.

She fingers her clit, wanting to be part of this dance, and together we take her to a full body climax. I cover her mouth with my hand and remind her to keep quiet. Her entire body goes limp and melts into the wall, my arms the only thing keeping her off the floor.

"Walt, what did we—"

I don't give her time to finish that thought. She doesn't get time to think or analyze or wonder what this means. No. I want her too much and I'm nowhere near done with this woman.

My mouth takes hers as soon as I flip her around, ending her words of caution and question. For a moment I wonder if she's going to call me on my shit and pull away, but instead her fingers comb through my hair as she pulls me to her in a bruising kiss. Our lips never part as my hand grabs at her arse. She takes the hint and pulls herself to me. I lift her into my arms.

That's all I need. I know exactly how this is going to end. I walk the few steps to her quarters and close the door behind us, turning the lock.

"Phone," she says, breaking the kiss.

"What?" I'm so high on lust I have no idea what she is talking about. Instead of repeating herself she reaches into my pocket and finds my mobile. She taps out something, then kisses my lips before dipping into my mouth. I groan as her tongue dances with mine.

"Finn. Coming to get the girls," she says between kisses. I walk us into her bedroom. There's a *swoosh* and then her tanks are nowhere to be found. She pulls the back of my shirt up. "Skin," she says before biting my lip. "I need skin."

The knowledge she's as with me as I am with her buckles my knees. Thank God, we made it to her bed already. She lands under me, her legs still wrapped around my waist. I'm full on humping her at this point, and if I don't get control, she's going to have a joggers-covered dick inside her at the velocity my dick is moving.

Pulling back to gather my wits about me I see this woman under me. Samantha.

My body immediately heels, waiting for my directive. Like me, it understands that this woman is to be savored and indulged. This is not a quick fuck.

Her brow furrows detecting my change, but I ignore the question I find there and kiss her lips slowly before sliding her joggers over her backside. I step from between her legs, so I can pull them off her and when they are, the woman lying on the bed is nothing short of spectacular. I lean back over her to offer another kiss, then mold my hands against her skin charting my way over her neck and the arch of her shoulders. Slowly and with each fingertip in contact with her beautiful skin, I learn every inch of her breasts and torso. She doesn't mind either. Her eyes are filled with patience and permission. My hands caress her sides, and I rake my hands down to her hips, pausing while my thumbs brush over her stomach. When her breath hitches, I glance up to see a hint of shock, maybe surprise, in her expression.

"What's wrong?" I ask.

"Your touch." She swallows. "It...it feels like home," she admits softly.

Yeah. I like that. A lot. And I show her by dropping to my knees and running my stubble covered cheek against the inside of her thighs. Up one and back down the other. Each time I come a little closer to where I know she wants me. Her body writhes with anticipation.

Just a little closer. I can smell her arousal. Just a little closer. My tongue grazes her crevices.

Just a little closer. My breath tickles the manicured patch of pubic hair just above her soft pink opening.

I dart my tongue out, but move in the opposite direction

of where she's craving it, my teeth nipping along her skin. Biting harder as I get to the thick part of her thigh.

"Walt." I can hear the impatience in her voice, and I chuckle.

"Walt." It's a warning. This time when I take another pass at tormenting her, she pulls my hair to the roots and places my mouth exactly where she wants it, grinding against me for her own pleasure.

And it's the hottest fucking thing I've ever experienced. A woman's confidence to ask for what she wants. It's like someone took inventory of every wet dream I ever had and rolled it into this one woman splayed out in front of me. And forget about it. Now that I've tasted her, I plan to make sure each one of them comes true.

My eyes scan her body, while my mouth makes a meal of her and my tongue laps up every ounce of elixir her body is offering.

She tenses, and I know her release is near. The thought of counting the number of orgasms I can give her before fucking her makes my heartbeat falter before I push to finish what I started. Pulling her tight nub between my teeth, I roll it back and forth before biting it—a little harder than I intended, but I just got so damn caught up in this woman. It doesn't matter though because her body is convulsing in an orgasm so intense it has her begging for my dick.

That was two.

I crawl up the bed, over her body, my lips leaving a trail of the evidence of her desire as they go. My tongue delves into her mouth and she kisses me without hesitation. Her eyes close and I slap the side of her arse cheek.

"Oh no, my crumpet. We have a way to go before you can rest." I glance at Finn's response. He got the girls a couple of minutes after Sam texted him and made sure to point out he would keep them until bedtime. I have four hours. Four hours to devour this woman beneath me. Fourteen-thousand-four-hundred seconds. And fuck if I don't plan to use every one of them.

"Finn has the girls until bedtime," I inform her so she can relax into the marathon.

Her eyes ask a hundred questions. If I'm honest, I'm not sure I know what the answer is. Not all of them anyway. She bites her lip and the depths of them go from questioning to decisive, and just like that she's moving. I've been flipped onto my back and she is straddling me. Starkers. Gloriously nude. Her arse bubbles up off my lap and when my hands snake around and squeeze her soft flesh, I know I will never want a skinny model again. The fact that it's more than my handful turns me the fuck on. Its soft dips and curves, so fucking sexy.

"What are you thinking?" she asks.

"That you are the sexiest woman I've ever known."

"Good answer," she laughs before turning thoughtful. "What are we doing?" Her eyes find mine and mine lock on hers. I want her to see without equivocation that I am not hesitant in the least.

"What do *you* think we are doing?" I ask, curious if she'll tell me where her head is. I have no idea why, because I have found her to be, in all things, brutally forthcoming.

"I think we are walking a dangerous line. I love the girls and I don't want to lose them." She doesn't stop touching me. My heart races. We can make this work. She's not shutting it down.

"The last thing I want is for the girls to lose you."

"I don't want anyone to know except us. Not until we know if this is just sex or if it's more."

"It's more."

She reaches into a drawer and pulls out a bottle of lube. I crinkle my brow, but don't speak as the cap snaps and she squeezes a few drops into her palm before tossing it to the side. Rubbing her hands together, she shimmies back a few inches and my dick makes an appearance from under her. Still hard as granite. She wraps her hands around it, lifting it upward as she lazily begins to stroke up and down. She applies a strong grip. Most girls hold it like they would shake someone's hand. Daintily. Not Sam. She holds it like she intends to make it hers. *God, let it be true.*

"You all are my family."

My dick grows in her hands. Her fingers find my balls and the skin beneath.

"You like hearing that." She doesn't ask. "That's good. Except if this doesn't work out, you still have your family. The girls. Finn. I would be the one to lose my family. Again."

How does she continue to surprise me? She's taken me to my knees and I'm not even standing. I flip her over, so I'm on top of her. I find her gaze and hold it. My shaft nudges its way to her opening, but then I hesitate. She knows why and whispers, "I'm on the pill and I'm clean. I've been tested, and I've never had sex without a condom." It's on the tip of my tongue to tell her the same, but the knowledge that I'm the only person who's been bare inside her, is more than I can sustain.

Without wasting another second, I slide my dick into true bliss. Her heat and arousal surround my cock, her walls rippling around me. This woman throws me a curve every time I think I have her figured out. I thought our first time would be two people fucking like animals. Instead, it's as real as it gets. I've never made love to a woman. With Sam, it's our first time.

I lay my body the length of hers, my hips pulling back and

thrusting in over and over. She's hooked her feet around my waist, my arms wrapped under her shoulders.

"I promise to do everything in my power to make sure that doesn't happen," I assure her. "I'd be your family, too, if you'll let me."

"You already are," she says, and there's a shine to her eyes. I want to tell her I love her. It's on the tip of my tongue. I want to tell her I am head over heels for her and nothing can change that. This woman is it for me. I know it. My body knows it. My heart knows it.

chapter twenty

Sam falls apart beneath me and I've never witnessed anything more beautiful. My pace quickens and with an arch of my back and whispers of encouragement from her, I empty inside of her, giving her every part of me in hopes she can see what I'm hesitant to say. I have to overpower the need to claim this woman in ways I never imagined I would.

Her eyes are glossed over; she feels it, too, but the fear I see there keeps her at bay.

"I know you felt it."

"Walt," she whispers, her head shaking back and forth.

"I'm willing to wait."

"Take what you want because this can't happen again after tonight."

I laugh out loud at her audacity to think one night would ever be enough.

Yep. That accomplished it. The Sam I see every day pops right back into place. I don't resist when she pushes me off her, flipping us so that she's on top again. Who am I to complain? I fucking love being under this girl.

"I'm serious," she says harsher this time, and her hands pin mine above my head. I lean up and suck her nipple into my mouth.

"Walt, I'm serious." She tries again, but her body has its own agenda. Her hips begin to grind against my cock as if I'm her own personal sex toy and it is fucking heaven.

Releasing her breast and freeing my hands, I pull her mouth to me and put every ounce of what I'm feeling into our kiss. My hands hold her hair back, showcasing her long neck. I stop to tell her that she is stunning, and there is no one walking this earth lovelier than she is. She blushes and tries to divert me with kisses, but I hold her in place.

"I won't forsake you, Samantha." The thought of letting her down makes my insides want to revolt. "Trust me."

She lowers herself onto me. It takes only a split second for our bodies to reconnect.

"There is no way you have ever felt this with anyone else. I know I haven't."

She doesn't respond. Instead she rises and falls, and I can see the shimmer of come on my dick as she rides me. Her bellshape curves making me want to fall at her feet in worship. She maneuvers herself around so that her back is facing me. She pulls my foot against the bed and leans against my bent leg, her legs straddling mine, her sex grinding against my thigh while my dick continues to claim her. She lays her cheek against my knee and the sensations coming at me are more than my mind can catalog. Just seconds ago, I didn't think there was a vision more appealing than watching her come apart, but this one is racing to be a close second. My hands knead her arse, helping with her motions. I slap her right cheek hard, leaving a handprint. My dick jumps in response. He likes that. So, I give him what he wants and slap the other cheek just as hard. Sam leans forward and grinds harder against my leg, increasing her pace. We're minutes away from another orgasm, and my soul easily imagines hundreds more. I feel Sam's wetness against my leg and over my cock as she comes in long violent shakes as number four rips through her.

"We should get up." Sam mumbles.

She's relaxed after hitting number six. Six orgasms over four hours. I mentally give my dick the thumbs up. He hasn't been this happy in a long time.

"Five more minutes," I murmur into her hair, leaving a kiss.

"Finn should be back any minute with the girls." She sits up but doesn't move off her bed. "I want you to take the next few days to think about this. We're still in the shallow end. We can walk away from this and still keep our relationship like it is."

"Who can?" I bite a little harder than I intended. *So much for showing her patience, jackarse.*

"We can. I mean it, Walt. I can't lose you all. It would take something from me that I'm not sure I would survive. I want you to think about this. We can still walk it back."

"One minute, one hour, one day. None of it is going to change how I feel. Trust me when I tell you that you don't have to worry."

She chews on her lip. I get the feeling that she would like to have it in writing. A guarantee. Something that gives her the assurance she needs.

"Sam." I release a breath. "I'm seconds away from saying

those words, but I fear it would freak you out more. I don't need to walk this back."

"All the more reason to take a couple of days." She leans forward and kisses me tenderly.

My heart and my mind are chanting over and over, "I love you". But I hold my tongue and try to see this from her perspective. That is the only way I will be able to comfort her and make her feel protected.

"I don't want the girls to know yet."

"Okay." I can easily agree to that one. The last thing either of us wants is the girls to get caught in the middle while we figure this out.

She slides off the bed and I yank her back for one more kiss. One more caress.

"Sam. I'm so in…with you," I say. "You take the days for you. For me. You're it."

There. I don't know how else to say it without saying it.

She leaves me without another word. I wonder if I should have just told her. My mind starts running through everything that just happened—every little thing. I throw the covers off me and pace around the room, obsessing. I throw on my clothes and head out of the room. I need to get out of here.

I practically run to Finn's floor, and fling open the door to see Poppy twirling around in front of Colin. She is wearing her pink tutu over her cupcake pajamas. She comes to a stop and tells Colin it's his turn. When his attempts fail, she critiques him, making him try again.

"Colin isn't as dainty as you are," I remind her. He gives me a flip of the finger on a turn that only I can see.

"Oh, I'm dainty," he protests right before he has to catch himself from falling over. Poppy pops a hand over her mouth to hide her smile.

"Bedtime, Miss Thing," Sam laughs, walking into the room. She must have been watching from the sidelines. I will her to look at me, but she doesn't.

"You, too, Zinnia," Sam says.

"You know I'm ten years older than her," Zinnie pouts.

"You do remember how many times I had to wake you last week. And that you received your second tardy on Friday."

"Sounds like you need more sleep, kiddo," Finn says, pulling her off the couch. "On with you. No back talk."

"I can take her," Sam smiles, poking at Zinnia as she levels us with kisses before heading to the stairwell. Poppy makes a minor production of her goodnights, taking far longer than necessary.

"If you need me to come in for the Seleske meeting, I can," Sam tells Finn.

"You have your first presentation this week. That is your focus. If I need you, I'll call you."

"Fine. Don't forget. Wednesday. Two o'clock."

"What's happening Wednesday?" I ask Finn once Sam and the girls have left.

"What was happening upstairs?" he asks. I quickly put a finger to my lips. I'm not ready to tell the guys yet.

"Well, I'm out. Got a hot babe waiting for me." Colin saunters out of the kitchen with a bottle of water. "She's the kind of girl that likes doubles. Fancy a go? Like ye good ole' days in uni? I mean how long has it been since you got any? I know Camilla wasn't giving it up."

"As enticing as you make that sound, no. And don't talk about Camilla like that."

"She was a bitch."

"She never misrepresented who she was. She didn't change. I did."

"Sorry, Zinnie forgot her book," Sam says, reentering the room with a slight blush. It's evident she heard our conversation.

"Of course, you could make me the happiest man in the world and I wouldn't have to seek out another," Colin teases Sam, pulling her into a bear hug. My fingers dig into my palms and Finn nudges me.

"You're growling," he whispers.

"Sorry, sweet Colin. I'm a one-man kind of gal. I never share."

Yep. That reaches the tips of my toes.

"I assume you know what you are doing?" Finn asks when Sam and Colin have gone.

"Yes, I know what I'm doing," I placate. "Sam is the one that has decisions to make. I know exactly who and what I want."

"Yeah, well, if this goes sour, she's the one that stands to lose the most."

"Why does everyone keep saying that? Jesus, I have never felt this way for a woman before. I assure you, if this goes sour, I'll be the one losing."

Finn clamps a large hand on my shoulder and gives it a squeeze, of...what? Support? Understanding? Warning? I'm not sure, and he doesn't say before sending me on my way.

"Come on, girls," Charlotte says, helping Poppy into her jumper. She is taking her to school today. I have a meeting I'm already running late for, and Sam went to bed only an hour ago. Her presentation is today. She stopped working on it last night just long enough to have dinner. After that, she insisted she was just putting the last touches on her PowerPoint. I checked on her every couple of hours, forcing her to go to bed when I knew there was nothing left for her to do. Even then, the only way I persuaded her was to point out she didn't want to look exhausted in front of everyone today.

Sam is presenting on paid maternity leave and why it makes both ethical and economic sense for developed countries to offer it. I was stunned to learn this country is only one of four in the world that don't offer it. Swaziland, Lesotho, and Papua New Guinea round out the other three. Somewhere along the way, her presentation came across the desk of the Dean of Business, and she sent Sam an email wishing her well and letting her know she would be in the audience, along with the department heads. If it goes well, the Dean would like to submit it for a TED talk.

Charlotte works from home and offered to help Sam and me out this morning, and for that, I'm grateful. I'm rushing to a meeting I have in five minutes. My responsibilities win out, but what I really want to do, all I have wanted to do since that night, is make love to Sam. We haven't spent more than five minutes alone since Sunday. I think it's purposeful on her part. I'm trying to respect her request for time and to give her space to get through today.

"This is my brother, Walt Nelson." Finn introduces me, and my day takes off from there.

"I'm heading to Sam's presentation. You want to ride with me?"

"What?" I question looking at my watch. It's 1:15. I went

to the apartment an hour ago to make sure Sam didn't over-sleep, but she was already gone.

"I'm heading—"

"I heard you. What I mean is, I didn't know we could attend?"

"I can. I'm listed as her mentor," Finn says as I stand and follow him to the lift. I tell Maria where she can find me, ig-noring the irrational jealousy I have even at the mention of Finn being her mentor.

I could have mentored her. I rather hope to in more ways than one, I muse. But I make myself stop. My dick is thicken-ing and this is hardly the place for it.

"Perfect timing," Quade calls out as we enter Finn's dark SUV.

"The girls are meeting us there. Colin and Pierce aren't going to make it," he says as he crawls in.

"Am I the only one that didn't know we could attend?" What the hell? I've been inside this woman. I think that gives me certain rights to know more than the others around me. I make a mental note to correct her. Hopefully, on her knees.

Traffic is heavy, and by the time we make our way across the campus, the auditorium is full. Charlotte, Zoe, and Grace are seated near the front. Here early, I presume. We get the last of the seats on the second row from the back.

The lecture hall is larger than I anticipated, and I wonder if Sam was aware she would be presenting to more than—my eyes scan the rows—seven hundred people.

A professor introduces a young man. He's presenting on the refugee crisis in Europe, and it's very enlightening. It's the sexier of the two topics, that is true, and I find myself wonder-ing how paid maternity leave can compare.

Professor Blume, the professor we met and Zinnie loved,

stands during the polite applause, and once he has spent an adequate amount of time thanking him for his presentation, he moves to Samantha.

"As a professor, you strive to impact your students. It's rare that a professor is graced with the fortune of meeting a student who impacts your teaching to its core." He makes a show of tapping his fist against his heart.

"Gag me," Quade says under his breath, and the girls in front of us let out a flirtatious giggle.

"This next presenter is that student for me. Her tenacity and her thirst for knowledge have impacted my teaching in ways I can't explain."

I tune out the rest of what the fucker is saying. I hate that it's his tongue her name rolls off of. He eye fucks her as she takes the podium and I imagine gouging his eyes out.

Sam thanks him for his introduction, makes a polite joke at his expense, then proceeds to school everyone in this room. If I didn't hate the fucker already, I would say that I now understand what Blume was saying.

She has the room in the palm of her hand. She's polished, well versed. She reads the crowd like a seasoned pro. She knows when to pause. She knows when to push. She knows how to captivate. By the time she finishes, I've already made a mental note to change our policy to include paid maternity leave. Finn is thinking the same; I see him typing a note in his phone about including a PR showcase. Like Sam said in her speech, companies must understand their moral obligations and step up to lead the way.

I wasn't expecting it, but I was not surprised to find she touched on areas of women in executive positions and equal pay. She makes a clever but retrospectively obvious connection between the pay gap and paid maternity leave, but she knocks it out of the park at the end when she argues that a move toward paid leave should include fathers and legal guardians, as well. That last bit is what blows the last presentation out of the water. By the time she finishes, the applause is boisterous, and the women in the room no doubt feel the empowerment Sam wanted them to. The Dean thanks everyone for attending and dismisses the lecture.

"Gentlemen." A deep baritone draws my attention to the row behind us.

"Graham." I shake his proffered hand and introduce him to Quade. "Quade, Graham Taylor."

"We've met. What brings you out this way?"

"I was wondering why all the co-eds were drooling in this direction," Emme Taylor laughs as she finds her way to her husband. Graham's arm wraps around her and he kisses her temple. "I should have known once I saw all the suits." She fans herself. "Samantha did an amazing job. So much so that I already typed an email to the head of HR for Taylor Enterprises with a directive to offer paid leave." She raises a brow to her husband as if to say, "Don't even think of protesting it."

"I saw that." Graham's smile tells me he would give every human paid leave a hundred times over if it made his wife happy.

"She did phenomenally well," Finn agrees. "I sent the same email. What brought you to the lecture?"

"The young man that spoke was in our intern program. We came out to support him."

"You should be proud. He did well," Quade states.

The Taylors excuse themselves, and we take a seat to wait on Samantha. She looks delicious in a navy-blue pencil skirt. Her hair is pulled into a smooth ponytail. The jacket to match her skirt has a large bow at the collar. It's chic and feminine while exuding power. At least that's what I heard Zoe tell her last night when she helped her decide what to wear. Of course, she's rocking her heels. She looks like a million bucks. The smile on her face is one that can only come from the relief of having finished a large project.

She's talking to the Dean and what appears to be other professors. They all laugh at something she says, and Blume uses the opportunity to rest his hand against her back. Slowly, he moves it to the curve of her waist. That's all it takes. I descend the stairs two at a time.

"Mr. Nelson," the Dean says, surprised by my attendance. "This is Walt Nelson of Nelson Financials." She introduces me to her department heads. When I make it to Professor Blume, he has to remove his hand from Sam to shake mine.

"To what do we owe the privilege?" the Dean asks. I imagine myself sliding my arm around Sam and kissing her temple, making it known that she belongs to me and every wanker in this circle can piss off. Then I imagine her cutting my balls off for disrespecting her, especially after her speech for women empowerment. So instead, I slide my hands deep into my pockets, insuring my balls stay where they are.

"Miss Abbott works for our company. My brother Finn is her mentor, and we have a vested interest in her career."

"With mentors like this, I can see why your professors are so enamored with your academia. You're getting firsthand experience from the best." The Dean laughs, and I make a mental note to pledge a donation to the school in her honor, because the look on Blume's face is worth every dime.

Finn and Quade have joined us, and after I get a warning look from my brother, we allow ourselves to be pulled into a quick tour. Sam excuses herself. She has to close down her presentation so that the class that has gathered behind us can begin.

This is twenty minutes of my life I can never get back, I think as the tour comes to an end. Finn deserves a medal for engaging them in conversation. I simply observed. Something I'm sure he'll be pointing out to me on the way home.

"I know what I heard," Quade says loudly. He wasn't on the tour, opting instead to chat up the pretty girls in front of us. We turn towards his outburst—his face is red, and Sam has her hand on his arm as if to calm him. I don't know what she's saying, but he immediately closes his mouth and crosses his arms across his chest. He says something back to her and then stomps in the direction of a closed door. Finn follows Quade.

"Everything okay?" I ask. Sam smiles, but it doesn't reach her eyes. "It is. I apologize, but I need to leave to make my next appointment. Thank you again for your time, Dean Tarver. I appreciate it more than you know." She smiles and shakes her hand.

I excuse myself quickly and follow Sam. By the time we reach the car, Finn and Quade are circling it like sharks out for blood.

"Don't insult—" Quade starts.

"In the car now," Sam says before he can finish.

We climb in and before the door is closed, Sam and Quade are going at it. Finn has to let out a sharp whistle to separate them.

"Quade." Finn looks to his left, holding a hand up to stop Sam from speaking.

"His hand was on your ass."

"And?" Sam retorts.

"What do you mean *and*? And it's not fucking supposed to be there."

"And?" she asks again.

"And he needed to be told."

"Not by you he didn't. I was handling it."

"Not fast enough." Quade slams back against the seat and glares at the woman in front of him. I can't remember when I've seen him so angry.

"You didn't give me the chance."

"What happened?" I ask. She hears the immediacy in my voice and she answers without any preamble.

"Blume made a pass at me. Quade walked by when it happened. Before I could make it clear nothing was going to happen, King Kong jumped in."

"King Kong. I like that." Quade loosens a little and considers the title.

"Good job, man." Finn clamps a hand on his shoulder. "Shut it," he tells Sam. "Doesn't matter if it's you, Zoe, Charlotte, or Grace. The response would have been the same."

"Can we go home first please? I want to change before picking up Poppy," Sam tells the driver. She doesn't respond or engage us in a conversation.

We drop Finn on the office level before Sam and I take the lift to our apartment. She drops her bag in exhaustion at the front table. "Go rest. I'll get Poppy," I tell her.

"No. I didn't get to take her to school today. I don't want to miss picking her up, too." She says removing her jacket as she moves down her hall. I tug her arm pulling her against me, my hand entrapping her wrists behind her. Leaning against her, I run my thumb down her side, inscribing my thumb print on her skin. Invisibly marking her. Branding her.

"I know you can handle yourself, but I have no problem making sure Blume knows it." I rub my hand across her arse, reclaiming what's mine. She begins to grind her sex against me, her skirt inching further up. "You belong to me. And I be-long to you." I add, because dammit, I want to. In any way she will have me. She moans and I lift the cup of her bra up expos-ing her breast.

"Do you think of me when you're alone?" I ask in her ear. I don't recognize my own voice. It's filled with a want and need for this woman who has turned my life upside down. When she doesn't respond to my possession I give it a slap as well.

Yep. She likes that.

"Yes," she whispers.

My dick turns into an iron spike behind my zipper. "Have you made a decision?" I ask. It's a risky question. I am hoping it's not too risky. Patience is not my forte, and the thought of going another minute without knowing makes me jumpy.

"No." There's a smile in her tone that makes me wonder otherwise, but before I can press her, she says, "You have ten minutes to convince me."

chapter twenty-one

"**I**f we don't throw away this candy, I am going to be as big as a house," Sam mumbles through a mouth full of chocolate. A week since Halloween and we're still going through all the candy the girls racked up.

I've never been one to dress up. The best part of Halloween was going with my boys to the local pub. I swear every woman, especially moms (something I never understood), who secretly want to engage their inner slut, dress in costumes to show their fetishes. We were always guaranteed pussy that night. Not that that was a problem for us at uni, but on All Hallow's Eve the girls were freakier and uninhibited.

As fun as those days were, they don't compare to Halloween this year. Who knew you could have so much fun with kids and friends when all you did was knock on doors and ask for candy?

Reid Beckett and Elise Donovan invited us to their townhouse for a family-friendly party. They live in Gramercy Park, an area sought after for its private park, and all the neighbors took their stoops at dark to hand out candy.

Poppy stayed true to her original plan and went as I love Lucy. She fell head over heels for Graham Taylor's sister, Lucy, who also came as her namesake. The two were the hit of every stoop they visited.

Sam and her girls went as the Spice Girls, using Zinnie to round out the five. I thought I would scream if I heard them sing "tell me what you want, what you really really want" one more time.

Even the guys dressed up and didn't waste a chance to chide me for being the party pooper. Minutes before we left, Zoe pinned a piece of paper to my lapel that said, "Nudist on Strike," when I sourly refused to participate.

"Here. We can throw mine away," Zinnie says. "I don't need it either." She's about to pour her bucket into the trash but Sam stops her.

"Just...let me get the Kit-Kats out. Oh," she holds up a mini box of Milk Duds and rattles them. "These too. Oh—"

"Maybe we should just keep it," Zinnie laughs and puts the bucket back on the counter.

"If you insist," Sam giggles.

"Okay, lights out," Zinnie says, hitting the button on the wall.

Today has been filled with crepe paper and homemade signs. It's my birthday. This morning the girls insisted I wear the aluminum foil crown while I ate the French toast they made. I had foil stars to wish on, but I didn't need them. I had my three wishes standing in front of me.

I blow out the candles as they finish an off-beat chorus of Happy Birthday. It's Tuesday, so our weekly dinner was converted into a celebration. Sam and the girls started celebrating on Saturday though. My birthday has lasted four days now.

I never knew I could enjoy a birthday. Ours were never

that special growing up, but it's clear all three girls have strong family traditions built around their special days. Sunday night, the four of us ordered in, spending the night to ourselves. They insisted we lay in Poppy's tent, the cover of it layered in star-shaped twinkle lights to mimic the sky. Zinnie and Sam each read aloud their favorite poem from *Leaves of Grass* while Pops held my hand. It is a memory I will always cherish. No one has ever celebrated me in the way these three girls have.

The lights come back up and there's a fury of cake cutting and laughter. I'm growing accustomed to the level of activity in this place on Tuesdays. Sam looks at me through the chaos and it puts me at peace. I'm not Superman or the world's best man, and that's okay, but I am the best man for her. Because, fuck, this woman is incredible. She must sense that I am seconds away from falling to my knees and asking her to spend the rest of her life beside me, because she winks and her eyes dance in a way that tells me my real gift will come after everyone has left and the girls are down.

"I'm ready," I tell Sam later that night while I'm balls deep inside of her. Finn gave me the best present of the night and shuffled everyone out the door at a decent hour. After bath and reading, Poppy is finally asleep and Zinnie should be by now too.

Sam moans as I circle my hips before pulling out and slamming back into her.

"Not yet. The girls need more time."

Circle. Out. Slam.

"Don't hide behind the girls. It's been a month now. I am not going to change my mind."

Circle. Out. Slam.

"I'm not."

Circle. Out. Slam.

"Fine. Maybe I am," she admits. "But right now, the only two people who could get hurt are in this room. If this doesn't work out, you and I can recover."

My circle, out, slam falters at her words and I stop moving all together. Does this not mean to her what it means to me?

"I'm past the point of recovering. I thought you were, too."

I hold still, waiting for her response.

"I lo—" She places a finger over my lips.

"I'm scared," she breathes, and a tear falls silently from the corner of her eye. "I need time."

"I can't fix it if you won't talk to me about it."

"Why do men think they need to fix women?"

"I didn't say fix you. You're lovely. I adore you in every way. I said fix *it*. If there wasn't anything wrong, you wouldn't be frightened. I would give my life to make sure you never have to feel that again."

Her body begins to tremble, and she visibly falls apart beneath me. I pull out of her. Sex is nowhere on my mind right now. I just need her to know she is safe and loved.

"I'm sorry," she says as I hold her, giving her every ounce of comfort I can.

"About what?"

"Crying is hardly part of sexy time."

"Don't you get it? I want you. In every way. There is nothing to be sorry for. I mean it, Sam. This isn't just sex for me. Or you. I know it. I see it in your eyes. I read it in the sweet texts you send me. I feel it when you kiss me." I pause and kiss her swollen lips. "I want all of you. Even during sexy time," I chuckle and move back on top of her.

Sometimes a moment's break is all you need.

chapter twenty-two

The next few weeks are a string of firsts for us. The girls had their first American Thanksgiving without their parents. I knew Finn would be here to celebrate, but I was shocked to learn the week before that my crew and Sam's squad all planned to celebrate the day with us.

We had several invites from my parents, Jenny's parents, other friends and families, but in the end the girls wanted to stay at our place and celebrate with whomever could make it. Pierce was the only holdout. Once Poppy realized he might not make it, she made it her mission to have him there. He never stood a chance.

The weekend before Thanksgiving Sam asked the girls about the traditions they had with their parents and which ones they wanted to keep. I mean, I had thought about it being hard for them because of the holiday and I even thought about it being different, but I didn't think to ask them how to make it the way they wanted it to be.

The decision was made that they each had to list a tradition from their past they hoped to carry into their future. If they had more than one that was fine. The point was to honor their parents. Then Sam encouraged us to think of new traditions we might start as a new family.

"Your turn, Sam," Zinnie instructed. "What tradition do you want to carry over from your family?"

By the time we had a growing list, there wasn't a dry eye amongst us. The three girls grieving for their loss and me for their grief.

Thanksgiving day started with Sam's tradition of making cinnamon rolls and watching the Macy's parade while we prepared dinner. Poppy got to write a word of her choice in marshmallows on the sweet potato casserole. Zinnie and I did the wishbone challenge, like she and Everett always did. We added a new tradition of saying one thing we are grateful for around the table before dinner and drawing names for stockings.

Stockings were Zinnie's idea. Since we have a large group, she suggested we draw names for stockings and exchange them during our Tuesday dinner before Christmas. The idea was well-received, and I found myself looking forward to being creative on what I might purchase to fit into a large sock.

That is how we found ourselves adding names to a bowl on Tuesday at six. Grace added the stipulation that the name we drew had to be kept a secret. Poppy enlists Finn to be her present helper, so he is the only one that gets to see her secret. She bounces with glee at the chosen name. She excitedly shows him, climbs into his lap, and whispers in his ear, clutching the name to her. A sheen of wetness shown on my brother's eye, and I know whatever Poppy whispered touched him. With his arms still encasing her, her legs dangling off his as she bounces in excitement as each person draws a name, he bends down and places his cheek against the top of her head.

"That little girl," he says to me after putting her to bed that night, his words catching in his throat. "How does a little girl who has seen more horror at the age of five than anyone should have to bounce with glee because she got a name of someone she thinks needs happiness?" He swipes at a tear and my hand rests against his back to comfort him. "She is always thinking of others."

"Like you," I point out.

My brother hugs me until he has his composure. He's a formidable businessman, but he has no problem showing his emotions. I was never comfortable with public displays of affection, but Finn changed that. He always showed his love in hugs, forcing me out of my comfort zone.

While we can't get through our day-to-day without our extended family, Sam wants some things to be just about us, so the following week, me, Sam, Finn and the girls picked out a tree before having frozen hot chocolates at Serendipity. By the time we made it back to the apartment, the tree had been delivered and was awaiting its transformation.

Tuesday night dinners soon became a cacophony of holiday decorating and taunts and tricks to figure out whose name we each have. This Tuesday, Quade, Charlotte, and Grace, show up to decorate and make sugar cookies. Cheers went up when we declare we are finished, and when I stepped back to take in the room, I am rendered speechless. There is an overabundance of twinkle lights, homemade garland, and ornaments. Missing were the stuffy, repetitive ornaments I was accustomed to growing up, where everything on the tree matched and looked like the designers did the decorating. It is perfect and for the first time ever, I find myself looking forward to Christmas with excitement I hadn't felt since I was Poppy's age.

Grace distributes stockings with our names on each one. She and Zinnie concoct a way to hang them since the fireplace doesn't have a mantel. There is Christmas music, cookies, and laughter. The night is perfect, ending with me inside Sam.

The girls are in high spirits going into their last week of school. Each of our friends are desperate to make the season as special as possible and it feels like every free minute is driven by an agenda of things to do.

Tonight, Colin paid what I assume is a small fortune to rent the skating rink in Central Park. Between the girls' friends and families and the friends we each invited there must be close to thirty people here. Finn's friends Blake and West join in with a group of kids West teaches. I love watching the dynamics of the group of kids. Their ability to come together with people different than themselves. It's a perfect ending to an agenda that was filled with seeing the tree, crepes in Bryant Park, and the famous storefront windows the city is known for this time of year.

Like I said, we haven't stopped and when I exit the lift the next day after work, I am more than ready for a night in. I start to announce myself but stop just short of interrupting. Sam looks to Zinnie with a raised brow and I see the look reflected on the teenager's face.

"I'm sorry. If I do it again, I promise I'll give you my phone," she murmurs. I have no idea what the offense was, but if Zinnie knows the repercussion is taking her phone, then it must have been serious.

"Deal," Sam nods. "Everyone deserves the chance to do over. Recognizing that you need one says you're winning in the decision-making process."

"I said I was sorry," Zinnie retorts.

"I heard you," Sam tells her with confusion on her face

that gives way to understanding.

"You are so After School Special." Zinnie rolls her eyes and I swallow my tea down the wrong pipe choking back my laughter. She taps me with a slight fist bump before she takes the seat next to me.

"What are we doing tonight?" she asks. Sam and I both answer, "Nothing."

Sam felt, and I agreed, that the girls needed processing time as much as they needed distractions.

"Tonight, we are going to enjoy the apartment being decorated and watch TV," Sam says, setting the take-out we ordered on the counter. "We have a lot going on this week. I have my final presentation. Poppy, you have your party. Zinnie, you have mid-terms. And Walt, you have a deal to finalize before Christmas."

"I don't like broccoli." Poppy turns her nose up when I offer her some beef with broccoli. Sam spoons some chicken fried rice onto her plate. She turns to hand the container to Zinnie, who she finds on her phone.

"You know the rules."

"I was texting Finn. There's a ton of food," Zinnie says. "I don't like thinking of him in his apartment by himself. Not when he could be with us."

"Yes!" Poppy exclaims gleefully. "I want Finn."

"Why doesn't he decorate his apartment?" Zinnie asks.

"It's just not something we've really cared about in the past," I answer.

"You mean before us you didn't decorate?"

"Nope. Those were the good ole days," I tease with a wink, but it falls with a thud on her serious expression. "What?"

"I don't like thinking of you by yourself either. Not anymore anyway."

"I'm not. I've got you three." As soon as my words leave my mouth, my eyes do a lap of the room to see if I've given too much away. Sam and I might not see eye to eye on how deep this relationship is right now, but we both agree that it needs to remain between the two of us. The girls are our main priority. The girls seem oblivious, so it must not have registered. Sam hides a smile as she turns to spoon more food onto her plate.

"Chinese," Finn says, entering the room. Poppy hops up and gives him a big hug before pulling him to sit next to her.

"We need to get you a boyfriend," Zinnie muses. The expression on my brother's face is priceless. Luckily, he is already lowering himself onto a seat, since his legs appear to falter momentarily.

"I don't need a matchmaker," Finn grumbles, narrowing his eyes at her. "Especially not by my niece."

Zinnie beams at the word "niece".

"That boy you liked is definitely not an option?" she presses.

"He definitely is not an option. He's getting married on New Year's Eve."

"Really?" I'm surprised I hadn't heard.

"He doesn't know it. Blake is taking care of everything. West thinks it's a regular party, but everyone else knows they are coming to attend the wedding. It will be at midnight."

"That is so romantic," Zinnie swoons. "Maybe you'll meet someone there," she says dreamily.

Finn rolls his eyes in my direction as if to say, "Please make it stop." I chuckle at his expense and bite off the end of an eggroll.

"Did you hear anything about the trial?" Zinnie asks.

"The date is set for January," I answer her softly.

"Did they decide to allow the plea bargain to be part of

the deal?"

"They did. Are you having second thoughts?"

"Every day," she admits. "But I remember what Sam said and try to make that my focus."

Sam winks at her.

"Well, it's done. The plea has already been entered. The trial in January is sentencing only. Try not to think about it. There's nothing we can do to change it at this point."

She pushes her food around, and Poppy must sense her distress because she sits back and watches her sister with concern.

"I know you said I need to forgive," Zinnie says, "but I haven't. Not yet. But I'm trying."

"You'll get there in your own time," Sam assures her.

"I just don't want my parents to think I abandoned them, ya know?" She looks up before adding, "Like I didn't fight for them."

"Your parents loved you, sweetheart. There is no way they would ever feel abandoned," Finn says.

As usual, Sam made a good call. The girls need time to process, not just activities to keep them from thinking about the changes they are living. Finn stays to help Zinnie study, while I take care of getting Poppy to bed and Sam works on her presentation.

Making my way back into the family area, Finn and Zinnie are in a heated debate about the impact of the Asian market driving up the cost of real estate in New York. Every rebuttal she has, I heard from Everett at one point or another. The thought makes me smile.

There are a pair of joggers clad legs just visible beneath the refrigerator door when I enter the kitchen. I glance over my shoulder to make sure Zinnie is still occupied before I slip around the refrigerator door, giving Sam a bit of a fright.

"Come with me," I whisper, biting her earlobe.

"But I'm hungry," she mumbles.

"I have something I can feed you." I pull her hand to my crotch. She slides her hand up and down my shaft.

"Maybe I want to feed you," she teases. I've never had a lover who got off on pleasuring me as much as Sam does.

"That can be arranged, too," I groan. Her hand is inside my joggers now, and I'm seconds away from losing my shit if I don't gain some control. But the decision is not mine to make. Poppy does it for me with blood curdling screams through the kid monitor I still turn on in her room at night.

Instinctively, I dash to her room, Sam and the others step in behind me. By the time I reach her, she's shaking from the sobs wrenching her body.

"I'm here, love. I've got you. You're ok. I won't let anything happen to you. I promise."

I chant these words over and over as I rock her back and forth. My arms hold her so tightly she's probably struggling to breath. She doesn't complain though; she just keeps sobbing.

"What is it sweetheart?" Sam asks.

"The man who took Mommy and Daddy," she hiccups and cries harder. "He took Walt."

"No one is going to take me. I promise."

"He can. You said he wasn't going to jail. That means he's out here. He can still take you." She cries harder.

"That's not going to happen." I attempt to soothe her, because really that is all I can do. There is no other way to make her understand. All I can do is reassure her.

And that's when the revelation hits me. I'm a father. Without a doubt. I love this girl more than I love myself.

"Zinnie come here." I pat the space next to me. "You two

are mine. You belong to me, and I will do whatever it takes to show you. You are the most important people in my life. Understand?"

Poppy shakes her head and Zinnie reaches for my hand.

"Trust me when I tell you I would never let anything hurt you. Most of all when it comes to your parents."

We shouldn't have talked about it in front of Poppy, but I don't want Zinnie to feel like she has to censor how she is feeling. I look up to find that Finn and Sam have quietly left the room, leaving me with the girls.

"Finish your studying." I kiss Zinnie and send her on her way. I lie down with Poppy.

When I wake, it's four in the morning and the lights are all dimmed. Sam must feel confident about the changes to her presentation because even she is in bed. I lift the covers and slide in next to her. She curls up against me. We have a couple of hours before the girls are going to be awake, and even though I think we both want sex, we're a little too tired to make it happen. It occurs to me that we have yet to spend a full night together.

"It was selfish of me to tell Zinnie she should forgive him," she says.

"Zinnie can't walk around with hatred in her heart. It will eat away at her until she is no longer recognizable."

"Like me," she whispers.

I sit up on my elbows and take her face in my hands. "I see you, Sam. You aren't unrecognizable to me." I kiss her with every ounce of love I feel for her before telling her. "I love you."

Tears fall down her face as she shakes her head back and forth.

"I want that more than anything, Walt. But you can't."

"It's like I told Zinnie in the weeks after her parent's death:

It's okay for her to laugh and live her life. I'm so sorry you lost your family, Sam, but you deserve to be happy."

"And what about you? Have you forgiven him? For taking Everett? Is that a struggle for you?"

Of course, Sam would see what I wrestle with most. "My joy is those girls and it came at the cost of my best friend. I…I'm still working on processing that. I just know I can't overthink it. The girls need me."

"I am so proud of the man you are." She kisses me, and her words are like a salve to my soul.

"I need to talk to Zinnie about the man who killed her parents."

"I think the counselor is working with her to forgive him." She misunderstands what I mean.

"I mean to not mention it in front of Poppy. She's just too young to process it."

"You're right. I thought you were talking about forgiveness."

"She needs that, too. For her. Honestly, I could give a fuck about this man. I wish I hadn't allowed the plea. No amount of forgiveness can undo the havoc he wreaked on those girls." Sam nods, and there's sadness in her eyes.

"Now, where were we?" I lean down to kiss her, but stop when I hear Poppy cry out.

I would like to tell you it got better, but Poppy struggles every night. The therapist said it is probably an overload of emotions from vivid Christmas memories and our conversation about the other driver. Whatever it is, the only thing we can do is ride it out. Poppy is five and her coping skills will eventually help her work it out. Until then, one of us sleeps with her each night.

Sam aced her presentation. I found out from Finn, who

heard it from Zoe, that Professor Blume tried again to persuade her to join him in some extracurricular activities. Sam promptly reported it to the Dean. Evidently Grace had been working on her the whole semester to report him. After Sam found out that a younger student had also been propositioned, I think she saw a pattern she could no longer ignore.

"She doesn't need you to rescue her from every man that hits on her." Finn tells me after I implode at the thought of that bellend putting his hands on her. I don't say anything because my anger is teetering at an irrational level.

"Oh my God. You're in this deep. You want to rescue her from everything, don't you? You love her?" he asks.

I don't answer, but he sees it in my eyes. I've only said it aloud to her once. It doesn't seem right to admit it to him yet. Right now, it's still something for only the two of us.

"Let's go." I stand, buttoning my suitcoat.

"Ready?" Quade enters the office doing the same.

The three of us make our way to Poppy's school. It's colder than I anticipated. We should have taken the car, but traffic is chaotic today and I was worried we wouldn't make it. As it is now, I'm not sure walking is much better. The city is under siege from tourists and shoppers. I've never seen this many people at two in the afternoon.

Poppy is a present in the school Christmas program. Sam finished her costume last night. She cut the bottom out of a large square box before carving holes for her head and arms. I helped Poppy wrap it in her favorite Christmas paper and glue the ribbon on while Sam created a large red bow to wear on her head. Zinnie had ordered her some red-and-white-striped stockings online, and all together she is the cutest package up there. She even has a couple of lines. If she hadn't spent every day repeating them, I probably wouldn't have understood when she says, "Christmas is more than packages," and "Peppermint is the mintiest of mints."

Nonetheless, each time she says her line, it's like a star was born. Sam threatened everyone within an inch of their lives not to cheer when she spoke, so that the kid with lines behind hers would be heard. But when Santa and all the misfit toys sing the last bar of their carol, our section explodes. We do have an entire row, after all.

Poppy happily poses for pictures, so everyone can have one with her. She is the hit of the play in our eyes.

Pierce greased some hands and was able to have a table waiting for us at the Black Tap where burgers and fries were a-plenty, and milkshakes looked like art pieces.

"Just keep your head down and don't look," Finn laughs at Zinnie, who is embarrassed that we are passing people who have been waiting in line for over two hours. Sometimes there are perks to traveling with Pierce.

We pass a group of carol singers on the way home, and Grace insists we stop to listen. By the time we get back to the apartment, we are frozen. Quade makes a large batch of home-made hot cocoa while the girls butter bread to dip in it.

By the time everyone leaves, we think Poppy might actually be exhausted enough to sleep by herself. I pray that's the case. I need to be inside Sam tonight. I would give all three of my foil star wishes from my birthday, but nope. Sam sleeps with Poppy.

But there is hope. Poppy has already begged Zinnie to sleep with her on Christmas Eve. She has the whole evening planned. After they go to bed, they will watch a movie in her tent and then sneak out to catch Santa in the act. Knowing Poppy can't stay awake ten minutes after her head hits the pillow, I know sleep won't be an issue. Sam and I both know it's our next best chance to have more than five minutes alone. And the naughty pictures started rolling in days ago.

Sam has decided to send me little teases every day, beginning twelve days before Christmas. A slight deviation from the original, but who am I to complain? On the top of her first naughty picture, she wrote, "On the first day of Christmas..." It was of Sam from the waist down, naked with a little cartoon partridge placed over her naughty bits. The next day, I received a text titled "On the second day..." That time, it was a picture of her naked torso with doves over her nipples.

After that, she went a little off script. I mean, what can you do for "four calling birds", but it didn't matter, because they got racier. I responded with a pic of my own, to which she photoshopped herself, swimmingly I might add, into the pic in such a way that it made it look like she was milking me. Then repeated it into eight squares. That has been my favorite so far.

I haven't received today's text yet, but the day is young, and I know Sam is busy with the girls preparing for tonight.

Tonight, is our Christmas exchange. I must admit, I'm looking forward to finding out who has my name. I have Grace and had the best time thinking of ways to fill her stocking. Admittedly, I had some help from my go-to personal shopper, Ms. Smith. Also, I've been trying to pay attention to things she enjoys. Like, I noticed that when she comes over, she dips her pretzels into the chocolate Nutella jar Sam keeps in the cupboard. Ms. Smith was able to get a dozen pretzel rods dipped in chocolate with edible gold from the confectioner in England that we grew up fancying.

Sam had posted a picture on Instagram of Grace and the girls that I had printed and framed. It's small enough to fit into her stocking. I got her a few other trinkets, but the gift I think she will love the most is the emerald earrings the exact color of her eyes.

"Let's call it a day," Finn says, entering my office. "I instructed the last group to wrap it up."

"I just need to send a couple of emails."

"Fine. Then let's have lunch with Quade. After, I have one more errand I want to run."

"That's right. You have to pick up your last gift for Pierce."

"Really? Again? No matter whose name you throw into that sentence, I'm not going to tell you who I have."

"He has Zoe," Quade enters.

"That's not going to work for you either."

The afternoon flies by, but before I arrive back to the apartment, I have my tenth picture. Fuck me, Samantha. Does she not understand how difficult it is to shop with a hard on? I show her as much, popping into a dressing closet in Saks to text a side view of my tented trousers, clearly displaying my discomfort.

There's laughter when I exit the lift to my home. People are already trickling in. The mood is cheerful and Christmas music plays in the background. The squad has been here for a few hours it seems. Zinnie and Poppy have been out of school for several days now.

"Look." Poppy pulls me into the kitchen to show me that she has been sprinkling sugar on cookies. It's easy to pick out her masterpieces: the sugar amount is double what's on the others.

"Sam, could you help me for a moment?" I ask casually.

"No telling," Charlotte yells from her end of the table. She and Zinnie are rolling some type of dough into balls.

"It's something for the girls," I assure her.

Sam takes a minute to assess everything in front of her. Once she's determined nothing will go wrong if she steps away, she looks at me and smiles. There's flour on her cheek, and I just stop myself short of grabbing her in front of everyone when she sneaks a wink at me.

She follows me to my bedroom, asking me what she can help me with. She must miss the click of the lock, because she squeals with surprise when I lift her and toss her onto the bed. Her head falls back onto the pillow, laughter spilling from her throat.

"We can't," she protests between kisses. I'm already lifting her shirt, licking my way across her body. I free her breast from her bra and pull it deep into my mouth. She moans, and her legs automatically wrap around my waist.

I love her nipples. They're a flawless shade of rosy pink and proportioned to her breasts perfectly. But I want more. I need more. I need her lips.

Finding them, she gives as good as she's getting and by the time we break for a breath, we are nearly dry humping one another.

"It feels like fucking forever since I have been inside of you."

"Because it has been fucking forever." She moans when my fingers graze her sex. I add a little pressure to where she craves it most.

"Twenty-four hours." Her hand jacks my cock through my trousers. "You can wait."

My hips are moving on their own and I apply more pressure in hopes to convince her otherwise.

"People," kiss, "are," kiss, "waiting." She squirms out from under me, and I make a show of falling onto the bed in frustration. Lowering my zipper, I pull my impossibly hard dick from my trousers. The pre-come I've been leaking makes it easy for my hand to move.

"You're not playing fair," Sam says, her hand inches from the door knob.

"No, I'm not."

Sam leans against the door and watches me pleasure myself. Her eyes glaze slightly and her breathing falters. She doesn't give in, but neither do I.

With my eyes locked on hers, my hand accelerates, chasing my release. My balls tighten to my body and electricity sizzles through it. Her name is on my lips when I close my eyes as my release hits me with the force of a two-ton truck.

"What the…" A warm mouth engulfs me just as the first rope of come leaves my body. My body spasms as Sam sucks me through my release, drinking every part of me she can. She stays committed to the cause, only stopping when I beg her to, my dick turning sensitive.

She crawls up and kisses me, letting me taste myself on her lips.

"Clean up. Dinner in thirty minutes." She says before leaving.

Christmas Eve is tomorrow. The girls and I are making a trip to Jenny's parents while Finn and Sam have a date to have lunch and to see the Rockettes. Then the five of us are meeting for dinner before catching Handel's Messiah at Carnegie Hall. A tradition of Everett and Jenny's we plan to carry on with the girls.

Finn is staying with us Christmas Eve night and I plan on having as much sex as I can with the woman I love. Let me repeat that. I plan on having as much sex as I can with the woman I love. The true gift that keeps on giving.

I can't remember having more fun with a group of people. Maybe it makes me old, but not even the days we spent in pubs were this enjoyable.

Everyone is in high spirits. Finn and Zinnie made crowns to wear. Everyone is a King on Christmas. It's an English tradition, along with crackers. It takes Poppy a few practices with the paper covered tubes, but finally she figures out how to pop them.

Dinner is filled with regales of how much each of us enjoyed shopping for our person.

Everyone pitches in to clean, and by the time we settle down to open our stockings, the buildings around us are lit against the night sky.

The fire is burning, and Pierce puts on an old Sinatra Christmas album he brought. Quade and Poppy play Santa and pass out the stockings. Zinnie is curled into Finn, and when Quade takes his seat, Sam curls next to him, his arm easily wrapping around her. Poppy climbs into my lap and Grace explains that we are going to go one at a time. She is not deterred at all by the groans, and no one argues back.

Poppy begs to see her person go first. She walks around like she is playing Duck Duck Goose, when she finally comes to a stop in front of Pierce. He blinks in surprise and looks down at her. This man who most people think doesn't have a heart. It's true he keeps his thoughts close to the chest, but I've known him long enough to know he is truly touched by the five-year-old in front of him.

"Finn took me because I'm five and I can't go by myself, but all of your gifts I picked out myself," she informs him.

"I'll tell you a secret," Pierce leans forward, pulling her onto his lap. "I was hoping you had my name." He smiles and she melts against him.

He reaches into the stocking that bears his name and pulls out a book. The cover is made of construction paper and is titled *Two P's in the City.*

"I wrote you a story about our special day together," she explains climbing off his lap to stand in front of him. "Each page cora, cora—what's the word again?" she asks Finn.

"Corresponds."

"Each page corasponts with a present."

"The word is mine—the idea and the presents are all her," Finn informs Pierce.

The book retells the day they went to *The Nutcracker.* It begins with their trip to Ladurée where they had macarons before the show. There's a crayon drawing of a window that spells "Ladurée." Beneath it are a little girl with curly hair and a man with dark hair and blue eyes.

She hands him a gift. It's a slender box with a sleeve of macaroons.

"You said these were your favorites." She motions to the chocolate mint.

"As a matter of fact, I did," he notes with wonderment.

He turns the page and it tells the story of the theatre the show was in. Poppy drew her version of the theatre across the bottom. She hands him gift number two. It's a framed picture of a selfie he took of the two of them. Poppy was in her tutu.

The next page displays the colorful nutcrackers she saw. She hands him this third gift. It's an actual nutcracker. This garners a laugh from everyone.

The last page is of them drinking hot-chocolate afterwards. The Bryant Park Tree is behind them and it's snowing. It was our first snow of the season that night. In the picture she drew, Pierce's nose is red, and he has blue lips. So, gift four is a lovely, cashmere scarf. I raise a brow to Finn, who winks back.

Poppy has good taste.

The last page is a picture of two arms from the elbow down. One is larger than the other and is in a suit. The other is small and wearing a plaid coat. She hands him his last gift, and his breath catches slightly.

Pierce holds up a red leather Cartier box that looks a bit worn. Inside is a pair of snowflake cufflinks with what appears to be a tiny sapphire in the middle.

"Those were Dad's," Zinnie says and Poppy nods. "Mom gave them to him on their tenth wedding anniversary. He loved winter."

"Poppy." Pierce is at a loss for words, and takes a minute to compose himself. "I'm so touched, but you should keep these."

"She wants you to have them," Zinnie nods, indicating to him that she does, too.

Pierce clears his throat and looks down at the curly-haired girl in front of him. Engulfing her into a hug, he lifts her onto his lap and tells her how much he treasures every gift. She asks which one is his favorite.

"I love them all, but the storybook is my favorite." He kisses the top of her head, and she looks like she was just given *her* favorite gift.

The night moves on. Grace cries when I tell her I thought the earrings matched her eyes. Clearly, I went above the budget, but what's the point of having a financial mogul draw your name at Christmas if you can't get a bit spoiled?

Zoe is spot on in her gifts to Finn. And Colin, in a *hilarious* nod to my outburst about Quade taking the kids to a ballgame a couple months ago, gives me season tickets to the Yankees.

Coincidentally, Sam picked Quade and Quade picked Sam. Am I irrationally jealous? Of course. Do I have to admit they know each other very well? Regretfully, yes. It's evident by the inside stories behind their gifts for each other. Quade's final gift is a trip for the two of them to a three-day music fest at Red Rock Park in Colorado. That plonker better have reserved two hotel rooms.

Grace has Poppy's name who has been playing with every item in her stocking while everyone was opening theirs. There's been a feather boa wrapped around her shoulders throughout the evening.

"There's one thing I wasn't able to fit into your stocking," Grace tells Poppy setting a box in front of her. Pops eyes expand into saucers at the beautifully wrapped gift in front of her. She looks from the large gold bow to Grace. "Open it sweetheart." Poppy takes her time, intrinsically sensing this is something special—just for her.

Pierce helps her lift the top off and when she folds back the tissue paper, she quickly glances to me. Looking for guidance. Sensing her distress, I slide onto the floor next to her and she sits in my lap. She's quiet and we all take our cues from her. Letting her process. She reaches into the box and pulls out a pink and orange crocheted blanket. It's large enough to cover her queen size bed.

Her little fingers inspect the yarn and when she's ready she looks to Grace.

"Do you remember this?" Grace asks her and Poppy nods.

"Mommy was making this for me before she died." Her eyes well, but no tears fall. "My favorite colors are pink and orange."

"That's what I heard. I ran into your grandmother," Grace says, pulling the blanket out of the box, "right after Thanksgiving." She drapes it over Poppy. "She remembered me, and we ended up having coffee. She was telling me about the blanket. I told her I would be honored to finish it. I hope that's okay with you?" Grace asks uncertain.

"I have a blanket too." Poppy says to Zinnie who nods.

"You sure do. Only the one mom made me was pink and blue. My favorite colors when I was your age."

Grace unfolds the rest of the blanket and points where the colors are inverted. "Your mom made almost all of it. See this corner where the colors are backwards from the rest of the blanket? This is the section I finished. I wanted you to always know where your mom stopped and I started. You can see, she made almost the whole blanket."

"Will you teach me?" Poppy asks Grace, who answers with a simple yes. Grace is perceptive and understands. She isn't expecting Poppy to jump up and down. Instead letting her work through her feelings on her own. Poppy doesn't leave my lap, but she leans forward and gives Grace a kiss.

The last person to open their stocking is Zinnie. Charlotte has it filled it with unique things she had been collecting from street fairs and boutique shops.

"One more thing," Charlotte says.

Zinnie digs to the toe of the stocking and pulls out a stack of business cards wrapped in a blue ribbon. They have a logo on the front, Eleven Hearts. Below is a web address. Charlotte hands her an iPad and Zinnie types in the address. Up pops a fully-created blog site loaded with pictures and posts Zinnie has already written. It's high quality. I knew Charlotte worked in web-design, but I had no idea she was this talented.

Zinnie reads the descriptive blurb then slings herself onto Charlotte, knocking her onto her back.

"I love it!" she says. "This is exactly what I would have wanted. I can't wait to show it to Jules when I start my internship."

"Remember—" Pierce states.

"I know," Zinnie says with a bit of exasperation. "I won't post anything that tells people where I am."

The girls don't know it, but Pierce has pretty much taken over their security. Ever since another billionaire's child was kidnapped several weeks ago, he is taking no chances. The girls have more security than the fucking president, they just aren't aware.

The night ends with a mix of traditions. Egg Nog from Zoe's family. Carols from Quade's. We each light a candle, from Grace's. Pierce asks to put Poppy to bed while the rest of the crew clean. Zinnie says her own good nights and when the last dish is put away and the last of the wrapping paper picked up, I take a minute to appreciate Sam's squad.

"You know," I tell Zoe, Grace and Charlotte, "when you invaded my house that first night, I had no way of knowing what you would come to mean to my girls. I certainly had no way of knowing what you would mean to me. Now, I couldn't imagine the girls' lives without you. You've sacrificed a lot of your time the last few months to get the girls to a place where they feel safe and empowered to be themselves. I couldn't have done this without my boys, but there's no way I could have done it without you women too."

chapter twenty-three

She skims her fingers over my skin in the way she traces the binding on her favorite novel before inhaling its scent. Reading every inch of me like I am a book that she reads over and over. My body writhes beneath her explorations and by the time she's turned every page and marked her favorite parts. I'm close to coming.

Handel's Messiah with just the five of us was perfect. Finn is bunking in the tent with the girls, giving Sam and me a few glorious hours to spend inside each other. This is better than any gift she could give me.

"Sam," I whimper. I need her. She's been driving me mad for the last twenty minutes. She shimmies down my thighs, giving her a better angle on my cock. She sucks just the tip before pulling me to the back of her throat. I've never told her this is what I crave. She just knows.

"Fuck yes." My hips rock toward her mouth. She moans her approval. Her left hand cups my balls.

"Turn over," she says, my dick falling to my stomach. Against my will, I do. It aches to not be in her mouth. She straddles my arse and massages every inch of skin she can find. Once she's convinced I'm too relaxed to move, she aligns her body with mine. She raises my hands above my head and her fingers entwine with mine. I've never been in a position like this before. She's not trying to dominate me, but I've never had anyone who focused only on me.

I can't lie. I'm a fan. It feels hella good to be loved.

Her hands clamped in mine, I can feel the pleasure from her sex leaving a trail as she slowly rides the curve of my arse. I love how uninhibited she is.

"I don't want you to get carried away," she whispers in my ear, her body gyrating against mine. "And I know your first instinct will be to flip me over and fuck me into this mattress, but I want your word you won't. Not until I say so."

Her voice is low and so full of desire that it's really all I need to get off. With her on top of me, I begin to grind my dick into the bed beneath me.

It's clear she likes the friction it supplies against her own movement, because she moans loud enough to wake the dead.

"Shh, baby," I chuckle, even though we are on opposite sides of the apartment as the others.

"You make me so hot, Walt. I want you so much." Her words tickle my ear and I start to roll over.

"No. Remember?" I do, but how she expects me to stay like this when she makes me feel like a fucking sex god, I'll never know.

She sucks on my neck and works her way down my back. The role reversal fogs my brain a little, because it feels fucking amazing.

My dick is leaking like a faucet at this point, and by the time her teeth sink into my arse cheek, I'm moments away from breaking my promise.

Her lips tickle the top of my buttocks before she bites the other cheek. But nothing prepared me for what she did next. I've never had my arse eaten out before. Finn, on more than one occasion, has tried to convince me that I'm missing out, but I never thought it would be something that happened. I had to beg Camilla to even put her lips on my dick.

But with Sam, it's like she wants every part of me as much as I want every part of her. She came apart when I did the same to her an hour ago. I thought I was going to have to resuscitate her. Now I understand why.

"Oh my God, Sam." I put my head into the pillow, making noises I didn't know I was capable of. This woman is totally ruining me for anyone else. Her finger massages my opening and before I can say, "I'm not sure about that," her finger breaches me. She curls it and when she does, she hits something that causes a full body explosion inside of me. My arse lifts into the air, and I hear her evil chuckle. She knows exactly what she is doing.

The bottoms of my feet feel like I have been fire-walking, and even though I am almost certain I could come just like this, there is no way that is how this plays out.

One ninja move later, Sam is wearing a large handprint on her arse and is flat on her stomach. I'm leaking so much I wouldn't need lube, but I do need a condom for this, so I take the time to grab the lube, applying it liberally to Sam before coating my dick with it. She doesn't protest or stop me. In fact, she urges me on with her dirty talk.

"Relax, baby." I say as the head of my cock breaches her arse. Her breath catches, and I kiss a trail up her spine to calm her. Slowly, I sink into her. Her heat incinerates me, and I have to lie still or risk coming on the first thrust.

We lie there. Neither of us moving. My fingers entwine

with hers, as hers were with mine moments ago.

"Move," she pleads, and I do. Each slide in and out, measured and intentional, shatter any remaining barriers between us. I'm not one to have dick measuring contests, but I've been in enough locker rooms to know that my girth and length is above average, but it doesn't appear to be an issue for her. She begs me to move faster, but I don't. Instead, I torture her and, in kind, myself, with slow precise undulations.

"I love you," she whispers. My entire body freezes at the words. Did I hear her correctly? Without thinking, I flip her over, remove the condom, and sink inside her. Her legs wrap around my waist and her wet heat swallows my cock. But that will have to wait, because the woman I love just told me she loves me.

"Say it again," I demand.

But she doesn't. Not yet. Instead, she leans up and plants the gentlest of kisses on my lips.

"I love you." It's an admission. Like it was embedded within her, bursting to get out, and she just couldn't control it anymore.

"I love you," I tell her. I don't want to make her wait even a minute to hear it again. My hips move, but I'm so beguiled by her that I'm not even aware of it until my cock swells deep within her, melding us together.

For the first time since we've started this affair, Sam and I sleep next to each other. I've wanted this as much as I wanted to hear her declare her true feelings. Each life can be measured by its milestones. Tonight, was a milestone in our relationship.

The alarm we'd set chimes, pulling us from our sleep. We're both a little too tired for Christmas morning sex, so we lie together through soft kisses, talking about the girls and the hopes we both have for today. I want to ask her about her family, to let her know her memories have a place in our lives, but she's so reluctant to talk about it. Instead, I take the easy way out and give her her gift while it's just the two of us.

I reach into my night stand and snag the ribboned box, setting it on her bare stomach. "Merry Christmas love."

"We're not exchanging until after breakfast," she chastises.

"Well, this one is just between the two of us." I nudge the box up her torso. She smiles and removes the ribbon.

Her face shows a combination of surprise and confusion. She sits up silently, pulling the ring out of the box and sliding it onto her right hand. When I don't protest the placement, she relaxes a little and smiles. Sam knows there's no way we talk engagement rings without first telling the girls. I know I'm ready, but I'm not sure she is. In some ways Sam is older than her years. She's seen more than any one person ought to. But in other ways, she's still young. She put her life on hold for so long, that she is really just now starting to live. I know she's ambitious and wants to finish school. Marriage right now, for her, would be pressing pause on her dreams again.

So, for now I'll settle for just telling the girls we are together. That I love Sam and she loves me. I plan to tell them tonight. There's not a single part of me that's worried about their response.

For now, this is the right ring for her. It's a bezel-set four-carat oval sapphire set in yellow gold. Simple and stunning. Just like her.

Despite our lack of sleep, Sam spends the next thirty minutes showing me how much she loves the ring. Fuck me.

I'll have a ring for her every day if it brings this kind of smile to her face and this kind of pleasure to my body.

Breakfast is full of pancakes and laughter and stories. I think about how different the holidays were just a year ago. I didn't know it at the time, but I was miserable. Disengaged. Living only for myself. Now, I live for these girls. Seeing all of them, Sam and Finn included, unwrapping presents, comparing gifts, oohing and aahing over their bounties makes me feel like a provider. Not because I buy them gifts, but because I can make them feel safe and cared for.

"Oh my God! Catch him," Sam yells to Zinnie, who grabs for Finn before he falls on his arse. Finn is not meant to be on ice skates. Zinnie goes down with him, but Finn braces her fall with his body. Sam doubles over. She and Finn are practically crying.

We put Finn out of his misery, leaving the rink to grab some much needed cocoa from the restaurant next door.

"Merry Christmas," the waitress says flatly. I don't blame her. She's working on Christmas. I order cocoas and warm croissants to heat our insides.

"They make you work Christmas?" Poppy asks the waitress, appalled.

"Someone has to." The woman smiles kindly to my inquisitive little girl.

"Don't you have family to be with?" asks Poppy, and I put my hand over hers. There's a hint of sadness in her eyes.

"My little girl isn't here anymore," the woman says softly.

"Are they sleeping in heaven like my parents?" Poppy

asks. The woman seems touched by her genuineness, but it's clear she doesn't want to talk about it.

"She is," she states, mustering a smile for Poppy.

Poppy. I think people can't help but appreciate her frankness, because it's so evident that it's from a place of purity.

"Did you two go home to use the loo?" I ask Finn and Sam.

"I forget how far away they are here." Sam slides into her chair. Finn is still laughing at whatever she said before they sat at the table.

"The waitress lost her little girl," Poppy tells Sam who props her arm on the back of her chair.

"I'm really sorry to hear that. So many people have lost some—"

"Samantha?" The waitress says her name and Sam's face pales before she even lifts her head.

"Samantha," she says again. Only this time it's filled with anger and a hint of malice.

"Mrs. Yates," Sam says with a pained look on her face.

"Is this your family?" The woman looks at Poppy and Zinnie. She looks from me to Finn, trying to figure out which one of us might be her husband.

Sam starts to introduce them, but she cuts her off.

"You were the one who left those flowers, weren't you? How is this fair? You stole my daughter from me. I loved her and you killed her. And nothing. No consequences for you. No. You get a happy family to go home to. I will never have a family again. No wedding for Kathryn. No grandkids to buy twenty-dollar hot chocolates for on Christmas day. You stole all that from me." Tears begin to stream down the woman's face. "You're a killer and you walked free."

Sam walks over to place her hand on the woman's arm. "Michelle, please. Kathryn wouldn't want—" None of us even see it. The woman's opened hand moves fast and with precision, slapping Sam across the face. Finn and I both jump up, but Sam holds out her hand to stop us.

"Don't you speak her name," Mrs. Yates spews. "Your choices killed my daughter. You killed your family. I wake up every day unable to breathe. And you're here, laughing and happy. I pray every day God would bring back my daughter and take you. I *hate* you," she says through sobs. The entire restaurant is silent, watching the horror play out in front of them. Mrs. Yates walks away leaving the hateful words that apparently have been stored inside for years.

"Samantha," I call gently. She looks like a cornered animal and I don't want to spook her. The pain across her face is enough to bring me to my knees.

"This is why," Zinnie says tearfully. Her face is red and splotchy. "This is why you pushed me to let that man walk. Because he is just like you. I didn't want to. I knew I shouldn't have, but I trusted you. And for what? You are just like him." She shakes her head in disbelief. "You made me break my promise to my parents. I promised them they wouldn't die in vain. That I would make sure the person responsible would pay for what he did."

"Zinnia," Finn says firmly and with a touch of warning.

"I can't undo that. You turned me into her!" Zinnia yells, coming to her feet.

"Zinnia, that is enough." Finn's baritone cuts the air.

In this moment, I'm not sure what to do or who to comfort first.

"I trusted you." Zinnie cuts deep one last time before running out of the restaurant. Finn calls her name and runs after her.

Before I can process or reach for Sam, Poppy darts through the tables after her sister. Her curls flying behind her, her eyes red from tears. She's five. I have no choice but to chase after her, leaving Sam standing alone at the table.

chapter twenty-four

Aping announces the arrival of the lift. It's dark outside. Sam steps off, a shell of the woman she was this morning.

This morning. It feels like a lifetime ago.

Finn and I both finally caught up to the girls, and by the time we had them safely home, they were exhausted from the emotions soaring through them. Zinnie was so upset she vomited, settling down only a couple of hours ago. Right now, Finn's in the middle of my bed with the girls under each arm. It was the only way we were able to quiet their tears.

"Where have you been?" I ask, coming to a stop in front of her. We're only a couple of feet apart, but it feels like we are separated by a canyon.

"I was trying to give Zinnie some time to process. How is she?"

"She's not good, Sam." Tears spill from her eyes and she takes a step towards the girls' wing. "They're in my room with Finn." She nods and turns in that direction.

I shove my hands in my pockets to keep myself from

reaching for her.

"I think maybe the girls need some time." My voice is like gravel.

"I'll let them sleep and talk to them in the morning," she says.

"No," I croak and then clear my throat and try again. "No, I think the girls need time to process. I, uh, I think it would be best for you to stay with one of your friends for now. The girls aren't ready to see you."

My heart splits in two. I only thought I knew what pain was. This is a bloodbath. "Sam," I press. "Why didn't you tell me?"

"You think I don't wake up every morning wishing that my family was still here? Wishing that I had been the one to go instead of them? That…" her voice quivers and my entire being wants to comfort her. I step forward, but she holds her hand up. "That I don't wake up every morning having to jump start my heart to make it through another day? Or at least I did, until I met these girls. Each morning was a little easier."

"You made me forgive him," Zinnie says from behind me. She looks like she hasn't slept in a year. "But not because I needed to forgive him but because you needed to forgive yourself. Don't you see how messed up that is? I thought that you meant it when you said that you loved us and that we were yours, but why would you do that to me? How could you not tell me who you really are?"

"Zinnie, go back to bed." There's no question in my tone that there is no room for arguing. Zinnie walks off. This is unconditional love. This is one of those moments when you have to sacrifice everything for your kids, even your own happiness. Because I'm about to send away the love of my life.

chapter twenty-five

"What's going on with you?" I ask Finn. It's been a couple of hard weeks for all of us, and I know it's weighing on him, too, but this is different. This seems unrelated to the disaster that is my life.

I've never experienced pain like I have the last two weeks. Pain I haven't even dealt with, because it's taken everything I have to focus on the girls.

Losing Sam has been like a blade to the gut. I really thought once Zinnie had some distance that she would be ready to talk about it, but she isn't. Her therapist is struggling to get her to open up, as well. When she's not crying, she acts as if nothing has happened, like if she ignores it, it will all just disappear.

"I don't know what you are talking about," Finn deflects.

Great. Two of them.

"What the hell did you do?" Pierce bellows entering the conference room where Finn, and I are having a meeting. He slams the door so hard, I'm surprised the glass didn't shatter.

"Don't start on him," Finn interjects on my behalf. "It was

an impossible situation. The girls had to be his number one priority."

"Oh, I know." Pierce goes deathly calm. The kind of calm you hear about before the tsunami wave crashes over you.

"You let her go."

"I made the decision to let her go," I tell him. "If you're looking to be angry with someone, be angry at me. Fair warning, you'll have to wait in a long line to get in your punches."

"You're not off the hook, by any means. I think you could have handled this differently, but you did what you thought was best for the girls. You have an excuse. You, dickhead…" he points to Finn, "you knew Walt didn't have a choice, so you should have been there for Samantha. You're her friend. You should have been there for here until Zinnie was ready." He turns to look at me. "And she *will* be ready."

"Look, it's not that easy. Zinnie is in a bad place," Finn says. "And we promised Everett to put the girls first."

"Fucking morons." Rage is radiating off Pierce. "And you think Sam not being in their lives is what is best for them? What's best for them is to be surrounded by people who love them unconditionally. What is best for them is to have people who love them enough to tell them when it's time to forgive. What is best for them is for Walt to be with the love of his life, so that he can be the best man for those girls."

"You know I love her?"

"Were you trying to keep it a secret? If so, you suck at it. It's been written all over your face for the last three months."

He releases a strong breath.

"Loving someone unconditionally doesn't mean they won't experience hurt. Zinnie is hurting because we haven't shown her another way. Do you think Everett walked away from Jenny every time she and Zinnie fought? You think they never let their girls down? Zinnie doesn't just get to choose who her family is. Sometimes life chooses it for you."

"You weren't there," Finn mumbles. He's torn between knowing Pierce makes a strong point and having had to pick up the pieces of Zinnie after Christmas day. Poppy is torn, too. She hurts for her sister, but all she understands is that her second mom went away.

"I understand she came back." Pierce crosses his arms. No way are we making it out of this unscathed.

"She did. Every day that first week," I admit.

"So, help me understand. She fought for the girls but you fuckholes won't."

"Enough." Finn stares him down. "He's hurting, too, and I won't allow you to talk to him like that."

"She's gone. Did you all know that?" The looks on our faces answer for us. He just shakes his head in disbelief. "Not one of you thought I needed to know."

"We were busy," I argue. "And you were halfway around the world."

"Let's get this straight now, because I don't ever," he lowers his voice an octave, "*ever* expect this to be an issue again. I don't care if I'm on fucking Saturn, you or these girls do not go through something like this again and not contact me."

"What do you mean Sam is gone?" I ask.

"No one has seen her in the last week. Not the squad. No one."

"She was staying with Charlotte."

"No, she wasn't. They were all out of town. She was staying at a hotel. When they got back, Sam had checked out and they haven't seen her since. She sent them an email telling them not to worry, but that was it."

"You mean she's out there all alone?" Bile rises to my throat as I stand. I'm met with a "now you get it" look. His confirmation is enough to break the barrier I built up to survive walking away from her. I empty my lunch into the trashcan.

chapter twenty-six

Another week goes by and nothing. No improvement with Zinnie and no luck locating Sam.

There's a knock on the office door and Finn enters.

"Poppy is at school." He took her this morning. I wanted to walk with Zinnie. She's really struggling. The therapist keeps encouraging me, telling me that she will make it through this, but when someone you love is hurting, days feel like years.

"Thanks," I nod, pulling up my email. "Maybe I should look into a nanny."

There's a knock on the door. "No. Don't start second guessing yourself. We can all help. The girls don't need anyone new right now."

"Mr. Nelson, there's a Mr. Thomas to see you."

"Send him in," Finn instructs. "Blake." He shakes his hand and peers behind him.

"School is back in session. West is teaching."

"Ah. Got it. West said the honeymoon was nothing short of spectacular."

"It's true. On an island with only the love of your life and servants is not a bad way to spend two weeks." He smiles like a man who knows love, and I find myself feeling a little bitter. "You could have called me, though. I would have helped from there until we got back to the States." Finn wants to hire Blake to help us locate Sam.

"I already know where she is," he says.

I stand up so quickly I almost knock over my chair. "Where is she?"

"She is staying in the apartment below ours. She met with Emme several days ago. Emme hired her and offered her a place to stay until she is back on her feet."

"Why hasn't she left a money trail? We've been looking for her for a week."

He shrugs. "Couldn't say. Maybe she was using cash? Maybe she doesn't have credit cards. Either way, she's not missing. She's hiding in plain sight."

"Well, at least we know she's not alone," Finn says.

But she is, I think.

The day rolls by at an excruciating pace. I want to go to her, to bring her home, but the unknowns keep me grounded. The girls are struggling, but we've finally found a groove this week. Zinnie spoke for the first time in a long time. She's still quiet and withdrawn, but she's trying to move forward. When I attempted to broach the subject of Sam this past weekend, she sobbed until she fell asleep.

"It's time." Quade enters the office.

"What's time?" I murmur, focused on the email in front of me. We have some things going sideways with our latest project.

"It's six."

"Is it?" I glance at my watch. "I need to get to the

apartment to pull dinner together. Plus, Zinnie has a school project due next week. I told her I would work on it with her tonight."

"I mean. It's Tuesday. At six," Quade says as the lift dings its arrival.

"Quade." I groan at his implication. "I don't think this is a good idea."

"The girls need everyone."

He's right, of course. They do. I close my computer, jotting down some notes for when I log in later.

When we enter the apartment, it's like a head on collision. There's music playing, laughter, and the girls are both smiling. It's a little forced, but it mimics the love that was so evident here just weeks ago. It's enough of a reminder that my chest constricts, and I'm not sure I can breathe. I excuse myself and dash to my bedroom to gain a moment of distance. With my back against the door, I try my best to calm my distress. There's a push on the door and I'm propelled forward. It takes Finn about a tenth of a second to assess the situation. Kicking the door closed, his arms wrap around me. It's too much. My brother's unconditional love pushes the last of my resolve and it breaks everything within me.

Finn's hand rubs up and down my back, soothing me. I gather his shirt in my fists as the pain of my sobs burst forth for the first time since this has happened. I miss Sam. It's like a death. One minute she was in my life and the next she was gone. "I don't know how to put the girls first and be the man I need to be for Sam."

I don't. I know the girls are my number one priority, and no matter how hurt I know Sam is, I know she wholehearted-ly agrees. She loves the girls like they were her own. She will always choose to do what is best for them. Even if that means she has to stay away.

"I promise it's going to work out," he assures me. "It's just taking longer than you want it to." He holds me until he's sure I'm ready to be released. "Wash up. Dinner is ready." He leaves me with a squeeze on my shoulder.

I wash my face and make sure I hide any evidence of despair.

"What's for dinner?" I ask, attempting to sound cheerful. I'm surprised I pull it off.

"I saved a seat for you," Poppy says. Colin is on the other side of her, trying to teach her to twirl her spaghetti against a spoon. I kiss the top of her head and thank Grace when she passes me a plate of my own.

Sam's friends engage Zinnie as often as possible. She likes to talk about her fashion internship. It's the only thing she's shown excitement for since the fallout. Everyone tries, but dinner is a struggle. The empty chair is a painful reminder of the gap in our lives. Dinner cleanup is assigned, and Colin makes a show of wanting to be the one to read to Poppy and put her down.

"Don't tell Poppy, but there's dessert," Grace says, putting a cake on the table.

"While we have our dessert, I wanted to talk to everyone," Charlotte says quietly. "About Sam."

"Charlotte," I say as gently as possible.

"It's okay," Zinnie says. "Say what you want to say."

"You and I both know there's more to this than meets the eye."

Zinnie's eyes widen, and Quade moves his seat next to her, his arm wrapping around her.

"What is this, an intervention?" she asks tentatively.

"Should it be?" Charlotte asks. "What's going on, Zinnie?"

"You mean other than Sam lying to me and causing me to break my promise to my parents? Oh, I don't know. Not much."

"Careful," Pierce chastises her, and I almost correct him, but I trust my friend to know what is right and wrong here.

"It just doesn't make sense to me," Charlotte continues. "You're a smart girl with a big heart. We've given you space to come to this on your own, but now I'm not sure that was the right decision. Because you're hurting, and you're not getting any better."

Zinnie starts to argue with her, but Charlotte doesn't give her the chance.

"So, I'm going to give you some background. About me. Sam and I graduated high school together. I was a foster kid. I didn't live with Sam's family, but I might as well have. My foster family wasn't abusive, just neglectful. I could be gone for days before they even noticed. Most of the time, I was at the Abbott's.

"Sam's family was like watching your favorite TV show. There was this banter between them, they had their own language. God, I loved being there. Eventually, I learned their language. It's something Sam and I still have today. Eventually we grew from two to four with Zoe and Grace. Then a few months ago it grew from four to eleven. With you all."

Charlotte pauses for a moment as if deciding something. I have no idea what she is about to say next, and even though it seems wrong to hear this from someone besides Sam, I know whatever she is about to tell us is going to give me insight into the woman I love. And right now I'm desperate for any connection I can get.

"Sam and I both applied to NYU. We got in on scholarships. When you are part of the foster system, you don't receive financial support after the age of eighteen. Sam's family had the basics, but that was about it. They struggled. Lived paycheck to paycheck like most families do. We roomed together and that's how we met Zoe and Grace." She points to her friends.

"I hit on her the first day of class," Zoe laughs, taking a sip of her beer.

"Sam or Charlotte?" Zinnie asks, shocked by her admission.

"Both," she smiles.

"Sam excelled in her classes. Just like everyone at this table is drawn to Sam, it was the same then, too. Sam never met a stranger. Everyone loved her. So, when it came time for her twenty-first birthday, there was a long line of people wanting to celebrate with her.

"The problem was, her family always celebrated their birthdays together. Her mom always made it a big deal, even for my birthday. They called, but we had talked Sam into staying in the city. The plan was that we would party, I would be the designated driver, and we would drive home in time to surprise her mom the next morning. Celebrate one day late.

"Sam's birthday was a Thursday that year. We all decided to go out Thursday night and celebrate. Our friend Kathryn from high school was at Columbia and decided to meet us to party, then catch a ride from us to surprise her mom for a long weekend.

"We danced, partied, kissed boys...and girls," she adds, glancing to Zoe.

"And I met a boy." Charlotte looks at Zinnie. "A boy I wanted to impress. I had been into in him for a while, but didn't think he knew who I was. When he asked if he could buy me a drink, I agreed. I was worried if I said no, he would get bored and move on. The more we danced, the more I drank.

"Sam as it turned out, only had a couple of shots at the beginning of the night. By the time we secured the rental car, she was sober enough to drive. So, I fell asleep in the backseat, and Kat slept up front."

"She was drunker than she realized," Zinnie says with disdain.

"Nope. She was sober. But a friend of ours sent her a belated birthday text and she glanced at her phone. I woke up in a hospital a week later. Kathryn was killed instantly. Sam was covered in bruises, but that was it. All three of us had to be cut from the car. The police told her they would contact her family, but she had to go to the ER to get checked out. Her family would meet her there."

The pain on Charlotte's face is more than I can bear. The thought of what she and Sam endured splits my heart in two. I go to stand, to move near her, but before I can, Pierce is holding her and kissing the top of her head. Tears slide down her face.

"It wasn't until it was time for the hospital to discharge her that she was told. The car she hit was her family's. They were on their way to surprise her in the city since she wasn't coming home. They all died instantly, except her brother, who died an hour before she was told."

The room is silent. I had no idea. As horrific as the story is, I'm not sure what Charlotte's intentions are. I don't think Zinnie lacks empathy for Sam. They share a loss that few understand.

Charlotte clears her throat, "I'm guessing you are wondering what this has to do with you."

Zinnie doesn't answer, but she's listening intently.

"The stories are different, but I can't help for wondering if there are two commonalities." She motions between Zinnie and herself. "Us."

"If I had kept my promise, I would have been the one be-hind the wheel. I was the denominator that changed every-thing. I started the domino effect. When I watch you and lis-ten to you, I see myself in you."

Zinnie looks at her, tears flowing down her face.

"I was being a brat," she says wiping her nose. "I was mad because my friends were all hanging out that night. Mom and Dad couldn't find a babysitter, so they made me stay home to keep Poppy." She pulls at the tissue in her hand. Her eyes shift down. "I threw a fit when they said they were going to stay a little later. So, they left." She looks at Charlotte. "They were on the road because of me."

"And Sam was behind the wheel because of me."

No one says a word. It's as if a physical weight had been removed from Zinnie's shoulders.

"Keep going," Grace says gently to Charlotte.

"When I was released from the hospital, I was grieving the loss of the Abbotts and Kathryn. The funerals happened while I was still in the hospital. I thought maybe if I had gone I might have some closure. I don't know. Sam visited me every day. Slept in a chair next to my bed every night.

"The community wasn't as forgiving. Especially once Mrs. Yates started spewing her hatred. She had lost her husband just six months before. Kathryn was her only daughter, and she couldn't handle a second loss.

"I mean, Christ, she was 21 and a day. A child herself. Accidents happen. She shouldn't have picked up her phone, but how many of those people do the exact same thing every day? And to sit in judgement of her.

"Like I said, her family didn't have a lot of money. They didn't have health insurance or burial insurance. Sam had to pay to bury them. Because she was ticketed for failure to maintain control of an automobile, her car insurance wouldn't pay any hospital bills. She had to pay for the care her brother received. My stay and her visit. The state charged her for the emergency services, and even though the courts ruled she didn't have to pay damages to Mrs. Yates, she did have to pay Kathryn's burial costs. By the time all was said and done, Sam owed a little more than three-hundred-thousand dollars. She had to give up her scholarship and go to work to pay the debts she owed.

"Sam has more than paid her penance. And I don't mean just the money. What you saw at the restaurant that day was the hurt and grief of a woman who never sought help to deal with her loss. She will always blame Sam. It doesn't matter that I know for a fact the only reason Kathryn went home with us was because her mom constantly made her feel bad for leaving her there after they buried her father. It doesn't matter that Kathryn could have easily offered to drive. She could have stayed awake. She knew Sam was as tired as we were. There's always someone to point the finger at. We can always play the 'if only' game. But you can't, Zinnie, it will tear you apart."

"How did you get better?" Zinnie asks her, like a drowning man searching for a buoy.

"Sam," she says simply. "I didn't know how to deal with the guilt I was feeling. So, I jumped on the bandwagon with everyone else. I mean, it's hard to take responsibility for your part when you are blaming others, right? But Sam knew. She heard I was drinking more than I should have, and she showed up to my room, knocked on my door, and told me to get over myself. That dominos are dominos, and they are going to fall, whether you knock them over or someone else does. We are all affected by decisions made around us every day. We can't control life. We can plan and influence it, but there will always be things truly out of our control."

"You make it sound like Sam is okay. I don't think she's okay."

"She's a work in progress," Zoe says. "Sam did the only thing she could do. She put one foot in front of the other until she found a pace that worked for her. She's never told a soul about her family until she visited their burial sites with you. You girls, and Walt, changed her."

"Sam wanted you to forgive the man who killed your parents," Charlotte explains, "because she knows what it feels like to hate someone. She hated herself for a long time. Counseling helped. We helped. Finn helped a ton when he hired her, but, ultimately, she had to let it go. I hated myself, too. Jesus, I had so many regrets, but Sam refused to let me wallow in them. She forced me to let it go." Charlotte's expression saddens more. "But with her, even though she had to forgive herself, I think there is a part of her that isn't sure she deserves happiness. It's why the three of us where so relieved to hear she didn't give up until she wasn't given a choice. For the first time since the accident, she fought for what she wanted. Forgiveness is for you, not the other person. Without it, you end up like Mrs. Yates. Driven by anger and hatred."

"What do you mean Sam didn't give up until she didn't have a choice?" Zinnie asks.

"Sam came by every day for over a week to try to sort this out," I tell Zinnie. "She didn't stop until I told her she had to. You weren't able to differentiate Sam from the man who took your parent's lives. I made a promise to never put you in harm's path. Sam was bringing you too much pain." The last part of that sentence makes me nauseous, because I know that is the last thing Sam would ever want.

Zinnie doesn't say anything. There's no revelation on her part. She just absorbs what Charlotte told her. Tears slip down her face, and she asks if she can be excused.

"Yes, sweetheart," I answer, and we watch her leave. Her shoulders slumped with carrying the weight of the world.

"Thanks for coming over tonight," I tell everyone. "It means a lot to the girls."

"We're not finished," Zoe says. "That was for Zinnie. Now, we have words for you."

"Zoe." I run a hand down my face. I look like I've aged ten years in the last few weeks. I feel it, too.

Quade takes the lead. "She's the love of your life, and you just let her go." Clearly Sam and I weren't doing as well of hiding it as we thought we were. Honestly, that's the least of my concerns.

"Jesus Christ, don't you think I know that?" I yell louder than intended, lowering my voice so I don't disturb the girls. "I know that. I didn't just *let* her go. I had to. I made—"

"Yeah, yeah, we get it. You made a promise," Zoe interjects. "It's a promise you shouldn't have made. You honestly think those girls are better off without Sam? Giving into Zinnie is not what is best for her. She has to work through this. Sam loves those girls like they were her own."

"How is she?" I ask.

"Oh, you know. Someone stood up in front of a crowd and screamed aloud the thing she hates most about herself. She lost the only family she's known since the loss of her own. She got kicked out of her apartment. Lost her job. And when I ask her about it she says that you were only doing what you know to be right, and we should cut you a fucking break. So, you know," Zoe shrugs, "she's peachy."

"Don't sugarcoat it for him," Quade says. "She looks like

her fucking heart has been ripped from her body."

"You've seen her?" I ask, ignoring his last statement. "When did you see her?"

Quade raises a brow. Shit, I've walked right into it. He can hear the jealousy in my voice.

"I've spent time with her every day," he goads. "Someone had to. You and Finn just dropped her."

"You've been with her this whole time? You didn't think that was something I needed to know?"

"You had the best fucking woman, and you deserted her." He stands to leave then looks back to me. "I once heard Jenny's dad tell Everett that the greatest gift he could give his daughters is to love their mother. Fix this."

"Or?" I bite back, still unreasonably pissed he's been with Sam every day.

"Or bro-code be damned man."

"Meaning?"

"Meaning, I'll do everything in my power to make her happy. I mean, if it's not me, it's going to be someone right? At least with me, you'll know she's taken care of." His eyes darken. "Her hair across my pillow. Her beneath me."

"Quade," Finn warns, but Quade is not to be deterred. He leans his closed fist against the table.

"My hands on her body. Skimming her hips before I make her mine. My name on her lips, when she—"

The chair I'm sitting in falls to the floor as I lunge at him, drawing up short when I'm pulled back by Pierce's arms. Quade doesn't so much as flinch.

"You fucking stay away from her or I'll rip your fucking heart out!" I roar.

He shoves his hands into his pockets and I think it must be to keep from punching me.

"Finally," he says. "This is the Walt I know." He goes to leave but turns around to make one point clear. "I didn't say all of that to bait you. It's a picture of what the future looks like. Fix this or step the fuck off."

Pierce pats my chest a couple of times to calm me down. "Where is she?" I ask.

No one answers. Instead they stare at me likely wondering if I am to be trusted with her heart again.

"If I have to ask again, it will get ugly," I promise.

"She's on a business trip," Grace offers.

"So, let me get this straight." Zoe leans back in her chair, her arms folded. "You've had, what? An epiphany?"

"Well, yes," I answer.

"What's changed? Don't go after her because you don't want Quade to have her. Don't go after without knowing what you are doing."

"Tell. Me. Where. She. Is."

chapter twenty-seven

This has to be the longest flight in the world. I'm pretty sure we've circled the earth twice to get my arse to London.

"What's our ETA?" I ask my pilot.

"The same as it was twenty minutes ago," he answers, not at all intimidated by my surliness. I grumble about firing his arse and check my watch on the way back to my seat. Another fucking hour.

"Another drink, Mr. Nelson?" Samantha, my stewardess asks. It had to be Samantha working this flight. Karma is fucking brutal.

"Yes. Please," I add after a beat, to soften the sting in my tone.

I spent last night talking with Zinnie, and I think that is how Sam would have wanted it. I made it too easy for Zinnie to hide behind the mess, but in my gut, I know Sam understands. She would be the first to say the girls come first.

I asked Charlotte to do it with me. As much as I wanted to be what Zinnie needed, it was obvious she needed Charlotte more. And there is a part of me that thinks Charlotte needed Zinnie just as much. My heart broke for the dark-haired beauty as she told her story last night. The pain still so fresh in her green eyes. I didn't want that for Zinnie.

Zinnie still has a long way to go, but I told her that it's a path we walk together as a family, and that Sam is part of this family. Then I told her that I intend to marry her.

This made Zinnie cry harder, not because she is against it, but she's missed Sam. She begged me to let her come to London, so she could make this right with Sam, but I wouldn't let her. Finn can bring the girls over if this goes well, but until I know for sure, I still have an obligation to protect them. And I have an obligation to protect Sam.

The truth is, I don't know what Sam is going to say or do when she sees me. It's an excruciating reality to know you obliterated the heart of the person you love.

Sam needed me, and I left her. I made mistakes and hid behind my own insecurities as a parent. I thought, *look at me, I'm such a great parent*, I even let the woman who gives me breath go. Instead, I should have been parenting Zinnie through her crisis. Not protecting her from it. It's a hard lesson to learn. The difference between protecting someone and controlling their surroundings.

I didn't sleep a wink last night. Zinnie and I agreed that the reason for my trip wasn't to be shared with Poppy. Not yet. It would be too confusing for her.

Fuck me over. When I fuck up, I really fuck up.

I was up with the sun. Zinnie hugged me until she stopped crying, then told me to go get Sam.

When Graham and Emme Taylor entered their office this morning I was waiting for them. Like so many others, Emme has already taken a liking to Sam and wasn't going to make this easy for me. I told her I didn't need another lecture, that I already knew I was a daft prick who didn't deserve her. When her lips twisted, I lost my shit and raised my voice. Not a mistake I will make again. I pray for the person who finds themselves on the wrong side of Graham Taylor. That man has serious protective issues.

"Pot, kettle," he stated when I told him as much.

"Mr. Nelson, we have started our descent," the pilot says overhead. Clearly, I am not the only one ready to get off this plane.

The flight traffic is a nightmare and it takes and extra thirty minutes of circling until we have the all clear to land. The wheels barely hit the ground before I'm standing at the door. Thankfully, my handler is used to me and has everything ready to go. The car is sitting on the tarmac, along with someone from customs to check me into the country and bypass all the lines.

It's now five in the evening. It's nearly dark. As the lights of the cityscape twinkle, I sit impatiently in the car until we arrive at my destination, only placated when the historic structure comes into view. The Milestone Hotel. The Taylors take care of their own.

I'm greeted by name when I exit the car. That's the kind of hotel this is. The staff knows the wealthiest in the city without having to be told.

"Samantha Abbott's room."

"Of course, Mr. Nelson. Let me ring her."

"No. Room number please. I want to announce my own arrival."

"That's against our..." I have to hand it to the young man behind the desk. He's giving it his best, acting as if he will not be intimidated. We both know that's not true, because this hotel understands power, and I have power.

The manager arrives just as I start to lose my shit and informs me that Miss Abbott was delivered to the Four Seasons for a meeting and isn't expected back until later this evening. I instruct him to please have the bell-hand pack her items and have them ready. We will be back to retrieve them.

The lobby at the Four Seasons is larger and it takes me a minute to spot her. She's sitting at the bar, engaged in a conversation with a man. He's my age, maybe a year or two's difference. He carries himself as someone with wealth does. I know she is here on business and I do not want to hinder her job, but when his lips touch her ear in a whisper, it's clear I'm going to dig my hole deeper before digging my way out of it.

"Samantha," I all but growl.

She's surprised to see me, but she holds her composure. She introduces me to the man next to her, but I'm not listening. The veins in my neck pulse and I think I might now understand what Bruce Banner physically felt before he began to Hulk out. The rage flowing through me at the site of his hand on her thigh is greater than I've ever known.

"Kindly remove your hand from her thigh," I say, my hands balled into fists. The man astutely reads my threat and picks his hand up.

"I look forward to seeing the numbers. If they match your proposal, we would be honored to carry the spring line." He shakes her hand and leaves his half-eaten dinner on the bar.

"We're leaving," I say to Sam.

"I'm eating." She turns back to her dinner and slowly cuts off a piece of steak. The bartender brings her a new glass of wine and she thanks him.

"I'm not playing."

No response.

I toy with the idea of carrying her out of here on my shoulder but that's not really my style. Instead, I sit, facing her. She doesn't face me, but when I cross one leg over the other as if I have all the time in the world, I catch an eye watching my movements. She's not unaffected by me, that's for sure. Attraction was never our problem.

She chews each piece of meat longer than necessary, and by the time she picks up the dessert menu, I've had enough. Throwing some bills on the bar to more than pay for the meals, I stand.

"Car. Now."

Two words. Simple, but effective. Or maybe it was my tone. Either way she's making her way to the entrance. I take her elbow and guide her to the car. I instruct my driver to take us to her hotel.

We ride in silence. I don't want to start a conversation that I can't finish in the fifteen minutes we have.

We arrive, and I shoot a menacing, albeit childish, look to the boy who refused me her room number, as we cross the lobby to an elevator.

Sam's room is quaint. It has a seating area and a bedroom. Smaller than the rooms I am accustomed to, but tastefully done.

"Why are my things packed?" she asks when we enter the bedroom.

"I had the staff pack them. We're going to my house."

"I assume the girls are okay or you would have led with that," she says kicking off her shoes. Her suitcase is packed, but left open on the valet stand. She digs through and pulls out something more comfortable than the dress she is wearing. Thank fuck, because she is spectacular in it, and it's hard to concentrate when she looks this good. She shimmies out of it, leaving herself in a lingerie set that has my dick a concrete rail.

She removes her bra, and when the breasts that I have adored since I first saw her spring free, there is no way my arousal can be hidden. She doesn't notice, or maybe she doesn't care. She slides on a plain white t-shirt then sits on the bed to slide off her thigh highs. Next, her knickers fall to the floor and she bends to pick them up. I wish she had her back to me so I could see her arse. Instead, the shirt billows out and I see nothing. She reaches in her case again and pulls out Finn's joggers.

She sighs when they are pulled up and in place. She puts everything she was wearing away in her case then grabs a makeup bag of sorts. Still not a word spoken. I follow her to the bathroom where she washes her face, then brushes out her hair.

I was wrong. She should have stayed in the dress. Here, in her natural beauty, when she is most gorgeous, she's more of a distraction.

Her facewash and lotions go back into her case, and I think she is ready to zip up and head out with me. Instead, she goes back out front, grabs a water and some chocolates from the mini-bar, and takes a seat on the couch. Her legs fold under her.

"We're leaving. Going to my house," I say again.

"I'm not," she says.

"I want to talk to you, Samantha."

"Then talk, Walt. But I'm not going anywhere."

I fume for about, oh, three seconds, then get to the real reason I'm here. Pulling a footstool from the chair, I position myself in front of her, my knees touching the couch.

"I'm sorry."

Shit. I've had almost twenty-four hours since I made the

decision to come after her, and it occurs to me only now that I have no idea what to say to her. How to make her forgive me.

"I'm sorry," I offer again, since I have nothing else.

"I know you are," she replies.

"That was too easy," I murmur. This woman. I'm always a step behind her.

She laughs, but it's not the easy-going laugh of my Sam. "What were you expecting? You were right Walt. You did the right thing. The girls come first. I would never hold that against you."

"I wasn't right. I should have listened to you that first week. Instead of giving Zinnie time, I should have made us work this out together. I love you, Sam. I won't choose between you and the girls."

"I don't want you to, Walt. Everything Mrs. Yates said at the restaurant is true. I killed her daughter. I killed my family."

"You had an accident."

"Texting is no different than drunk driving. I chose to pick up my phone. I chose to look at the screen. I took my eyes off the road. No one else. I'm sure Charlotte has put a tale in your head that she's at fault because she was supposed to drive. She's not. I am."

"The girls need you," I blurt, because I'm beginning to panic. There is a resolute calmness about her that I had mistaken for hurt or anger earlier. I was thinking she was going to make me grovel, make me fight to prove to her, but that is not what is going on here at all. She's given up. She believes what she is telling me.

"Walt." She turns and lowers her legs to the floor, only I'm right in front of her, so they part, trapping mine between hers to accommodate me. She takes my hands in hers and holds them against my thighs. "Jenny and Everett left the girls to you. They entrusted you to do the right thing. You are a wonderful father and I am so proud of the man you are."

"The man I've become. Because I wasn't this man before you."

"You were. You just needed someone to show it to you. The girls did that."

"You did that," I plead. Forget arguing. I'm scared. I've lost her. It's so evident in her eyes.

"Sam." I clear my throat. "Sam, I was wrong. Please don't do this." The tears I struggled to hold back spill over the brim. "Please don't. I love you. I didn't know how to be what Zinnie needed and to be there for you."

"Walt, I love you. With all my heart, I love you, but you were right. This will pass. The hard times fade, and you realize that you are where you are supposed to be. I don't get a free pass because I'm a good person who made a mistake. I took the lives of six people. Six people who are no longer here. There's no telling how many countless others I affected. A man whose soulmate was meant to be my sister, but I took that from him. A co-worker who lost their job because my father wasn't there to help protect his. Mrs. Yates who will never have grandchildren because of me. It's a ripple. My actions caused a ripple that none of us can fathom. That's what our decisions do. They affect others. I have to be responsible for that."

"Sam, you can't possibly carry that weight around. It's destroying you. And it's not how it happens. You fought for the boy that killed Everett. You didn't even know him, but you fought for him to get a second chance. Why don't you believe you deserve one?"

"It's time for you to go," she says. But this time she's not so calm. There's a hint of emotion there, and I hurl myself towards it like a lifeboat. She's breaking. And I'm not going to stand by and let her stay glued together.

"I'm not leaving." My face morphs into stone. This. Digging in. This I can do.

"Walt," she pleas, her voice quivering.

"I'm not leaving."

"Then I will." She stands to step around me. I let her clear the foot stool before pulling my shirt off and wrapping my arms around her from behind, using her surprise to my advantage. I pull her to my body, holding her in place.

"Get off me," she demands.

Anger. Now we're getting somewhere.

"No."

"Walt, get the fuck off me."

"No." She thrashes her body back and forth in an attempt to free herself, but I'm not giving up. I stay glued to her back. I need her to feel me. To know I'm really here and not going anywhere.

"You're hurting me." I'd release her in a heartbeat if that were true. The truth is, I have hurt her. Just not physically.

"No. I'm not."

"Walt." She tries again to free herself.

But it's working. I can hear it in her voice. It's seeping from her body into mine. She's breaking. Her emotions are on the cusp and it's exactly where I need her to be.

"I am going to marry you. So, do whatever you need to do to wrap your head around that, but I'm not leaving here without you."

"Walt," she sobs. Finally. She needs this, but it tears my heart in two.

"Samantha, how can you expect to teach Zinnie to forgive if you won't even forgive yourself?" I whisper into her ear as her body begins to convulse. I release her arms and her hands

cover her face as gut-wrenching sobs rip through her. The fight
is gone. All that is left is her grief. I roll her over and pull her
into my lap, propping us against the pillows. Her arms wrap
around my back, her face buried against my neck. Even after
she's fallen into a disturbed sleep, I hear her whimper. Her
body has finally given out.

I don't move. I just hold her, pulling her closer to me.
Praying my love is seeping into her, infusing her with the
knowledge that she is more deserving of love than anyone I've
ever met. She stirs briefly, and the tears are back.

"I love you," I tell her.

Her shoulders visibly sag, and I watch her release the last
regret she was holding on to.

She's holding onto me like she's desperate for me, and in
this very minute, I vow to protect this woman with everything
I have. Even if it means protecting her from herself.

My thumb runs the length of her jaw. I dose off, and when
I wake a while later, she's still asleep. The tremors have ended,
and she looks peaceful.

Another hour goes by and I feel her stir. She doesn't fight
me. She doesn't attempt to move. She just looks at me, a tear
escaping down her cheek. "I killed my family," she says.

"I know, love. I know."

chapter twenty-eight

A fter Sam's breakthrough last night, I put her to bed after pulling her joggers off. By the time I returned from the loo, she was on her stomach, asleep.

I undressed and joined her, draping my thigh and arm across her. It took a strong conversation with my dick, but it finally got on board and settled down. Not an easy feat when it's resting against that glorious body.

We sleep through breakfast, both of our bodies healing from the chasm that's been there since we split.

The winter sun is setting when I wake again. Sam was crying in her sleep, and when I drape the weight of my body against hers, she shimmies into the protective nook I'm offering her and sleeps again.

I wake sometime later and order room service. My hunger winning out over watching her sleep. She doesn't stir and my attempts to wake her are futile so I eat in bed next to her, not wanting to leave her side.

She seeks me out in her sleep when I lay back down. My hands comb through her hair. I tell her she's forgiven. I tell her she's a wonderful mother. I tell her she's deserving of a life. I tell her she's smart. Funny. Sexy. Beautiful. I tell her she's loved. The last one gets me a kiss on my chest where her head is resting, and just that easily, she's asleep again.

Sam stretches next to me. She lets out a soft moan of someone who's been in bed too long.

"I'm hungry," she mumbles. When she turns to face me, she has sheet indentions on her face and a horrible case of bedhead.

"Ah. There's my girl."

She doesn't correct me, or protest, but she doesn't smile either.

"What time is it?"

"Almost noon. On Friday," I add.

"What?" She sits up too quickly for someone who hasn't eaten or moved in way too long. I help her to her feet and escort her to the bathroom. I pick up a complimentary toothbrush on the counter and brush my teeth. Man, does that feel good. Sam watches me as she pees. Not taking her eyes off mine, she wipes, flushes then washes her hands.

She steps up to me and my body reacts to hers, thinking it's about to be kissed, but instead, she pulls the toothbrush from my hand and puts it in her mouth. She brushes her teeth.

But then, she smiles.

We're going to be okay.

Neither of us says anything. She grabs a brush from her case and begins the task of detangling her hair. When she comes out of the bathroom again, I've laid out the only causal clothes she packed—jeans and her white T-shirt. When they delivered dinner last night, they brought up the bag my driver had left for me. I pull out a jumper that buttons down the front and lay it on the bed as she slides into a pair of knickers.

"Whose cardigan is this?" she asks.

"Mine."

She smiles, picks it up from the bed, and puts it on. That's it. There are no other words spoken. I find a casual jacket in my bag to replace the one she stole. We ride the lift to the lobby and I shake off the car, opting instead to walk. Sam takes my hand in hers, and we walk several blocks before coming to the restaurant I wanted to take her to.

Snagging a table in the back corner, we eat fish and chips, and drink a local ale. Sam tells me about her job with Emme. What she was doing over here and how she plans to make it work with her school schedule. I fill her in on some of the projects we were working on before she left, letting her know her hard work paid off and we signed the clients.

She asks me about London and I tell her what I love about it. We make plans to see some places that interest her after we finish our meal. We don't talk about the girls, or our friends, or what our next steps are. We just talk like a couple who is on holiday.

Sam is still processing, and I'm okay with giving her that time, as long as she understands that we are leaving here together. I don't press or start an argument. I just show her my city, and she holds my hand.

We eat dinner in the room. I don't move us to my house or even to a larger suite. I leave us in her room, in hopes she will feel safe and that she is in control. My thoughtfulness falters a bit when we get back in bed. I want to be with her. Make love to her. Help her feel my love. I tap into every ounce of reserve I have and wait for her to initiate. She doesn't. So, I tap down my desire and settle for holding her. It's not long before her breathing evens out and she sleeps.

There were no tears today.

Saturday is much the same, only I leave her in a bookstore for the afternoon, going to Harrod's to pick up more items for us.

We dress for dinner and I take her to a Michelin-rated restaurant, one of my favorites.

Sam is dressed and leaning over me Sunday when I wake. "Going back to the bookstore. Want to finish my book."

I nod, and she leaves me with a kiss. On my lips. Who knew it could be such an exciting thing.

The door to the bookstore jingles, announcing my arrival. It's Sunday, so they will be closing earlier than yesterday. I go through the stacks at the front of the store. The middle of the store has coffee and tea. I lift a biscuit from the plate. I search the stacks, my pulse accelerating as I near the end, wondering if she left. I turn into the last aisle and there in the corner is Sam. Curled into a chair, legs folded under her. There are a couple of biscuits resting on her thigh and a cup on the arm of the plaid chair. She turns the page of a book. A different one than yesterday. A couple of random people occupy the other chairs, oblivious that they are sitting next to the most remarkable woman. If they knew, they would be soaking her in like I am. She turns the page and my body stirs, remembering her fingers skimming my body in the same manner.

When the clerk comes back to let everyone know the

store is closing she looks up for the first time and sees me. A shy smile flickers across her lips and she stands. I've been sitting for more than thirty minutes in this hard chair, my legs crossed. I'm wearing worn jeans from uni, a white collared shirt under a navy V-neck jumper, with the shirt sleeves rolled up over the cuffs. My sunglasses are tucked into the V.

Her hand lands palm up on my crossed knee. It's the easiest decision I've ever made. I accept and walk out of this store, my hand in her hand.

Later that night, we order room service. I'm cutting into my salmon when Sam says, "Salmon was Rory's favorite."

I recognize the name from one of the grave stones she visited. My only response is to cut another bite. I chew, and she keeps talking. I gather this is the first time she has discussed her family at length since the accident, and I wonder if it's because she didn't think she had the right to before.

Once she starts, it's like a reel of family movies are playing in her head. I order dessert for us a couple of hours later. We laugh at the funny stories, cry at the harder ones. I ask some questions, and she hesitates for only a minute before answering.

I tell her about Charlotte talking with Zinnie, and what Zinnie has been feeling since the accident. We talk about therapy sessions, and I encourage her to go back to hers. I remind her that she is worthy of love and good things happening to her. We talk about what the girls need and how to begin to heal our family. When we look up it's two in the morning.

We climb into bed, exhausted from the emotions sitting just beneath our skin. She gives me a soft kiss on the lips before falling asleep with her head on my chest.

chapter twenty-nine

The water from the shower flows over me, matching the weather outside. Today is the day I take charge. But not yet. Sam is behind me in this shower testing every ounce of strength I have. So far, I'm winning. I bend my head to rinse the shampoo, when her arms wrap around my waist. She just stands there, holding me, sucking streams of water off my back.

"Thank you," she says.

I turn and kiss her. A full kiss for the first time in almost two months. My heart soars at the contact of my tongue against hers.

Little by little, my Sam is coming back to me.

"We'll be there tomorrow night," Finn says. Sam is people watching from a chair at the café we stopped at for lunch. I stepped out when my phone buzzed so as to not disturb the other patrons.

"Perfect. I have the main suite reserved for you and the girls, so you will all be in the same space."

"You and Sam aren't already in there?"

"No. I didn't want her to have to move. I plan on keeping us separate. And you're sure Zinnie is ready?"

"Yes. She and Charlotte have spent a lot of time together while you've been away. I went with her to two therapy sessions. The therapist agreed she was ready. She's been begging me to fly us over earlier, but I wanted you to have the time you needed."

"Finn."

"I know." I don't have to tell him how grateful I am. "Hang on," he tells me, and Zinnie gets on the phone.

"You're not waiting for us, are you?"

"No, sweetheart. This has to be about the two of us."

"I know," she says, and I can tell she means it. "It's how Dad would have done it."

Sam hasn't been the only one thinking the last few days. Being away for the first time since the funeral has given me time to process and remember my friend. The things he said, the stories he told.

One in particular resonated with me the first night I was here. The night I decided to stay as long as necessary to bring Sam back to herself.

"Jenny and I are going to Vermont for the weekend. The girls will be with her parents. If you need me, call someone else," he jokes, lifting his beer to us before taking a sip. The five of us are in a circle of leather chairs. The bartender brings us each a couple of fingers of Macallan.

"Didn't you just get back from taking the girls to Paris?" Colin asks.

"*Yep. But this trip is just for me and Jenny. Gents, once you man-whores finally take the plunge, you'll learn, kids grow like weeds. They're gone before you can blink an eye, living their own lives. Jenny is the love of my life. By taking care of her, I take care of the girls.*"

None of us understood what he meant. It wasn't possible for us to. But now, now I understand.

"I need to call Emme," Sam says as we walk the streets downtown.

"Okay," I respond. I don't tell Sam that Emme is more than aware that she is taking time off. I told her as much when I rang her Friday.

"This is the place." I step into a building, holding the door for Sam to follow.

"Where are we?"

"I need to pick up some papers from a friend of mine."

We exit the lift on the fifth floor. The door reads "Sir John Weatherly".

"Walt Nelson to see…"

"Get your arse back here," my friend calls from his office door. Fitting his name is Weatherly, because he's starting to look it. Too much booze and too many women.

We clamp hands before hugging.

"I must say, I was rather shocked to hear from you yesterday. This must be Miss Abbott." He kisses the back of her hand. She laughs when he tries to kiss a little further up, and I bop him on the back of his head. Hard.

"Piss. That hurt. But I get it, I wouldn't want anyone kissing my wife."

"Oh, I'm not his wife," Sam tells him before turning to me. When she does I'm on one knee, holding out the ring my grandfather gave to my grandmother. It's modest at two carats, set on a simple gold band. Sir John is an arse, but an old friend. He's slips out of the office, leaving us alone.

"Sam, you are my everything. I promise to never make you feel otherwise. I know I've been doing this backwards. Hell, we were a family before we were a 'we'. But I know the difference now. I know that you are my priority. The girls are the love of our lives, but you're my soulmate, and I promise to always treat you as such. Please spend the rest of our lives as my wife. Will you marry me?"

"Walt," she says gently, and I see the reluctance in her eyes. The hesitation. But it's not at my love or her love for me. It's with her own demons. I don't push. I just wait.

"Walt," she starts again, lowering to her knees. "I promise my love to you. I promise to never make you feel less than. I promise to love you more than myself."

"Say it," I assert for the first time since she broke down.

"Yes. I'll marry you."

My hands encase the sides of her face, pulling her to me. My lips glide over hers in a kiss of love and adoration.

"We've been doing this backwards, Sam. We've been raising daughters and we never dated. You are a wonderful mother and I can't wait to see the impact you will have on our girls, but this is about us. You and me. I want to marry you today."

So, Sir John marries us in front of his secretary and an assistant. He pulled the necessary paperwork for us when I rung him yesterday. It helps to have friends in the right places.

When it's time to exchange rings, I give her the simple gold band my grandfather wore until he died. She slides it onto my finger with a promise to be mine. Always and always. The same promise I made moments ago to her.

There's soft clapping from his secretary when I kiss my bride. Even a tear. She laughs and hugs Sam as if she would her daughter.

"Your bride is beautiful," Weatherly smiles. "I spoke with Finn. They just left New York. Go enjoy your wife while you can." He smiles and for once, my friend has some good advice.

When we finally get back to the hotel, Sam is in a daze. "I can't believe I'm married." Sam stares at the ring on her finger. "I never thought this would happen for me," she admits. "I love you," she adds softly.

"I adore you," I reply stripping out of my clothes.

Sam watches me with curiosity. "I think we need to wait," she says quietly. I halt in mid air, my sock not even fully pulled from my foot. Are you kidding me? I'm not sure I have the ability to keep myself in check much longer.

Suddenly, she bursts into laughter. I narrow my eyes, furrowing my brow. "That is just cruel."

"I'm sorry, baby." She's still laughing as she begins taking off her clothes. "You held out longer than I ever thought you would." Her jeans drop to the floor. Her knickers close behind. "I really thought this morning I would be bent over in the shower as you took what was yours." She drops her shirt and steps toward me.

"On your knees, husband. You have an apology to make."

"But I said I was sorry. Last week. When I got here. We've moved on, haven't we?" I grin.

"I never said I accepted it."

"Well, you married me, so I'm kind of thinking you've forgiven me." I say, lowering to my knees, "But let's make certain."

about the author

KJ is a novelist, hot tamale-addict, and an abolisher of grammar. When not writing, you can find her reading at the beach, exploring New York City, or hanging out in her hometown of Memphis, TN. She started hitting Amazon's top 100 lists with her first novel, *Taylor Made*, in 2016. She is currently working on the next installment in the Sunday Love Series.

www.kjlewisbooks.com

also by
kj lewis

Taylor Made

Taylored to Perfection

Sunday Love

Mondays with You